A LOVER FOR LADY JANE

WELSH REBELS

VIRGINIE MARCONATO

OLIVERHEBERBOOKS

Cover art by Dar Albert at Wicked Smart Designs

Published by Oliver-Heber Books

0 9 8 7 6 5 4 3 2 1

Prologue

N ow what was she to do? Jane wondered.

Her sister, Siân, along with her new husband and the rest of the family, had left the day before. Barely a week after the wedding, the newlyweds had elected to depart for their new home in Wales. Alone, Jane had decided to stay behind at Sheridan Manor to welcome her new cousin. Her aunt, Branwen, was to give birth to her fourth child in a few weeks' time and would no doubt welcome the help. This, of course, had been the official excuse. In reality, Jane dreaded going back to Castell Esgyrn and finding herself on her own. With her beloved sister married to the love of her life, and living in her own cottage, she would be lonely, and well...

Jealous.

Jane hated herself for the sentiment, but she couldn't help it. Things would change, inevitably. With a husband and soon, a family of her own, Siân would have less time for her. That was bad enough, but her sister had married none other than Christopher Harrison, the man who had made Jane's life a misery as a child. Unfortunately, she wasn't sure she would ever be able to fully forgive him for the pain he had caused her, constantly mocking her for being too "perfect," in his own words. Of course, they had grown since then and he had explained that he'd only been jealous of her happy upbringing, so different from his lonely, miserable one. He'd even asked for her forgiveness, which she had granted, but the fact remained. She feared she would never be fully at ease with her brother-in-law.

Shaking her head, she steered her mare toward the town. Perhaps a visit to the market would do her good and distract her from her maudlin thoughts. It was worth a try. What else was there to do while she waited for the birth anyway? Nothing.

As she was approaching the river, four men sprang in front of her. Before she had time to react, they had pulled her down from the saddle and surrounded her. Their snarling countenances did not bode well. She already knew they would not be satisfied with being handed the contents of her purse. They might well make her surrender an infinitely more precious possession.

"Who are you? What do you want?" she asked, doing her best to calm the beatings of her heart. Why oh why had she not agreed to William's offer of an escort? Just because she was on her father's land didn't mean she was safe. A woman alone was never safe.

Instead of answering her questions, the bearded man in front of her lifted his arm. Jane's eyes widened in horror. Was he about to...

The question never fully formed in her mind, as a heartbeat later, his fist connected with her head, and she fell into a black hole.

Chapter One

England, Winter 1310

"*Ydych chi'n siarad Cymraeg?*"

Do you speak Welsh?

Oh yes, she did speak Welsh, just as well as she spoke English, in fact. But Jane was not about to admit as much, not to a man who had hit her and also, by the looks of things, abducted her. She had just woken up alone, with a splitting headache, in an unknown room decorated with the finest tapestries. There was no prize for guessing what had happened to her.

She had been taken to one of the local lords' castle.

But why? It made no sense. If the men had been after a noblewoman's money, then they could have robbed her while she lay unconscious. If they'd been intent on raping her, then they could have done it on the forest floor. There had been no need to take her to a comfortable room. If they'd wanted to kill her, they could have sliced her throat, run her through with their blades or strangled her instead of merely hitting her.

Doing her best not to betray her fear, Jane stood up from the bench they had placed her on and stared at the bearded man towering over her, the one who had hit her earlier. Geraint, she had heard the others call him while they waited for her to acknowledge their presence. A Welsh name, which explained why he had asked his question in Welsh. This only added to her puzzlement. What were Welsh men doing here?

"I am Lady Jane Hunter," she said, pointing at herself. They would assume from this answer she thought they'd asked for her name. "Lord Sheridan's daughter and Matthew Hunter's niece."

If ever there was a time to make herself sound like someone of importance, this was it. They might let her go when they understood who their captive was. Though he now mainly resided in Wales, her father was well known round these parts and renowned for being fiercely protective of his family. Her uncle was the administrator of the domain and respected for his fairness.

The man, however, didn't seem impressed by her answer. Or perhaps he knew so little English that he hadn't realized she had just given her name. It was possible. He didn't seem able to utter a single word in her language.

"Leave it," grumbled the man by Geraint's side, a giant with a thick mane of brown hair. "She thinks you asked her name. Of course, she's English, what did you expect? Why would the high and mighty lady bestir herself to learn a barbaric language?"

Why? Because she'd spent the best part of her life in Wales and, save from her father and her uncle Matthew, all the people she loved were either Welsh or half-Welsh. She hadn't *bestirred* herself to learn Welsh, she had embraced it. But it seemed to her that it would work to her advantage to pretend she could not understand what they were saying. That way they might let slip some vital pieces of information about who they were and what they wanted. Besides, she was in no mood to make their life easier.

She stared at them blankly.

"Go get Griffin," the giant instructed the blond man by the

door before turning back to Geraint, his irritation barely concealed. "I told you we would need him. Why isn't he here already?"

"I sent him to deal with the lady's mare. I didn't expect her to come to so quickly, if you must know. No matter, just make sure you bring him to me as soon as Tomos finds him. I'll take our guest to the blue chamber. She can wait for us there"

Guest.

Jane remained impassive but the choice of word had taken her by surprise. Was this just a misunderstanding then? She didn't dare hope it was. No one struck their guests to force them into their home, did they? Abducting her meant they intended to ransom her at the very least. Her father was not at Sheridan Manor at the moment but there was no cause to worry. When the message reached him, her uncle would do whatever was required to ensure her safety, pay whatever sum was demanded.

In no time at all, she would be free.

She placed a tentative finger over the place on her temple where she'd been struck and found it tender and swollen. No doubt she would sport a bruise for days. Geraint, as could have been predicted, didn't appear concerned by the fact. He gestured that she should follow him. No need of an interpreter to understand what was required of her this time, or that she had better obey without delay. Two of the men—she'd counted six in total, including the one who had gone back outside in search of the man who spoke English—had placed themselves behind her, blocking her retreat.

No, she was most definitely not a guest, but a captive.

She followed the man up the spiral staircase.

❦

Jane stared at the closed door. How long it would be before the men were back with this Griffin who would act as translator? Not long, probably. A plan had started to form in her mind when Geraint had left her on her own, but she had to act quick if she had any chance of it working.

There was no guarantee it would, but it was worth a try. In any case, she had nothing to lose. Keeping an eye on the door, praying the men did not choose this moment to come back, she unhooked her cloak and started to remove her dress, then finally her shift. Shivering in the room where no fire had been lit, she wrapped the delicate garment around her waist, then stuffed the overhanging material inside the makeshift belt she had created. Once she was satisfied the padding sat in the right place, low over her stomach, she donned her gown again, making sure to smooth the creases over the bulge. It was done, and not a moment too soon. As she was putting the finishing touches to the arrangement, she heard footsteps in the staircase. Three or four men, at the very least, coming up. Leaving her cloak on the bed, Jane took her place by the window. A moment later the chain was removed and the door opened. Heart thumping hard in her chest, she waited.

Finally, she would know why she had been abducted.

"There she is. Ask her when that bastard Sheridan will be back."

Jane winced inwardly. Clearly she had underestimated the difficulty of pretending she didn't understand what was being said. If they were going to call her father a bastard in her presence, she would find it extremely hard to remain impassive. But she had to try, as reacting would alert them to the fact that she understood Welsh perfectly well.

"My lady, when do you expect your father to be back at Sheridan Castle?"

The interpreter's voice was soft and deep, his English unac-

cented. In short it was nothing like the aggressive, barely under-
standable bark she had expected to hear. And there had been
proper respect in his voice when he had called her "my lady."
But her relief was quickly forgotten as the implication of his
words hit her.

Had she heard that right? She had only told the men who
she was a moment ago. And yet they knew her father, Connor,
was away. So... Had they kept themselves abreast of what was
going on at Sheridan Manor? Had they targeted her because she
was Lord Sheridan's daughter, not just a hapless woman or a
rich lady perfect for ransoming? Had they known who she was
all along?

"I know not when he will return," she answered, keeping
her back to the men. "He spends most of his time in Wales, now
that he's married to a Welsh woman." If the men didn't know
that, they could not be very familiar with the family's habits.
She hoped it was the case, as it would make it easier for them to
believe the lie she was about to utter. "He said he would be back
before the birth, but that is still some months away."

Griffin dutifully relayed her words to Geraint, who barked
his reply. "What birth? What the hell is she talking about now?"

Jane forced herself not to move. This was going to be very
difficult indeed. How long before she forgot she wasn't
supposed to understand what the man was saying and answered
the questions directly? Only when Griffin translated the question did she turn around, one hand resting on her belly, now
made bigger by the shift hidden under her dress.

"The birth of my child."

Three men stared at her in shock. She stared right back
because between Geraint and the giant she had seen earlier was
the man she assumed to be Griffin. And he was...

She could not find the words to describe him, or the feelings the sight of him provoked inside her. Saying that he was

tall, had long blond hair, blue eyes and a manly jaw, while true, seemed woefully inadequate. Saying that she had been struck dumb at the sight of him would be understating what had happened within her. The man had taken her breath away.

With a measure of shock, she realized that he reminded her of Christopher, Siân's husband. How could that be? She would never have thought anyone resembling the man she had despised for so long would appeal to her. But appeal he certainly did. They stared at one another a long moment, then the spell was broken.

"The birth of your child?" Geraint erupted in Welsh.

"The birth of your child?" Griffin repeated in English.

Where there had only been loathing in the other man's question, his voice was colored by concern. This was interesting. If he thought her condition meant she should be treated with care, or even released, then she might be able to use him to gain her freedom.

If he'd only been brought here to translate, he might not be one of Geraint's friends. Everything seemed to indicate he was not. His manners were different to that of the other men, he was calling her "my lady" with deference, speaking in a soft voice, looking ill at ease. Yes, this man could well be an ally.

"Please," she said, addressing herself to him. "You must see that it is impossible for you to keep detaining me in my condition."

He cleared his throat before turning to Geraint to translate her words. He'd added a detail of his own, she noticed. The pregnancy was a difficult one and she'd been ordered to rest. This meant two things. First of all, as she had suspected, he was on her side and secondly, the other men didn't understand a word of English, otherwise he wouldn't have dared risk them picking up on any discrepancies. Jane took heart from this. She was not alone, she had an ally, an ally with whom she would be able to converse privately.

"Who's the father? We weren't told she was married!" Geraint roared. "This might well complicate matters, because now we'll have an angry man looking all over the place for her."

"I am not married, and the father's identity is none of your concern," Jane told Griffin, who had relayed the heated words in his usual calm manner. This was the only answer she could give, for who could she name at the risk of exposing him to the men's violence?

Besides, not naming her elusive lover had given her another idea.

"Tell the men that if they think to use me to pressure my father into coming to them, they are wasting their time. He cares naught for me since..." She placed a hand on her fake stomach bulge. Loath as she was to paint her father as a ruthless lord who would spurn his daughter for going to a man before marriage, she had to do what she could to get herself out of this, and making the men see that keeping her captive was useless was one way of doing it. "He was incensed to see me dishonor myself and will have nothing to do with me."

"Were you forced?"

Jane arched a brow. This unexpected question had come from Griffin, not from Geraint. Why did he want to know that?

"What difference will it make to your master if I were?" she murmured.

"To him, probably none. To me, it—"

"What are you two blabbering on about now?"

The interruption made Jane jump. For a moment she had forgotten where she was and why. Lost in Griffin's blue gaze, comforted by his concern, she had allowed danger to fade away.

"I was trying to ascertain whether the lady's child was imposed on her by force," Griffin answered.

Geraint made an angry gesture, not in the least impressed. "Who cares about that!"

"I do."

"Why?"

"What do you mean, why? Can't you see it would be an outrage if she—"

"I see nothing. Are we going to have pointless discussions when we should be deciding what to do now that we have found out Sheridan is gone to Wales and will not bestir himself on behalf of his wayward daughter? It seems we've abducted her for nothing! We can't even use her for bed sport. I will not soil myself by touching a woman carrying someone else's pup."

"Will you not? I'm not so fussy," the giant laughed, eyeing her up and down with ill-concealed longing. "Not when there are ways to ensure that stomach of hers doesn't get in the way. Besides, she's not that big yet. Yes, I'd fuck her."

"Yes. But you'd fuck anything with a pulse, wouldn't you?"

"I can't deny it!"

The two men laughed, and Jane focused on breathing and ignoring the vile words. *Remember, you're not supposed to know what they're saying, unless Griffin translates it to you.*

He did not.

Thank God the lady could not understand what was being said, Griffin thought, gritting his teeth at the men's crudeness. How the hell had he ended up in this nightmare?

When Geraint and his men had come to his village the previous month to recruit someone who could speak English, he had immediately volunteered. He'd been considering leaving the place at the time and this had sounded like the perfect opportunity. The men had offered to feed him and even promised to give him a small sum of money once the mission was complete. He'd imagined he would be asked to translate property deeds, oversee meetings with a disgruntled English lord, or some such.

But this morning he had discovered he was actually here to relay threats and insults to a lady who had been abducted by the band of men—and he was horrified.

Not only was the lady innocent of any wrongdoing, having been taken in order to blackmail her father into surrendering himself, but she had been injured. There was no mistaking the reason for the large bruise discoloring her temple. The men had hit her. As if that were not bad enough, he was now finding out that she was with child. How could the men be so cruel as to keep her captive in those conditions?

He looked at her, so brave in her predicament.

She was stunning, unlike any woman he'd ever seen, and he wasn't sure what was more remarkable about her. Her eyes, of a clear, piercing green that rivaled the most precious gems. Her hair, falling in a sleek, dark sheet over her shoulders and all the way to the small of her back. Her lips, red, full and inviting. But it was not just her beauty that captivated him. It was the contrast between her otherworldly perfection and the vulnerability—or was it actually strength?—he could see running underneath. She was alluring and innocent at the same time. Yes, innocent...if you forgot her swollen stomach of course. *Had* she been forced?

He could not help wanting to know. Geraint had said that he didn't care about the circumstances surrounding this baby's conception but he, Griffin, needed to put his mind at rest. He needed to know if there was someone out there who should pay for his villainy. Lady Jane had said she was not married... He doubted she would have found herself a lover. Well born ladies didn't do that. So, unfortunately, the possibility of her having been assaulted was all too real.

And it bothered him.

"Listen," he said, putting an end to the men's vile discussion. "I will try to get to the bottom of this, find out if we need to worry about seeing the father of her child descend upon us with all his might. It will be quicker and easier to get an answer out of her if I don't have to stop to translate all the time, and she might open up more easily if she doesn't feel under threat."

He hated making the lady sound like a witless female who could be fooled by false reassurances, but the important thing was to be alone with her and assure her he would do what he could to help her.

"You want her for yourself, don't you, English?" Cynan snarled. The man had taken an immediate dislike to him when he had explained how it was he spoke English so well, but Griffin was not going to let it worry him. He'd heard the same comments and faced the same disapproval all his life. He would not let a man of the crass giant's ilk intimidate him.

"I don't want to bed her, I only want to be able to tell Geraint what the situation is," he said as calmly as he could. "Besides, I'm hardly going to touch her with all of you within hearing range, am I?"

"Why not? I would not let it stop me, and I would make sure you all heard her screams of pleasure while I—"

"Enough!" Geraint interposed. "This is not helping. Griffin, make sure she talks, find out what the situation is with the father of the brat. We'll see you in the hall when you've finished. And make sure you bolt the door when you leave the room. She is not to go anywhere."

"I will."

A moment later, Griffin was alone with the lady. Oddly ill at ease, for he had never been in such close proximity to noble people, he waited.

"Please, I am detained here against my will. Are you willing to help me?" she asked, lifting her extraordinary eyes to him.

His heart skipped a beat, and he remembered telling Cynan he didn't want to bed her. It had not been a lie. This was not why he'd asked for a moment alone with her, and he knew she would not let a man like him touch her in a million years, but still, he was a man. He could not stop his loins from heating when he imagined how it would feel to hold her in his arms.

He shook his head and focused on answering her question. She would understandably be worried to find herself alone with a rebel. He had to reassure her.

"You have nothing to fear from me. I'd like to help, but it will have to be our secret. You must understand that I'm risking a lot simply by disagreeing with Geraint." This was true, even if he wouldn't let it stop him. He was alone against six ruthless men. If they understood he was working against them, he would not last long.

"I promise I will not betray the fact that we have an understanding." To his relief, Lady Jane seemed to appreciate the gravity of the situation. Besides, it was in her interest not to compromise the safety of her only ally. Even with him on her side, she had little chance of escape. Without him, she had none. "I don't want to put you in danger."

He nodded, satisfied. Now, on to the reason why he was here. "Are you going to tell me who the father of your child is?"

A brief hesitation. "No. I'm sorry. I can't."

Griffin nodded again. He had not expected her to say anything else. "Will you at least tell me if you were forced?" This, he had to know.

She flushed a delicious color that gave him his answer—and sent spikes of desire through his spine. Dear God but she was delicious. "No. I was not forced. I chose to go to him."

Well, then. If she'd gone to her lover's bed willingly, then there was nothing more to say. Lucky bastard, Griffin thought grimly. Not only had the man made love to this beautiful woman, but she had been the one going to him. That surprised him. He'd imagined nobly born ladies did not behave as simple villagers might and valued their virginity highly. Apparently, he'd been wrong. Either that or Lady Jane Hunter was like no other, which was a possibility. From the start, she had struck him as different and bold. Hadn't she been brave enough to ask for his help, not knowing how he would react? Wasn't she standing up Geraint despite her fear? A woman like this could well have gone to a man of her choosing to demand to be bedded. What he wouldn't give to have been that man...

"We should perhaps start by telling Geraint that he is a powerful man," he said, pushing those unhelpful considerations aside. "A mighty lord who will mount an expedition to get you back when he sees you've been abducted." It was most likely the case anyway. Who in their right mind would allow his woman to be taken? Especially when she was carrying his child? Or perhaps her lover didn't know he had irredeemably compromised her. She was hardly showing after all, perhaps she had not found the courage to tell him about the babe yet. Still. The man would be mad not to want to keep Lady Jane. If she were his, he would—

No. He would nothing. Thinking like this would lead nowhere. He might as well try to imagine what he would do if the English King decided to hand him the crown.

"Do you think it will be enough to make him release me?"

Griffin's chest collapsed when Jane's eyes lit up in hope because he knew it would not be that easy and he hated to disappoint her.

"No. But it could not hurt to try. The more obstacles and impediments to his plan Geraint has to face, the less likely he is to continue in this madness. He was already disappointed to be told your father was not at Sheridan Manor. Then he discovered you were with child. When I join him in the great hall, I will tell him he will now have an irate nobleman to contend with." Griffin was only the interpreter. He had no idea why the man was so intent on getting his revenge on Lord Sheridan, but surely Geraint would see that there were better ways to get to him than to threaten his daughter, especially if, as she'd said, he didn't care about her now that she was with child. "And if you could start behaving like a shrew, he might start to rethink the wisdom of keeping you captive."

Jane's lip wobbled. Not quite a smile but at least she didn't seem afraid anymore. "I can behave like a shrew if need be."

"Very well. Then I suggest you do your best to make him regret taking you."

Chapter Two

"So?"

Griffin settled himself in the chair opposite Geraint and tried not to wince at the sight of his beard shiny with the juice from the roasted goose leg he was holding. The man was eating with as much delicacy as a dog gnawed at a bone.

"So the lady refused to name the father of her child."

"There's a surprise!" Cynan growled through his mouthful of pie. "And naturally, you didn't insist, allowed her to avoid answering and simply walked away. But why would you cause her a moment's discomfort, hey? You're English as well!"

"Only half-English," Griffin corrected, helping himself to a slice of suckling pig. He'd heard the slur enough times that he knew how to handle it. It hadn't lost its sting, exactly, but he now managed to appear unaffected, thereby denying his tormentors' satisfaction. It was all that mattered.

"Only! That's one half too man—"

"As I was saying, she did not divulge the baby's father's name. She did, however, let slip that he is a powerful lord with men and means at his disposal. She is convinced he will mount a veritable expedition as soon as he notices her disappearance. Which is why, I think, she is so intent on hiding his identity. She doesn't want you to know where you will be hit from," Griffin added as inspiration struck. "She wants you unprepared when he finds you."

"You should have insisted," Cynan barked. Really, the man's resemblance to a beast was uncanny. All this gnawing, growling, and barking... Was he surrounded by a pack of snarling dogs? It seemed so. "There are ways to make her talk."

Griffin swallowed his mouthful of meat without tasting it. Did he mean torture? Rape? Nothing would surprise him coming from the man. "I will *not* hurt or even consider intimidating her into—"

"Fair enough. If you're not man enough to do it, then I will."

The giant stood up; intent written all over his face. Before Griffin could protest, Geraint stood up in turn, blocking his friend's way. "No. I will not have her damaged. She is to reach her father intact. Hywel's orders, you will recall."

"Why? What difference does it make?"

"Sheridan is hardly going to surrender himself for a woman already half dead, is he? It would hardly be worth it."

"I don't mean to damage her!"

"No. But I know you," Geraint was not so easily convinced. "You might not *mean* to but that's what you'll do. You can't control yourself when your blood is up, for whatever reason, and having a beautiful lady under you will definitely make you lose all restraint."

Ice replaced the blood in Griffin's veins. He put his knife down, knowing he wouldn't be able to eat other thing tonight. Jane was in even more danger than he had supposed if Cynan intended to go to her. With his bulk and his rough manners, the bastard would hurt her if he touched her, whether to punish her for her defiance or bed her for his selfish pleasure.

Silence descended into the room, heavy as a shroud.

"There's only one thing for it," Geraint eventually decided. "We'll have to take the wench back to Wales. If her father won't come back to her, then we'll take her to him."

The men around the table looked at one another in consternation. Evidently, they had not thought this mission would end up being so fraught with complications. In their mind, they would capture the lady on the Monday and be rid of her and in possession of her father on the Tuesday.

"Wales? You mean, we'll have to take her all the way from whence we came?" The look in Osian the miller's eyes made it obvious he was hoping to have misunderstood.

"That was not part of the plan," Tomos the farmer's son added.

"No. But it makes little difference in the end. Hywel wanted us to bring him Lord Sheridan, and we will. Only, instead of traveling with a dangerous, captive warrior in our midst, we will have a more easily controlled female with us. I say it is even better, all things considered." He nodded, as if satisfied, sat back down and reached to another goose leg, which he attacked in much the same way he had attacked the first one. "Yes, it is the best solution. Going away will also have the added advantage of making it a lot harder for the father of her brat to find her—and us. We leave at dawn."

Griffin was aghast. His and Jane's plan had failed, spectacularly. Far from deciding she was not worth the trouble, Geraint had concluded he was better off with her than with her father.

"You cannot mean to take a lady with child all the way to—"

"Listen, you English half-breed, and listen well," Geraint snarled, leaning across the table. Behind him, Cynan snorted, no doubt delighted to see him put back in his place at last. "You leave the decision-making to me. You're only here to relay my words to the woman and hers to me. Don't forget it or you might end up on the end of my sword. I will not tolerate rebellion from anyone, least of all you, who I only met less than two weeks ago. Are we clear?"

"Of course."

There was nothing else to say. Though his appetite was well and truly gone, Griffin picked up his knife and urged himself to calm. He could not protect the lady Jane if he was dead. And protect her he would. Or at least, as much as he could.

Later that evening, Geraint and two of his men came back to the blue chamber, accompanied by Griffin.

Jane had been bracing herself for the confrontation and she decided not to stand up from the chair or even turn to face them when they entered the room. Let them make what they would of her scorn. They didn't deserve anything less, and that way, her stomach would be concealed from view. She was not convinced it was quite the shape it was supposed to be, so it was better the men didn't get too many opportunities to scrutinize it.

Fortunately, they didn't seem to take issue with her act of defiance and only Griffin came to stand where she could see him. The look on his face was enough to tell her their plan had failed. Geraint had not come to announce he would let her go. Quite the contrary.

"Here's what we're going to do," the rebel said, before starting to expose his change of plan.

Her insides tightened when he announced his intention to take her to Castell Esgyrn. She had not imagined she would have to spend so long in the company of the rebels. The more time she spent with them, the more likely it was they would realize she was not with child—and able to understand Welsh. Being on her guard for days on end would be exhausting as well as dangerous. She was not a guest, contrary to what Geraint had said, but a captive. Who was to say they would treat her with respect?

Griffin seemed to share her consternation. Though he was doing his best, as agreed, to behave coldly toward her, she saw concern swirling in his blue eyes. She guessed he would have argued against taking her all the way to Wales and had been ignored.

"If your father won't come to you, then we'll go to him," Geraint concluded. "You say he cares not about you or the babe, but we'll see what he does when we bring you in front of him and threaten to slice your belly open to remove his bastard grandchild from your womb if he doesn't surrender himself."

Fortunately, Jane was sitting on her chair and looking out the window when he uttered the awful threat, for she knew she had gone the color of whey. Griffin, the only one whose face she could see, arched a brow at her reaction. Damnation, he was wondering whether she had understood what had just been said. She had to be more careful. But how to remain impassive when they were talking about doing such things to her?

"He says your father will have no other choice but to surrender himself when he sees we have you captive," he said eventually, his voice even deeper than usual. "He cannot be as indifferent to your fate and that of your child as you think."

Though, in effect, he had told her what Geraint had said, he'd left out the part about slicing her open to get the babe out of her. Jane would have been grateful to him for the intention if she had not been frozen in place by horror. These men were even more dangerous than she had first supposed. True, they had brought her to a comfortable room and had asked for a tray of food to be brought to her earlier, but they would not hesitate in hurting or even killing her to get what they wanted—her father.

Why? What did they have against him?

As if to answer the silent question, the men started to argue between them in a low voice, making it clear that this was not meant for her and Griffin was not to translate what they were saying.

"Should we send a message to Hywel to inform him about the delay?" a man with a nasal voice asked. "He'll be expecting Sheridan to be brought to him within the week. Traveling with her will take longer than with him."

"Yes. He should be told, though I can already tell you he's not going to like it." She thought she recognized the giant's voice. He sounded mightily aggrieved.

"He will like it even less being kept waiting for no reason." This came from Geraint.

"Aye. That's true."

From her place on the chair, with her back to the men, Jane didn't miss a word from the conversation. This Hywel was clearly the man who wanted her father. Geraint and the others had only been sent to England to do his bidding, so as to ensure Lord Sheridan's disappearance could not be traced back to him. Who was he and what did he want with her father? Hywel was too common a name for her to immediately identify him, even if at the back of her mind, something was niggling at her. She had the impression she should know the man.

"When do we leave?" she asked. The sooner the better where she was concerned.

"Tomorrow at dawn," Griffin answered without translating her question first. "I will ask for a fire to be lit in your room," he added, eyeing up the empty hearth in disapproval. 'Tis too cold in here, you should at least wear your—"

"What the fuck are you talking about now?" the giant interrupted. It was clear from the snarl and Griffin's reaction that the two of them didn't see eye to eye. No wonder. Jane couldn't think of two more different people.

"I'm informing her that we will leave at dawn and telling her a fire will be lit for the night."

"And who allowed you to make such a decision?"

"Didn't Geraint say she should reach her father intact? That includes her health, I should think."

"Methinks you're far—"

"Enough," Geraint interposed. "Griffin is right. It's too cold in here. Tomos, come with me, we have preparations to oversee," he added, making for the door before addressing himself to the giant. "You will lock the room behind us. Stay here a while before you leave though. I should think a moment with you will be enough to convince the lady she had better not try anything foolish while she's with us."

"Shall I stay as well?" Griffin asked, worry etched all over his face at the idea of her being alone with the man. Jane could not blame him; she was worried herself. "To make sure that whatever he says—"

"No. She will understand well enough we won't tolerate any trouble when she sees his face."

Insisting would only have placed himself in danger, so Griffin had no choice but to obey. After one last look at her, he left the room. A moment later Jane was alone with the giant. She stayed where she was, with her back to him, rigid with fright. What would he do? She could tell he hadn't moved yet. What did he intend to do?

Finally, after what felt like an eternity, he made his way toward the chair. Then he bent over and started to talk, placing his mouth at her ear.

"The English pup won't always be here to take your defense and Geraint will be made to see that there is no harm in me taking my pleasure with a hostage." A finger lifted the mass of her hair from her neck, grazing the flesh as it did. She shuddered when he brought the lock to his nose and groaned in appreciation. "Make no mistake about it, lady, I will have you under me before we reach Castell Esgyrn."

Jane would have given ten years of her life not to understand the threat but alas, she did understand it, all too well. How she managed not to react, she would never know. She remained still, playing her role to the best of her ability. Only when the door closed on the vile man did she allow herself to crumple.

Oh, lord. What mess had she gotten herself into?

Chapter Three

"Are you sure that's a good idea?" a blond man called Osian asked Geraint, a hand rubbing at his unshaven jaw.

All seven men were getting ready for departure. Jane had been awoken before dawn, instructed to eat something while she could, and dragged into the bailey none too gently. As it was bitterly cold, she had decided to wear her shift under her dress to protect herself as best she could from the wind, knowing that once they were on the road, she would spend most of her time wrapped in her cloak anyway.

"Yes." Geraint answered, barely looking at his friend.

"You really mean to make her ride the stallion Hywel sent Lord Wills?" Osian insisted, gesturing at the magnificent dappled gray horse standing behind him. Jane had heard two men say earlier that the mysterious Hywel had sent the precious gift to the English lord as a reward for his help. In exchange for him providing a shelter for the rebels and their captive, this Lord Wills had been given a priceless mount.

"There is no other horse available. He doesn't mind, as he

agrees it is the best solution. We will return the horse in due time, don't worry."

The man looked unconvinced. "Even so, stallions can be unpredictable, and Taran is still young. Are you sure she will be able to—"

Geraint stopped him with a raised hand, his patience finally snapping. "Taran is the only horse we have. You have seen for yourself that, apart from his own mount, Lord Wills only keeps brooding mares in his stables, and they are all about to foal. I won't endanger them at this time or buy another horse for a captive who's already proven more troublesome than antici-pated. The stallion will have to do. In any case, I'm sure it won't be a problem. The daughter of a mighty lord, English as he may be, will know how to ride better than most men."

As ever, Jane was careful not to betray the fact that she had understood every word of the conversation because another plan was forming in her mind. Geraint was right. She could ride better than most people, knights included, her father had made sure of it. But the men weren't to know that. If she acted all nervous at the sight of the beast and then, at the opportune moment, urged him into a frenzied gallop, surprising her captors by her ability, she might be able to escape. They would conclude something had spooked the animal and not suspect her of deceit if she didn't manage to flee. It was worth a try at least.

Besides, pretending she couldn't ride properly would only annoy the men, who no doubt hoped to reach Castell Esgyrn as quickly as possible. If only for that, she would have pretended not to know what she was doing. She hadn't forgotten her promise to Griffin to behave like a shrew.

"Now let us go. We've lost enough time already."

When they brought the stallion in front of her, Jane arched her brow in disbelief mingled with an alarm she didn't feel.

Taran, which meant Thunder in Welsh, seemed just as impetuous as Osian had hinted. Had she not been the rider she was, she might well have taken fright.

"I hope you don't expect me to ride him?" she asked in a whisper.

"It's a bloody horse," Geraint replied once Griffin had translated the question, even if in truth there had probably been no need. Her unease had been obvious. "Of course I expect her to ride him. What else would she do with it?"

"I'm sure you'll be fine," Griffin told her. As ever, he'd taken it upon himself to soften the tone of the answer—or rather to change it completely. Geraint had not offered any reassurances, far from it. "Taran is as good natured as can be for a stallion."

"I'm not a good rider at the best of times," she lied. "With a horse I don't know, and a stallion, I'm not sure how I will fare."

"Well, she'll just have to manage, won't she?" was the actual answer.

"Worry not, we probably won't gallop anyway," was the version she was given.

Despite her situation as hostage, Jane could not deny a flutter of pleasure. Griffin was being unflinchingly protective and kind. In her misfortune, she had at least found a reliable ally. Never had she been more grateful for someone's presence by her side. What an inspired idea it had been to pretend she didn't understand Welsh, because if Geraint had realized she could converse with him without an interpreter, then Griffin would have been sent away. She wrapped her cloak more tightly around her to protect her other lie from being discovered. The men had to keep believing she was with child.

"Take the lady to the mounting block," Geraint ordered. "We're leaving."

Taking the order as their cue, the rest of the men vaulted onto their horses. After holding Taran steady for her, Griffin went to his own mount, a magnificent gray stallion he seemed to cherish. Jane was surprised. It was an unusual beast for someone of his position to have. Who was he that he could afford such a mount? Cynan had called him "the English pup." Was he English then? What was certain was that, like her, he spoke both languages with equal ease.

"Let's ride."

The retinue set off, her in the middle, the seven men surrounding her. It seemed that despite her claim that she was not a competent rider, they did not trust her not to try to escape. Geraint was leading the group, the giant was bringing up the rear, and Griffin was just behind her.

They traveled all day without them finding the opportunity to have any sort of conversation.

By the time they stopped for the night, Jane was exhausted. Pretending to be a nervous rider as well as with child and unable to understand what was being said around her had taxed her brain to its limit, but she thought she had done a credible job of it. That first day had gone without mishap—if one forgot she was a captive under surveillance and not a lady traveling back home of her own accord. The most difficult part, strangely enough, had been not letting her interest in Griffin shine through and resisting the impulse to look at him at every opportunity. She should not be drawn to him thus but how could she stop herself?

He was unfailingly attentive to her, protective and kind. When they had stopped to eat something toward the middle of the day, he had made sure to select the most appetizing cuts of meat for her and fill her cup with ale before she'd even thought to ask for anything. Every time he talked to her, he did his best to sound cheerful even if it was obvious the situation weighed on him. She was grateful for his efforts, as it helped keep her own fears at bay.

After two days on the road, she was thoroughly convinced he was a good man at heart. What he was doing with a band of ruffians was a mystery. The problem was, she couldn't see any way of contriving a conversation with him to find out and besides, as she kept reminding herself, she was not supposed to want to have anything to do with any of the men responsible for keeping her captive, even the ones going out of their way to make her comfortable.

Due to her feigned inability to gallop or even canter unless they were in a flat, open field, their progress was much slower than Geraint had wished. Still, on the morning of the fourth day, they arrived within sight of the border.

"It won't be long before we cross into Wales," Cynan said with satisfaction. "I will admit I cannot wait. England really is a foul country, inhabited by foul people."

It was just as well Jane was not required to answer, because such a remark did not deserve any comment.

Later that afternoon, she saw the opening she had been waiting for. Up until then, Geraint had led them along a different route than the one she and her family usually took when going to Sheridan Manor, so she had not been able to get her bearings but now she knew exactly where she was. On the other side of that hill was a village where the Hunters stopped every time they traveled that way. If she could launch Taran into a gallop while the men had dismounted to water the horses and reach the woods a short distance ahead, then she would be hidden from view. There, she would turn at a sharp angle, and head for the village down below.

Once there, she would ride straight to Mistress Blodwen, who always made them welcome. No ride from Castell Esgyrn to Sheridan Manor was complete without a halt in her cottage, where they would invariably be met with refreshing ale and the most delicious bread. Jane was certain the kind woman would hide her and the stallion until the men had gone past.

It would be as if she had vanished into thin air.

Yes, it was as good a plan as any she was going to come up with. There would never be a better opportunity to escape her captors. She could not afford to wait because she did need a place to hide. She would never outrun six men; the most she could do was give herself a head start to reach a place of safety.

Griffin could help with that, even unwittingly, and ensure they stopped now instead of when Geraint decided to.

"I'm tired," she said, bringing her horse next to his. "We've been on the road for days. Could you ask for a halt? We need to water the horses soon anyway so it will make no difference."

He nodded and called out to the head of the group. "Let us stop a moment, please. I think Eryr has gone lame. I'll check him while the horses have a drink."

Jane's chest squeezed. Once again, he'd made sure not to expose her to Geraint's ill temper by pretending he was the one requesting the halt. He had no idea she could understand what he was saying, so he was not doing it to earn her favor, but simply out of personal kindness. She would miss him, she realized with a pang of anguish. But she could not stay a captive just to be near him. It was not only her safety and comfort that were at stake, but her father's life as well. Because, contrary to what she had told the Welsh rebels, there wasn't any problem between them. He loved her and would agree to the men's terms, whatever they were, just to get her out of their clutches, and be handed to Hywel. And then what would happen?

The idea of him ending up at the mercy of a man she imagined intent on killing him strengthened her resolve. This was not about her. She had to save her father. If that meant being taken away from Griffin, then so be it. Perhaps once this was over, he would visit her at Castell Esgyrn? He knew he would be able to find her there or at Sheridan Manor, so it was not impossible.

She shook her head. No. She was getting painful ideas into her head. Why would he bother to see her once he was finally free of the trouble she'd caused him? He would be relieved to be able to carry on with his life unencumbered by pregnant English ladies who needed constant supervision.

"A halt is an excellent idea," said the giant whose name she still hadn't been able to establish. "I need a shit."

Jane reminded herself too late she wasn't supposed to understand and wrinkled her nose at his crudeness. Griffin saw her reaction and frowned. Drat, it wasn't the first time he'd looked at her that way. Evidently she wasn't doing as good a job as she thought at hiding the fact that she understood what was being said. At least he hadn't spoken about his suspicions to the others—that she knew of.

Well, if all went according to plan, in a moment, she wouldn't have to worry about betraying herself to the rebels. She would be out of their reach.

"All right, let's stop."

Geraint was the first to dismount, quickly followed by the giant, who instantly headed for the nearest bush. Excellent. If he was busy relieving his bowels he would not be able to rush out in pursuit when she launched her mount into a gallop. Neither would the other two men who had headed the same way to relieve themselves, even if they'd had the delicacy not to announce out loud their intentions. Griffin, she suspected, would do nothing to stop her flight. That meant if she left now, only Geraint and the two smallest, slowest of the men would be able to mount and come after her. It was unhoped for.

Before she could lose this advantage, she kicked Taran into action.

The stallion, only too happy to comply after days of near

inactivity, tore through the field stretching in front of them. Shouts were heard in the distance, but Jane focused on the woods ahead, which were getting closer with each powerful stride of her mount. A little bit more and she would be under cover, able to veer off the obvious course and lose the pursuers. Her heart lifted. She could already taste freedom on the tip of her tongue. It tasted like Blodwen's bread.

It all happened in a heartbeat.

One moment she was thundering through the clearing, the next she was rolling on the ground, wondering if the horse would not crush her under his hooves. Realization settled in her chest, as heavy as a boulder. Taran had tripped, sending her to the ground. The men were hard on her heels, ready to capture her.

She had failed. It was over.

Chapter Four

*N*o!

The word exploded in Griffin's mind. He'd seen the frightful scene as if it had happened twice as slow as normal. Taran, flying over the clearing like a bird with the dark-haired Jane perfectly balanced on his back. The horse, stepping into a hole, and falling, sending his rider rolling at his feet like a dislocated rag doll.

Damn Geraint's eyes! This could have been predicted all too easily. Griffin had warned him only the day before that he thought the horse needed re-shoeing. The man had waved the comment away, snarling that they had lost enough time already. They would shoe him once they'd reached their destination, not a moment before. There was no need, as they were only walking or trotting anyway.

Well, look at the result!

The poor horse might be injured beyond repair—and Jane might be dead.

He was the first to reach her, since he'd not been far behind. Because he'd been busy checking Eryr for an injury that wasn't there, he'd been the only one next to his horse, and therefore able to mount and gallop after her in a heartbeat when the stallion had bolted off.

When he'd heard Taran scarper away, he'd not imagined for a moment that Jane had been the one kicking him into action. His first thought had been that the animal had taken fright, surprised by a flock of birds bursting out of the branches or a sudden smell no one else had detected. It had quickly become obvious, however, that the woman sitting on top of the galloping stallion was an expert rider. Had she been as inexperienced and nervous as she had led them to believe, she would have been unseated immediately. No. He now knew the truth. Jane had been the one kicking Taran into action. She had been trying to flee. And why not? She was a captive after all. It was what clever, determined captives did.

How had he not guessed that was what she was about to do? Just before Taran had vanished in a thunder of hooves, she'd thrown him a piercing look. Something like an apology had gleamed in her amazing eyes. Now he understood. She was saying goodbye before disappearing.

Damn it all, she would have made it, if the horse had been properly shod!

Heart in his throat, he jumped off the saddle. Panic had caused his lungs to seize in his chest, and he wasn't sure how he would react if he saw that she was dead.

"My lady!" He fell on his knees by her side. She was not moving. Why was she not moving? He could not shake her, not when he didn't know what, if anything, was wrong with her. "My lady, please, say something. It's me. Griffin."

"It's over," he heard her say after a while.

Relief swept through him, stronger than any emotion he'd felt in his life. If she was speaking, even if she sounded dejected, it meant she wasn't dead. That was the most important thing. Now he had to know if she, or her babe, were injured. He placed a hand over her shoulder, when he wanted to put it on her stomach. "Don't move. You might have a broken bone. How do you feel?"

"It's over," she repeated, sounding on the verge of tears.

So he'd been right. This hadn't been an unfortunate mishap. She had meant to escape, and she was crushed not to have succeeded. "Are you injured?" he asked again.

That was all he worried about at the moment, and he needed to know. She shook her head, a tear rolling down her cheek. He desperately wanted to wipe that tear away, because he understood her disappointment all too well. He would have done the same in her place, tried to flee. When he had launched himself in pursuit, it had not been to stop her. He'd intended to pace Eryr, so as not to catch up with her up until they'd reached the cover of the trees. Once hidden from view, he would have asked her how best he could help in her attempt. Let him face Geraint's fury later for not being able to stop her, he cared not. He'd wanted her gone, he'd wanted her safe, even if seeing her go was tearing at his heart.

But now, as she'd said, it was all over.

"I know you tried to escape," he whispered in her ear, though no one could have heard, least of all understand him.

Her green eyes pierced him, but she did not deny it. "Please, don't tell the men I—"

"What the devil happened here?" Geraint boomed, bringing his horse to a skidding halt behind him.

Griffin nodded imperceptivity at Jane. She would not be able to understand what he was saying in Welsh, of course, so he was asking her to trust him. Her secret was safe. No one would know she had attempted to flee; she would not face retribution for the failed attempt.

"What do you think happened? As could have been predicted, Taran spooked and then tripped when he couldn't control himself in his panic. He's now likely lost a shoe, if not injured himself, by stepping into a hole. I told you he needed to see a farrier." He stood back up, bristling with intent. This time, he wouldn't be denied, not when Jane's safety was at stake. Let the man do what he wanted to him, but he would not allow her to get injured in any way. "It is not safe for the lady to continue riding him. A rider as inexperienced as she is should not be allowed to ride such a young, unstable stallion. I thought you wanted her to reach Castell Esgyrn intact?"

He hated using that word, which made her sound like a possession, but the argument seemed to convince Geraint.

"Very well," he agreed. "We'll have to find a solution. Get her up. We've lost enough time already."

He didn't get down from the saddle, never once asked if she was hurt from the fall. Griffin's blood was galloping in his veins as fast as the horses' had done a moment ago. How much longer he would be able to hide his irritation was anyone's guess. His patience was quickly running out.

He bent down to lift Jane up, but she pushed him away and wobbled back on to her feet unaided. Far from being offended, he was relieved to see that she was determined and able to stand on her own. It showed that her spirit and her body were both intact.

"Go get Taran back," Geraint told him next. "You'll lead him back to the men and ride with him in hand. I will take the wench on Tywysog with me."

There was no choice but to obey. Griffin turned to Jane to explain that she was to go with the man and sit on the horse with him. She swallowed and nodded, visibly bracing herself at the idea of being in such proximity to her enemy. The idea of Geraint wrapping his arms around her upset him as well. It felt wrong, and his fault. Perhaps he should not have suggested she stop riding Taran, but he'd panicked and thought only of her safety. He could not have her on a restless, injured horse.

"I'll be back soon," he whispered, before hastening over to where Taran was waiting, munching on some lush grass in the distance.

Jane watched Griffin head to the edge of the woods to retrieve the stallion, leaving her alone with Geraint. What would the man do once she was in his arms? To her relief, he seemed angry at yet another delay rather than suspicious about a possible escape attempt on her part. She knew she had Griffin to thank for that. Reliable to the last, he'd done exactly what she would have asked him to do if she'd had time to talk. He'd pretended the flight had been an accident caused by Taran's nervousness and kept her real intentions secret even though he'd guessed she was attempting to flee. She would have to find a way to thank him once all this madness was over.

Geraint guided his mount to a piece of rock that would act as a mounting block and gestured at her to come closer.

"Come, sit in front of me," he instructed, pointing at the pommel of his saddle.

Determined to be contrary, and knowing she was not supposed to understand the instructions anyway, Jane stood on the rock and hoisted herself up as best she could on the stallion's rump.

This, unsurprisingly, did not go down well.

"I told you to go in front!" he snapped before muttering to himself. "Bloody hell. Will there be no end to this torment? Why couldn't we have abducted the other sister, the one who actually speaks Welsh? It would have been fitting she served a second time to get to Sheridan."

A second time. In that moment Jane understood who Hywel was, and what he wanted with her father.

Revenge for his dead father.

The man had to be none other than the son of the rebel who had forced her mother to hand over her English husband to his group of men all those years ago. Gruffydd ap Hywel, his name had been. Evidently, he had named his son after his own father, as was common practice. That was why the name had niggled at Jane's mind. The whole family had heard about how the old rebel, who'd been a friend of her father's, had blackmailed Esyllt into opening the castle to him shortly after her wedding. By using Siân, who'd only been seven at the time, he'd forced her to hand over her husband to men intent on killing an English lord. Only her uncle's timely intervention had prevented the murder. Connor Hunter had been saved and, after months of searching, the two brothers had finally located the rebel who'd gone in hiding. Together they had put an end to the monster's life. Everyone had thought it had been the end of it. They had been wrong. Now *she* was being used to get to the mighty Lord Sheridan.

Despair made her choke. Why had she failed in her escape attempt? There would not be another, not if she was to ride pillion with Geraint.

Just then, Griffin arrived with Taran in tow. Leading him by the reins, he brought him back to the men, following behind Tywysog. As soon as they were reunited with the group, they set off again,

"Hold me tighter!" Geraint instructed after a while, drawing her hand across his waist to compensate for the fact that she could not understand his words. "Damn it all, do you want to fall and break your neck this time?"

Knowing he wouldn't see her smirk or understand what she was saying, Jane delighted in voicing out her feelings out loud, taking care of sounding confused by what he'd said. "Oh no, believe me, I would much rather break *your* neck. I hate you and your ill-mannered, stupid, crass—"

"Shut up and hold me, damn you! You're going to fall if you carry on in that way, and I would like to trot, to try and make up for lost time."

She carried on as if he had not said anything, making sure to hold him as loosely as she dared. "Your brutish men who agreed on this mission, all the while knowing I was innocent of any wrongdoing. Your despicable men who are about to hand my father to a man who—"

"Enough of this blabbering!" Geraint exploded, bringing his horse to a halt. "Griffin, you take the damn woman with you on Eryr. At least you'll be able to tell her I don't want to hear another word from her lips until we reach Castell Esgyrn."

Everything within Jane relaxed and she almost jumped down from the saddle there and then, forgetting she wasn't supposed to have understood the command. At the last moment she stopped herself and waited for Griffin to dismount and translate the instruction.

"My lady," he said, sounding as relieved as she felt. "You are to ride with me on Eryr now."

She accepted the hand he was offering and slid down. A moment later, she was sitting in front of him, after he'd explained it would be more comfortable for the animal to carry the extra weight on his shoulders rather than his rump. The care he had for the stallion's well-being warmed her. She gave Eryr a caress, sorry to be adding to his burden. Mercifully, the animal was built for strength, and Griffin was nothing like Geraint. Though he was tall, his body was lean and taut as a lance, he would not weigh as much as the rebel, who had started to run to fat.

"Eryr. It's an odd choice of name for a horse, don't you think?" she said once they had resumed their walking.

"Is it?" Griffin sounded surprised. Jane mentally kicked

herself. Of course she wasn't supposed to know that the word meant eagle. "Why do you think so?"

How was she going to get out of this?

"Because it's very hard to say," she improvised. "You would do better with a shorter, easier name, I think."

"It's not hard to say for us Welsh, and he's not a dog we need to bring to heel." He still sounded puzzled. "Anyway, Eryr means Eagle. I suppose it could be considered odd to choose a bird name for a horse."

"Not odd at all to me. My uncle's favorite horse is called Raven."

"He's black, I imagine?"

"You would think so. But he's white as snow." She could not help a giggle at Griffin's splutter. How was it that being with this man could make her forget the situation she was in? This morning, escape had been the only thing on her mind and here she was, enjoying her conversation with him, basking in the warmth of his embrace. "He called him thus because his wife Branwen's name, as you will know, means 'white raven'."

"Is she Welsh then?"

"Yes, like my mother Esyllt. They've been friends since they were children."

"And you spend half your time in Wales?"

"I do. I only stayed at Sheridan Manor when my family went back to Castell Esgyrn to wait for the birth of my cousin."

"So..." He sounded cautious, as if what he was about to say made no sense. "How is it you don't speak the language, or even understand anything?"

Damn and blast. Jane could have kicked herself. Why had she relaxed her guard? But perhaps she shouldn't be surprised she had. Cradled in Griffin's arms, she could not think straight.

"We always speak in English at home. It was easier that way. When my father married Esyllt, his second wife and the woman I consider as my mother, she and her daughter Siân already spoke English and once the habit was taken, it was hard to go back. We spend a lot of time in England anyway. How is it that you speak English so well, with no accent?" she asked to steer the conversation away from dangerous waters. Besides, she was curious. The giant had called him the English pup. Was he English then? His mastery of the language was certainly good enough.

"My mother was English. That is why I am called Griffin. Had I been fully Welsh, I would likely have been called Gruffydd."

Yes, of course... How had she not thought of that? Still, she shivered at the thought of him sharing a name with her father's enemy. Griffin was much better.

"Your mother was English, then?" she prompted. She wanted to know more about his family.

"Yes. She was the maid of the local lord, who had come to settle on the other side of the border after the invasion in '77. Shortly after her arrival, she met my father, a farmer living next to the castle. They married in secret, knowing their union would not be seen favorably but she was sent away in disgrace when her belly started to swell with a babe—my sister." He let out a snort. "The little English maid was despised and dismissed by the mighty lord for marrying a Welshman, when it is common knowledge that he fathered at least a dozen bastards on the local women. The hypocrisy and cruelty of people will never cease to amaze me."

"Yes."

Jane's heart constricted. She could well imagine what his family had endured from ill-intentioned people. It was one thing for noble Englishmen to marry Welsh women on the King's orders to enforce his domination over the country, quite another for ordinary folk to follow their heart and fall for someone who was seen as the enemy. Such unions were still viewed with suspicion now, so she could well imagine how it would have been seen almost thirty years ago.

"I think it is a beautiful love story," she murmured, not daring to turn her head to speak in Griffin's ear. "Two people who were brave enough to ignore what people said and decided to be together despite the odds stacked against them. It is not an easy path to take."

"No, it isn't."

He sounded pensive, so much so that she didn't dare ask anything for the rest of the day, simply enjoying the feel of his arms around her.

~

When they stopped for the night later that afternoon, Griffin was still pondering on Jane's remark about Eryr's name. It was not the first time he'd wondered if she understood his language. She often behaved in a way that betrayed a knowledge she was not supposed to have, starting to respond before he'd translated Geraint's instructions to her, reacting to something one of the men, usually Cynan, said within her hearing. He was certain she knew more Welsh than she was letting on.

Well, no point asking her again. He'd already tried to find out the truth this afternoon and she'd denied being able to speak or even understand his language. After so long pretending, she wouldn't betray herself so easily. Besides, she might not want to risk him finding out such important information about her. As far as she was concerned, even if he was doing what he could to help her, he was one of Geraint's men, which meant she could not trust him fully. No, if he wanted to know the extent of her knowledge, he'd have to trick her into revealing she understood what he was saying.

And he thought he knew just how.

Once he'd removed the saddle, Griffin leaned in to speak into his horse's ear, making sure she was still behind him. "You're a lucky boy, are you not?" he asked Eryr softly, "spending the best part of the afternoon with the Lady Jane's legs wrapped around you. I would give the fortune I don't possess to be in that position. But believe me, if I ever got between her perfect thighs, *I* would be the one doing the riding."

When he turned to the lady, he had the satisfaction of seeing that her face had gone a crimson color. As he'd suspected. She might not be able to speak Welsh fluently, but she understood it well enough.

"Ah, my lady," he said in English, feigning surprise at seeing her so close. "I was just telling Eryr here that he was lucky..." He paused, eager to see if she would panic at the idea of him repeating the lewd words to her.

She didn't panic, exactly, but her eyes widened ever so slightly, betraying alarm. "I'm sure you don't need to tell me what you tell your horse in confidence."

Her effort at breeziness was commendable, but he was not fooled.

"It's no confidence," he said, keeping his gaze fastened on her. He could have looked at her beauty all day. "Just some silly nonsense about having earned himself an extra portion of food tonight."

"Of course. All that riding..."

"As you say. Though, if you must know, as a man, I've always found riding an enjoyable activity."

His mouth said riding, but his eyes suggested something different—and she didn't miss his meaning. The color on her cheeks reached alarming proportions. If she could have vanished into a hole in this moment, he guessed she would have gone in head-first. What had possessed him to provoke her so?

"Well, good night," she said. "I will admit, the day has been rather trying and I'm ready for sleep."

"Of course."

He, for one, knew he would find it hard to get rest tonight, plagued by the memory of her soft body cradled against him. How would he stand the same torture all day tomorrow? Then he decided that anything would be better than being without her.

Griffin hated himself for the thought, but he was glad Jane had not managed to escape, as he was not yet ready to be parted from her.

Chapter Five

Griffin woke up to a sky full of stars. The clouds must have cleared while he slept, uncovering a stunning tapestry woven with glittering diamonds. In the trees overhead, two owls were answering one another. Over by the fire, Cynan and Tomos were talking in hushed tones about a woman. It did not take Griffin long to understand who that woman might be.

"She is with child. You know what that means," Cynan said, satisfaction dripping from his voice.

"Do I?" Tomos had never been the brightest of the lot but this time Griffin could not blame him for not understanding what the big man was getting at. He didn't either.

"It means she is no virgin." It was obvious Cynan had expected a reaction of some sort, which Tomos failed to provide, because he carried on, in the same tone he would have used to explain something to a three-year-old child. "Which means that there will be no harm in us amusing ourselves with her. Do you see? She will not be the worse off for offering us some well-earned relief."

"Oh, yeah." There was wonder and hope in those two words.

"She's a tasty piece, for all her defying ways, and not fat from the babe yet. A moment in her arms should prove a welcome distraction from this dreary ride."

"She is very beautiful," Tomos agreed.

"Beautiful, aye, and nothing like your average village wench or pox-ridden whore, that much I can tell you. Just imagine how soft her breasts will be and how white her thighs. Jesus, I'm hard just thinking about it." He grunted and adjusted his position. "I'll have to have a word with Geraint tomorrow. He was adamant we shouldn't touch her on that first day, but I doubt he will refuse us the boon now. I can tell the wench's attitude is getting on his nerves, so he'll agree she needs to be put back in her place. Hywel wants his bargaining tool and he's going to get it. He didn't say we could not amuse ourselves with it before he uses it himself. As long as she is not too badly damaged, then I say we should be allowed some reward for our pains."

"Aye. I too want between her soft white thighs."

"You'll get in, my friend, but after me. I'll be the first to plough that sweet little furrow and fill it to the brim."

Griffin bunched his fists when their coarse laughs pierced the night, replacing the calls of the two owls.

What he had heard was horrific but the worst of it was, Cynan was right. After days on the road, getting increasingly irritated by his bothersome captive, Geraint would give his agreement to the foul scheme, on the condition that the men did not hurt her too badly. Which did nothing to ease his worries. A single stolen kiss would have been more than she deserved to endure. Having her at the mercy of lust-crazed brutes was unthinkable.

All thoughts of sleep forgotten, Griffin stood up and walked over to the two men keeping watch. From the moment he'd seen

Jane in that blue room, standing up to her captors with courage, he'd been battling with his conscience, and this had finally given him the kick he needed. He would not stand by and let her be hurt. He would not be less brave than she was and force her to risk breaking her neck to escape her tormentors.

He would help, and what was more, he would succeed.

With the threat of rape hanging over her head, failure was not an option anymore. Her safety and his sanity depended on this escape.

"What are you doing here, English? Heard something suspicious?"

"No, but I can't seem to sleep, so you might as well make the most of it and get some rest," he told Cynan, doing his best to sound calm when his blood was boiling. Now was not the time to get confrontational. Tomos was not so much of a worry, but the giant, for all his villainy, was an astute man. It would not take much to raise his suspicion, and Griffin needed him gone. "No sense in all of us being awake. I'll take over with Tomos a moment, then he can go get Osian to replace him in a little while."

Cynan stood up and stretched his arms over his head, groaning in relief. "Well, if you're offering, I won't say no. I didn't sleep well last night and I plan to be well rested on the morrow."

Yes. So he could rape Jane to his heart's content. Griffin clenched his jaw.

Over his dead body.

~

Jane was woken up by a man's hand over her mouth, muffling her cry of surprise. Panic instantly flared in her chest. Who was that? Geraint, who'd come to the conclusion that she was more bother than she was worth after her attempted flight and had decided to kill her? The giant, who was finally making good on his threat to have her? Another one of the men, intent on sampling her charms in secret before delivering her to her father? Before she could grab the arm to try to uncover her mouth a voice reached her ear, a voice that instantly cut through the panic.

"Hush, it's only me."

Griffin. She instantly relaxed, indicating she would keep quiet when he released her and was rewarded with a caress over her hair. The gesture, more intimate than she should allow, but tender, moved her.

"I'm sorry to have startled you, my lady, but there was no other way. I could not risk you making a sound."

He uncovered her mouth and brought his head lower, his face now so close to hers that she could feel the hairs on his jaw against her skin. This time she was not moved, she was... She wasn't sure what she was, but heat had started to bloom in her chest and her breathing had gone rather more shallow than usual. Griffin stilled, his cheek a hair's breadth away from hers. Had he noticed her reaction to his proximity, even in the dark? She swallowed, hoping it was not the case.

"Come." He straightened up, taking his wonderful scent with him. "We need to leave."

Leave? Now? Why? It was the middle of the night. Had the men decided they would reach their destination faster if they traveled by night as well? The muscles in her tired body protested as one when she made to move. After more than four days spent constantly on her guard, she was exhausted, and her fall from Taran earlier today had not helped.

"Keep silent," he urged, helping her to stand up. "You and I are escaping. We don't want to wake anyone up."

At the words, her fatigue vanished, and the stiffness in her limbs was forgotten. Anticipation shot through her veins. If they were truly escaping, then she was ready. Sleep could wait.

"Let's go."

Hand in hand, she and Griffin made their way to the bushes where the horses were tethered. With his pale gray coat, Eryr was easily spotted in the darkness. Never had she seen a more welcome sight than that of the mount which would take her to safety. Jane went to untie him while Griffin retrieved his saddle and set about getting him ready. They were about to walk away, when an idea struck her.

"Shouldn't we set the other horses free before leaving?" she whispered. Dawn was still some time away. Untethered, the beasts might wander away in search of grazing spots, delaying the pursuers even longer when they had to retrieve them in the morning.

"Good thinking." Griffin pressed her hand in approval. "Let's be quick and silent about it, though. Our priority is to leave unnoticed."

The horses were only too happy to be freed and nudged away from the camp. Once all the beasts had been scattered, she and Griffin went back to the waiting Eryr. They led him away from the sleeping men before climbing on. As soon as they were settled, Griffin kicked him into a comfortable canter.

Little by little, as the distance between them and the camp grew, tension started to leave Jane's body. Had she made it this time? Was she really free from Geraint and his men? The steady beat of the hooves on the ground seemed to answer the silent question.

Yes. Yes, you are.

In spite of the reassurance, it was a while before she dared to talk and shatter the silence of the night.

"Why are we escaping?" she asked at last, turning to look at

Griffin over her shoulder. "I mean, I know why *I* would want to escape the men, but you? Why are you leaving them as well?"

He could have stolen a horse for her, covered her flight, sent the men in a wrong direction in the morning. He didn't have to actually go with her to save her, and they both knew it.

"Because there is no other choice. From the moment I found out why I had been recruited by Geraint I've felt ill at ease. I had no idea he and the men meant to abduct a woman, or I would never have agreed to follow them. I thought I would only be required to act as intermediary in a sale, a dispute over land or some such." He shook his head in obvious disgust. "For days I've been debating with my conscience. Then tonight I heard Cynan—"

"The big one with the wavy hair?" Without knowing why, she knew he was talking about the giant who had threatened her.

"Yes. I heard him talk with Tomos by the fire. He plans to hurt you."

Hurt her? She frowned. Why would he risk injuring her when they meant to use her as a pawn? It made no sense. Unless... She stilled. Unless Griffin had used the word "hurt" in lieu of another, much stronger one. Jane took a deep inhale and asked. "He has no intention of inflicting a wound with his blade. That's not what you mean, is it?"

There was no answer, and she knew she had guessed right. Cynan didn't really mean to *injure* her, but rape her, as he'd threatened to do on that first day.

Jane started to tremble and burrowed further into Griffin's arms, more grateful for the protection he offered than she had ever been for anything in her life.

"It's all right," he soothed. "I won't let him get to you. That is precisely why I'm taking you away."

"You know they will come after us," she whispered.

As soon as their absence was detected, the men would set off in pursuit, and they both knew it. Griffin had placed himself in terrible danger by helping her, when nothing obliged him to. The rebels, Geraint and Cynan especially, would make him pay for betraying them. He must have known what he was risking, and yet he had not hesitated.

"They will. But they will have to retrieve their horses first and then come up with a plan. As they don't know what direction we've taken, they will most likely split into two or three groups. Some will ride back toward Sheridan Manor and others will push on to Castell Esgyrn, because it is the obvious thing to do."

"But not what we will do," she finished, catching on to his idea. He had obviously thought this through while they rode.

"No. As I said, I cannot risk them getting to you." Griffin's arm tightened around her waist, betraying his determination. "We will head north for a while, riding at night and hiding during the day. If we are not out in the open when they ride past, they will not see us."

Yes, simple enough. Ingenious even. Jane relaxed further against him. This second attempt at freedom would work, she sensed it. But there were still some questions she needed answers to.

"How did you dispose of the men keeping watch?" Geraint had ordered that two men should guard the camp at all times, presumably to ward off any ill-intentioned people and prevent her escape.

"I sent Cynan to bed, arguing that I could not sleep anyway, and took his place. Once he was asleep, it was easy enough to hit Tomos over the head. He never saw anything coming."

She nodded, heart in her throat. He had done all this for

her, at great cost to himself and with no expectation of a reward. He had saved her and her father. How could she ever thank him? She wasn't sure. *Was* there even a way to reward such a deed?

After a while, he brought Eryr back down to a walk. Jane could not blame him. The poor horse would be exhausted.

"We should have taken one of the other horses for me," she said, straightening up in dismay. How had she not thought of that before? They would have been able to ride faster that way—and also put one of the men out of action.

"I thought about it but after what happened yesterday, I preferred not to risk it," was Griffin's answer. "Your fall from Taran was bad enough."

Though she knew he had not meant to disparage her, she was piqued in her pride "I'm actually a very good rider. I lied about my lack of ability, thinking to lull the men into a sense of false security—and annoy them."

Griffin gave a little laugh, as if he approved of her deceit. "I thought you might be. The way you rode Taran in that field made it clear you knew what you were doing."

She was pleased he had noticed her ability. "My father made sure his children were competent riders from a young age. My sister Siân is probably even better than me, though he started teaching her later in life, when he married my mother."

"You said yesterday that Lady Sheridan was not your real mother?"

Griffin realized that he knew very little about Jane Hunter, and suddenly it bothered him. She had opened up a little the day before, but only to reveal that she spent some of her time in England, and that her uncle had a white horse called Raven. It was not enough. He wanted to know everything.

"No, she's not. I only met her and Siân when I came to

Wales, aged seven. Esyllt is my father's second wife. He was ordered by the late king to marry her."

"I see. It was one of those political alliances made to reinforce his hold over Wales." Somehow, he'd hoped for a more satisfactory alliance, for her to be raised in a loving environment, as he had.

"Yes. Only, the two of them fell madly in love and found happiness in their marriage."

He was relieved to hear it. "Do you have other siblings?"

"Two sisters and a brother. My real mother died in childbed when I was six, along with a baby girl I never knew." She paused. Though she was not looking at him, Griffin sensed the list of losses was not finished. "I also had a twin sister, Elspeth, who died shortly after that. It was very hard. I still miss her very much, even if meeting Siân helped me get over the worst of the grief."

Her voice was barely above a whisper. Griffin wasn't sure what to tell her. Losing a sister would be bad enough, but a twin would be even worse. He could only offer belated condolences, which felt inadequate.

"I'm sorry," he said, wishing he didn't sound so bland.

"Thank you." Mercifully, Jane didn't seem to think his response inappropriate, and he felt her nestle herself closer against him. Soon her body went limp, betraying her exhaustion.

"Try to get some rest now," he suggested, resisting the urge to place a kiss over her hair. Never had anyone raised his protective instincts thus. "You didn't get much sleep tonight."

"Neither did you. In fact, you woke up before me. I'm not that tired anyway."

A smile teased the corners of Griffin's lips. Protesting that she did not need to sleep when her words were already slurred from fatigue, she sounded more like a sulky child than a mighty lady. It was endearing.

"I'll be fine. There will be plenty of time to rest when we stop later."

There was no answer.

Chapter Six

It was only when Jane was jolted awake that she realized she had fallen asleep in the saddle, held in place by Griffin's arms. She immediately straightened back up, even if it was too late to pretend she had been awake all that time. Dawn was not far; she could see the sky above the horizon becoming the lightest shade of pink. Today would be a glorious winter day, there would be no mist to wrap them in shadows or drizzle to blur their pursuers' vision. Atop a gray horse, they would be visible from miles around.

"We have to find cover," Griffin said, reading her mind. She was grateful he had not commented on the fact that she had woken up because she felt rather ridiculous. Hadn't she protested that she did not need any sleep while they were discussing her family, only to collapse in his arms a moment later?

"Let's try and see what we can find amongst those rocks," she suggested.

Apparently agreeing with the idea, Griffin nudged Eryr into a trot and headed that way. After a while they found a crack between the rocks, not quite a cave, but ideally suited to their purpose. Only people actually entering the crack would see them.

"We will have to bring Eryr in with us. He's too distinctive not to be recognized from a distance," Griffin ruled, dismounting first. "It might get a bit cramped with him in the hole, but it will be safer. A horse tethered outside will signal the presence of its rider to everyone."

"Of course," she said, jumping down in turn. Did he really think she was so spoiled she would put her comfort above their safety?

The three of them made their way inside the opening. It was covered in leaves, most of which were dry. Jane smiled. It was the best they could have found at such short notice. While she kicked the few wet and moldy leaves out of the way, Griffin removed the stallion's saddle and bridle, whispering soothing words all the while. He always did that when he was tending to his horse, which only endeared him to her further. It was obvious the animal was more like a companion to him than a tool. Not for the first time, though, she wondered how the son of a poor farmer could own such a horse. She made a note to ask him some time.

"Good boy. We'll get you something to eat, never fear. I've seen a patch of grass not too far from the cave," Griffin was saying. "I'll get you some in a moment."

Jane had seen the patch in question. Moved by gratefulness, she went outside to gather food for the animal who had whisked her and Griffin away from Geraint's camp. Eryr would be hungry after carrying them both all night long, and he deserved everything she could find for what he had done. She soon reached the spot she wanted. There was not much growing in this season, but it was better than nothing. Gathering the folds of her dress in front of her, she filled the pouch she had created with as much grass as she could.

Back at the cave, Griffin watched her deposit what she'd found in front of Eryr, who started munching straight away.

"So. You do understand what I say." It wasn't a question, and it was uttered in Welsh.

"I do," she answered in the same language.

He crossed his arms over his chest and leaned a shoulder against the stone wall. "I've had my doubts for a while. Do you speak Welsh too?"

"Yes. Siân taught me as soon as I arrived at Castell Esgyrn all those years ago. Now I speak as well as a native, or so I've been told."

"You do." He nodded, looking both shocked and impressed at her fluency. "Why did you hide the fact?"

"Wouldn't you have, in my place? I thought that keeping my knowledge of the language a secret could only be an advantage. My abductors might let slip important information in front of me if they believed I couldn't understand what they were saying." And indeed they had done just that. She had everything she needed to identify them. Her father would be able to track the men down and make them pay for what they had done. "I also thought it would reduce the time Geraint wanted to spend with me. It worked. The less time he spent with me, the better. You saw how irritated I made him."

"I certainly did." The gleam in Griffin's eyes was appreciative. "That was clever of you, as was pretending you could not ride well."

"Yes. If only I had actually managed to escape, it would have been even better."

Or would it? Now she was not certain. Had she fled on Taran's back yesterday she would now be alone on the road, vulnerable to other attacks. She had not let the idea worry her, as this had been the only option at the time, but undoubtedly, being with Griffin was far safer. With a man like him by her side, nothing would happen to her.

In the absence of anything that would serve as seats, they sat on the floor opposite one another, with their backs against the stone.

"So, if you understand Welsh, you know why the men abducted you and what their plan was."

"Yes. I know they were taking me to a man called Hywel." She paused, then decided she might as well tell him everything. After what he'd done for her, he had earned her trust. "And I think I know why. He must be the son of Gruffydd ap Hywel, the man who abducted my sister Siân fourteen years ago."

Griffin recoiled in horror. "He abducted a *child?*"

"Yes. He wanted to force my mother, who'd only just been married off to her English husband at the time, to hand him over to his group of rebels. They threatened to hurt Siân if she didn't open the castle one night. She had no choice but to comply, even if she knew they intended to kill my father just for being English."

And they had gone full circle. Now she, just like Esyllt had been, was being used to get to Lord Sheridan But once again, the rebels' plans would be thwarted. She had the man sitting opposite her to thank for it.

"Jesus." Griffin paled. "This Gruffydd really was a bastard. And clearly his son is just as unhinged. What happened to Siân?" he asked after a while.

"Don't worry about her. In the end she wasn't hurt. She barely even understood what was happening. She is married to Christopher Harrison, an Englishman, and happier than I've ever seen her." Her chest squeezed in the now familiar feeling of envy. Her sister had someone to care for her, someone who was more important to her than she was. A new era was dawning.

But...for the first time since Siân's wedding, Jane didn't feel despair. She was currently sitting near a man who made her heart beat faster, a kind, intriguing man who had saved her from a dire fate and seemed determined to protect her with his life. This was something no one else had ever done. He also, even more importantly, saw past her supposed beauty, to the person she was underneath. Instead of praising her alluring figure or the color of her eyes, as other men were wont to do, he remarked on her courage, valued her ideas and suggestions, made her feel like they were on an equal footing, behaved as if she were as brave and resourceful as he was himself. And she, in turn, saw beyond his finely chiseled features to the generous, beautiful soul hidden underneath.

That had to prove the attraction was real. Siân had seen something in her husband no one had seen, and she had been right to trust her instinct because, despite what Jane thought of him, Christopher was obviously the man for her sister.

Jane turned to look at Griffin, who was leaning back against the wall, eyes closed, looking spent after his sleepless night. She ought to let him sleep, but there was something she needed to say before that.

"Thank you, Griffin. I owe you my freedom, my father's life and my...dignity."

She had sensed from the moment she had met him that he was a good man, and not like the others in Geraint's band of rebels. He'd been respectful, attentive from the start, done his best to make her comfortable, and alleviated her fears while they traveled. Still, she had not expected him to go as far as to place himself in danger for her. He had to be aware of what the men would do to him if they ever found them, and yet he had not hesitated. This went beyond what she had the right to expect from him or anyone and she couldn't prevent a sense of guilt.

He let out a long sigh before opening his eyes. "You don't need to thank me. I wish I'd had the courage to act on the first day and spared you days of fear and discomfort. How do you feel after the night's events?"

A glance at her stomach made his meaning clear. Jane reddened. Even now, when he was in danger of facing the men's wrath, he was thinking only of her and the babe. The babe that didn't exist. She had to tell him she was not with child; it was not fair to let him worry unduly now that she knew she could trust him.

"I'm fine. In fact I—"

A rustling sound in the leaves outside their hiding place interrupted her. The horse started to stamp around and snort nervously. In the blink of an eye, Griffin had jumped to his feet and placed himself in front of her, shielding her from view.

"Who goes there?" he called out, his voice strong and assured, even though he was unarmed.

No one answered. A moment later, a flash of red crossed the opening in the rocks.

"A fox, nothing more," Jane said, relieved beyond measure. The men had not found their hiding place, they were safe. For a dreadful moment she had feared seeing Geraint or even worse, Cynan, jump on them.

"A fox," Griffin confirmed, sounding just as relieved. He ran a hand through his hair and sighed. "Let us get some rest. It's the best thing to do for now. We only slept a few hours last night and since we won't set off again until tonight, we might as well make the most of the opportunity. There's naught to fear. Eryr will wake us up if anyone approaches. You heard how he reacted to the fox."

"Yes." He was right. They needed to rest to be able to ride safely tonight.

"Go see to your needs first," he instructed her, nodding at the opening's entrance. "I will go after you."

Though she had snatched a moment of sleep on the horse earlier, Jane was so tired she fell on the carpeted ground as soon as she walked back through the opening in the rocks. She didn't even hear Griffin return.

~

The smell of roasted meat was what woke Jane up, or so Griffin supposed. This was good timing as he had just decided that the rabbit was cooked enough. When she opened her eyes, she found him crouching by the fire, spit in hand, ready to remove it from the flames.

"Good evening."

The unusual greeting for someone who was just waking up melted his heart at the same time as the sight of her set fire to his loins. In her reclining position, with her eyes half closed and a smile floating on her lips, she was a picture of sensuality.

"Good evening," he answered, mouth dry.

"Have you even slept?" she asked, rolling to her side.

This proof of concern for his welfare reduced his rapidly melting heart to a puddle. "Yes. Don't worry about me. I feared I would wake you up when I brought the wood in and got the fire going, but you never even stirred."

"No. Like my father, whom I take after in every way, I always sleep soundly." She twisted her lips, as if she would have preferred to be a light sleeper. "At least, I do when I feel safe. As Geraint's captive, I haven't been able to get enough sleep so this was sorely needed."

Of course. She wouldn't have been able to relax since her

abduction, constantly wondering when Geraint or the men would come to her, always on her guard and looking out for chances to escape. With luck, a whole day spent sleeping would have helped with her exhaustion. She sat up, looking impossibly neat, when he felt each and every day he'd spent on the road keenly. How did she do this? Who didn't look mussed upon waking up from a sleep on the forest floor? Jane Hunter apparently. With her hair falling in its usual sleek sheet over her shoulders and her miraculously uncreased dress, she appeared ready for an audience with the King himself. Only one dried leaf had dared come mar the effect.

"Wait. You have... Just here." He reached out to remove the offensive leaf from the side of her head. Their gazes locked, green against blue. Griffin's breath caught in his chest. By the saints, but she was beautiful. Dizzyingly so. How had he ended up alone in a cave with a woman like this? It could only lead to trouble.

"Thank you." She reddened and set about smoothing her hair. There was no need. With the leaf gone, she looked just as perfect as usual.

Griffin shuffled back toward the fire, fearing what he would do if he stayed too close to her. He might brush the side of her cheek, pretending there was dirt on her face, he might reach out to straighten the bodice that was perfectly fine. He might draw her into a hot, passionate, decadent kiss, a kiss he had no right dreaming about. She was a lady, damn it all, and not for the likes of him.

"I put a snare outside before going to sleep," he told her, clearing his throat. Much better to explain what he had done than imagine how her mouth might taste. Like honey and rose petals, probably. "When I woke up, there was a rabbit caught in it. I roasted it, to go with the bit of bread I had left in my saddle bags. I also filled the wineskins. There is a river not too far. Are you hungry?"

"Yes."

Her enthusiasm wrenched a smile from him. She was so artless, sitting on the ground without complaint, when she was probably more used to carved chairs and plump cushions. Without further ado, they started eating.

Griffin could not believe what was happening. Watching this elegant lady eat the simple fare he'd prepared as if it were the most prized delicacy sent flutters to his chest. She ate like no one he knew, with small, precise gestures. The straight, white teeth bit into the bread as if it

were the consistency of a cloud, the dainty fingers held the rabbit leg as they would a delicate object about to shatter, the pink tongue licked the juice from her lips with swift, maddening flicks. Damnation, he wanted to take hold of her hands and lick them clean, he wanted to taste the sweetness of her lips, he wanted...so much more.

He swallowed his last mouthful of rabbit with difficulty. His body had gone as taut as a bow string, and he wasn't sure how long it would be before the roaring in his blood dissipated.

"Night is falling," Jane observed, glancing toward the slit between the rocks.

"Yes. I think it's safe for us to ride and start heading west."

"Us?"

She whispered the word, as if she'd not imagined he would accompany her to her destination. He bristled at the mere suggestion. What else did she think he would do? Abandon her here with no money, no horse and no protection? As if he could do such a thing! Or was there another reason behind her question? Now that she was free, was she saying that she would rather he did not stay with her? Everything within him rebelled at the idea, and he forced his answer through gritted teeth.

"Yes, us," he said, forestalling any discussion. "I will escort you back home, if you allow me."

Allow him?

Jane's whole body collapsed in relief. She had been about to beg Griffin to do just that, even if it was not fair of her to ask such a thing. After having spirited her away from the camp successfully, he might think his role over. With his conscience clear, he could now leave her and return to his own life.

Though she didn't want to be parted from him, she forced herself to offer him the option. "You've done enough already. I cannot ask you to—"

"You didn't ask. I offered. And I won't take no for an answer. You need protection, not just from Geraint's men. The roads are not safe for a woman on her own, and you are not a villager but a rich lady, which is to say you are twice at risk. And of course..." He threw a furtive glance at her stomach and lifted his chin, determination etched on his face. "I would have escorted you even if you had not been with child."

Jane blushed. They had been interrupted by the fox earlier, but it was time to tell him about her lie. After what he had done for her, she could not carry on with the pretense. Not only was he doing all he could to protect her, but he also worried about the safety of her supposed child. The least she could do was to ease his mind on at least one account.

"There is something I have kept from you," she started, as she stood back up.

"*Yet* another thing, you mean, like the fact that you speak Welsh?" He smiled, standing up in turn.

Heavens, but he really had a beautiful smile, Jane reflected for the tenth—or was it the hundredth time? His lips were perfect, full and firm. How would they feel against hers? Soft or demanding? Jane had kissed a few men in the last two years, or rather she had been kissed by a few men whose heads had been turned by her dazzling beauty, or so they claimed. And it had always been a disappointing experience, nothing like she had imagined. They kissed her in triumph, not real desire, like victors claiming a prize everyone had been after. Griffin wouldn't do that. He would kiss the woman she was inside, not the pretty face he wanted to parade to the world. With him, she would not be disappointed. What was more, she knew she would not simply let him kiss her, she would kiss him back, and live the moment to the full.

"Yes. There is yet another thing," she breathed, pushing such thoughts from her mind.

"Let's hear it then."

"I-I am not truly with child."

He blinked, and looked at her stomach once again, though it was covered with her cloak. "But how...We all saw—"

"The day I was captured, while alone in the blue room, I placed my shift around my waist to make it appear as if my waist had thickened, and I've been careful to always wear my cloak ever since. Thankfully, as it is the middle of winter, Geraint saw nothing odd in that, and no one thought to keep checking if my stomach was still the same shape."

"Yes, of course they wouldn't." He ran a hand over his face, as if he could not believe what he'd just heard. "You're really not with child then?"

"Really." He didn't seem to believe her, but she wanted to reassure him. There was only one thing to do. "See for yourself."

With those words, she opened her cloak and placed one of his hands on her stomach. Under his palm he would feel softness, nothing like the taut stomach of a woman carrying a babe.

"No," he croaked, looking at the fingers splayed over her middle. "You're most definitely not with child."

It was only when his hand slid around her waist to draw her closer to him that Jane realized her mistake. She should never have put his hand on her. But it had seemed the natural thing to do. It was as if this man had been born to touch her, as if he owned her, and she him. It was a ludicrous thought but how else could she explain this connection between them? Under his palm her skin was heating up, in her chest her heart was quivering like a trapped bird. Could he feel it?

"I'm relieved to be able to stop pretending," she said in a whisper, staying in his embrace when she knew she should draw back. "I was dreading one of the men seeing me without my cloak before we reached Castell Esgyrn and understanding I had lied about the babe. I'm sure Geraint would not have been best pleased to know he'd been tricked."

"No, he would not."

Griffin sounded relieved as well, but for a slightly different reason. After days worrying about her child's welfare as well as her safety, he would be able to relax marginally. Now he only had one person to protect.

"So, my lady. You ride as well as any knight, you speak Welsh like a native, and you're not with child." He tilted his head in mock concern. "Is there anything else you are keeping from me, I wonder? Is Jane even your real name?"

"Yes, my name really is Jane." She tried to smile but could not because indeed there was something else she was keeping from him. Something she could never reveal. How attracted she was to him, had been from the start, how ardently she wished he would kiss her now that they were alone and he was holding her in his arms.

She reddened. What would Griffin think if he knew what she was thinking about right now? He was still holding her tight against him, but he'd made no move to lower his head. He was not interested in kissing her, only in establishing what secrets she was keeping from him.

Well, she would have to keep that one at least.

When she stayed silent, he drew back and cleared his throat, as if suddenly realizing he should not have held her so tightly against him. Jane swallowed, bemoaning the loss of his warmth against her side, of his hand on her waist. This embrace had been like none she had ever experienced but he seemed to think he'd taken unforgivable liberties.

"Come," he said gruffly. "It's dark enough now. We should go."

Chapter Seven

Directly in front of them, framed by rows of dark, skeletal trees, the full moon rose from under the blanket of clouds, as red and glowing as a fire ember, almost shimmering with evil intent. Jane shivered. There was something unsettling about the whole scene, ominous almost.

"What is it?" Griffin asked, his voice low and reassuring in her ear. He would have felt her tensing against his chest.

"The moon... It's like the eye of a devilish creature. A dragon of some sort, looming over us, ready to pounce."

He let out a soft laugh. "Ah, my lady, such fanciful musings. 'Tis the moon, nothing more. Surely you've seen it many times before?"

Of course she had, but tonight it appeared different, swollen and menacing, glowing over the horizon, bursting with malevolence, nothing like the usual benign presence guarding them from up above. She shivered again when it slid back under the veil of clouds.

"It's all right," Griffin murmured, tightening his hold around her. "I'm here, I will not let anyone, even devilish dragons, get to you."

"No. I trust you."

What would she have done, out here on her own, Jane asked herself for the tenth time? Thank God he had fled with her.

To distract herself from the unease the moon had created inside her, she asked him what she had wanted to ask him for days.

"How is it that you own a destrier?"

With his powerful rump and strong neck, Eryr had obviously been bred to carry knights in armor to battle, not to work in a farmer's field. Even Geraint, who was clearly a man of some means, had not possessed such a splendid stallion. As Lord Sheridan's daughter, Jane knew just how expensive a warhorse could be. A man like Griffin would never have been able to afford a mount destined for a nobleman.

"One day, about six months ago, the local lord organized a tourney," he started to explain. "The English knight who won it was a young, proud man. Though he was gravely injured in the last melee, he refused to let it be known for fear of dimming the prestige of his victory. He rode away from the castle, pretending everything was fine. I found him outside my cottage the following morning, lying in a pool of his own blood. He'd fallen from his horse straight into the geese pen."

Jane almost laughed at the undignified image. "What a fool. It is not as if there was anything shameful in sustaining an injury during a melee. It happens all the time."

"I wouldn't know. I have never been to a tourney."

"No. Of course," she mumbled. Why had she said something like that, which only highlighted the distance between the two of them? "Well, I'm telling you, he was a fool for hiding his injury and riding away before he could be seen by anyone. What prestige is there in ending up lying face down in a geese pen? None, I should think."

Griffin let out a snort. Evidently he agreed with her. "I

brought him in, but my efforts to save him were in vain. As he lay dying, he urged me to take good care of his horse, who was his most precious possession. I did, as I had no idea where to send him anyway. His original name was Conqueror. Not wanting to keep such an unfortunate, English name, I renamed him Eryr, though I'm not sure why."

"It was a good decision," she said with a smile. "Conqueror is indeed an unfortunate name for a Welshman's mount."

"Yes, I thought so."

Just as they had last night, they set up camp as the first sunrays pierced the horizon. The risk of discovery being considerably less than it had been the previous morning, they didn't waste time trying to find a hole like they had the day before, instead choosing a place buried deep in the middle of the woods. Unless Geraint and his men scoured every bush they came across, they would never see them where they were. Besides, as she knew, they were not on the obvious route.

All night they had traveled in happy companionship. A lord's daughter and a farmer's son should not have anything in common, but Griffin was surprisingly easy to talk to, mischievous and sharp, and she found herself laughing out loud more than once.

Though this was not something she would have dared admit to anyone, it was refreshing to be able to enjoy a man's attention without worrying about hurting Siân's feelings. Jane had started to feel self-conscious from a young age, when she had seen how people treated the two of them differently. Men usually ignored her shorter, clumsier, supposedly less beautiful sister whenever she was around, praising her elegance and poise instead, not sparing a glance for Siân, who was relegated to the role of observer. It had been embarrassing, even if, fortunately, Siân had never seemed to mind the men's lack of interest. Of course, now, Jane knew why. Her sister had not been interested in catching anyone's attention, for she had been biding her time until Christopher, the man she'd elected to marry from a young age, finally fell in love with her. Mercifully, he had. Ignoring her slightly unpolished exterior, he had seen her sister for the gem she was and married her. Her new brother-in-law had never even spared a glance for her, Jane, the much praised "beauty of the family." He was the only man who'd never given her the impression he wanted to bed her, for which she was grateful. It would have been unbearably awkward otherwise.

As to Griffin...

Griffin might well want to bed her. Jane had not missed the gleam in his eyes when he looked at her, but unlike the other men, he did his best to hide his desire and never caused her any unease. From the start he'd wanted to protect her. He had saved her from a dire fate, seen to her comfort, was doing everything he could to alleviate her fears, and he was even making her laugh. With him, she could be herself, or rather, a more accomplished, more complete version of herself. She was not reduced to the way she looked, and she did not have to worry about hurting her sister's feelings.

It was very satisfying.

"Why did you end up with men the likes of Geraint?" she asked once the fire was roaring. It was not as cold as it could have been, but a light breeze had picked up and the warmth of the flames was welcome.

He sighed, as if he'd asked himself the same question too many times. "He came to my village a few weeks back, asking for someone who could speak English. No one was better placed than I was to do that. As I wanted to leave anyway, and had my own horse, I jumped on the opportunity to go with them. Obviously, I had no idea what he needed an interpreter for, or I would never have agreed to have anything to do with any of them."

Still, it would not have taken him long to see what kind of men Geraint and his companions were. They could not have inspired trust in him with their rough manners and hostility, especially Cynan. Why had he been so desperate to leave his village that he'd ignored all the clues?

The question was out before she could wonder at the wisdom of asking it out loud.

"Did you leave because of a woman?" Wasn't that always the way? And Griffin was far too handsome not to have attracted female attention.

"I did," he confirmed, his voice raw. "A woman I thought to marry, if you'll believe it. Only it turned out she didn't want me."

"Was she ma—" Jane stopped before the word "mad" could escape her lips. But really, what woman in her right mind would refuse to marry Griffin, especially if they were lovers already? "Was she married already?" she improvised. "Was that what the problem was?"

"No. But she never wanted me. All she wanted was a child." He threw a few branches into the fire while he pondered on what to say next. "I took precautions when bedding her at first but then she told me that she was taking plants to prevent conception, and I did not question it. I had seen her drink various potions, so why would I? In any case, I thought that we could always marry if there was a babe, because fool that I was, I had started to have feelings for her. And soon, I started to suspect she might indeed be with child, despite the potions she took in front of me. I confronted her one evening and she admitted she had never tried to prevent anything. The potions were just a decoy destined to fool me. She had planned it all from the start and she was now a few days late."

How awful to be deceived thus. Jane could only imagine his

reaction. She threw a twig in the fire to avoid meeting his gaze. "So, what happened?"

His answer was crushing. "Nothing. The morning after our discussion, she vanished. That same day another man from the village disappeared. I was told by a neighbor that the two of them had been seen kissing many times. By all accounts, I was the only one who wasn't aware of their relationship."

"Oh, Griffin, I'm so sorry." Jane was horrified because he was right. The woman had never wanted him, only to become a mother. She'd started to bed him with the sole aim of getting with child, abusing his trust, pretending to take potions to make him give her by stealth what he didn't want to give willingly. Then once she'd achieved what she wanted from him, she had fled with another lover, a man who would get to raise the child instead.

It was a terrible betrayal.

Griffin shrugged, as if he cared not one way or another but she was not fooled. The woman had hurt him deeply, so much so that he had agreed to follow Geraint in a bid to get over the pain.

"Perhaps the two lovers had found out that the man was barren and would never give her the child she craved. Perhaps she only met him after she'd met me and thought she'd rather raise the babe with him, I know not. Only... I confess that for one night I imagined myself as a father, and it was—" He stopped but she could all too easily guess what he had not said. He'd already fallen in love with his unborn child, and he felt the loss of it in his bones. "I'd always thought I would name a son I would have Llywelyn, after the last prince of Wales, who by coincidence was killed in December '82, the same month I was born. It seemed a good way to put an end to the taunts about me not being a loyal Welshman."

"Yes," Jane agreed, though in truth, she doubted the fools

who despised him for being half-English could be made to see reason. "What about your sister? Where is she now?"

He'd mentioned an elder sister the other day. Had the woman left the village before him, in an effort to flee the taunts she would have been exposed to as well, and rebuild her life in a new place?

"In her convent. She became a nun about ten years ago." The way Griffin said that told Jane he disapproved of the choice. Why? Had the woman been forced into the holy orders, even if she didn't have the calling, as some sort of penance for her parents' supposed sin? As if he'd heard her musings, Griffin carried on. "She decided it was best if she never married and never bore children who would be mocked for their English heritage."

"Oh. That seems..." Jane wasn't sure what to say. A shame? Harsh? Cowardly? She could not speak her mind, not when Griffin seemed upset enough already.

"Yes, exactly," he said as if he knew better than she did what she meant. "From as far back as I can remember, she's been ashamed of our parentage. We never really got on as children. As youths, it was even worse. She is intensely religious, and rather judgmental. I often think it is a good thing our parents died before they saw the sort of woman she had become. I wouldn't be surprised if she had told them that their union had been a sin."

Now Jane was sorry she had asked about his sister. After the woman who had betrayed him, this was another painful topic. Perhaps it was best to put an end to this conversation and try to get some rest. She was not really tired; the light of the timid winter sun dancing through the leaves and Griffin's body next to her made her feel more alive than she had felt in months. Nevertheless, she suggested they slept a little.

"That way we can perhaps set off later in the afternoon."

"Yes," he agreed, settling himself in a shallow depression that seemed made to offer travelers a well-deserved rest. The whole forest floor was carpeted in dry moss, making for a surprisingly comfortable bedding, much better than the hard stone floor and brittle leaves of the previous night.

Jane found herself a suitable spot a few feet away from the fire, underneath a majestic oak. It was not long however before she realized that, as soft and welcoming as the hole was, there was a major problem with it.

"Is anything the matter?" she heard Griffin ask when she turned over in search of what she needed.

"I'm cold," she finally admitted. Yesterday between the rocks, they had been sheltered from the wind but today, despite the cloak wrapped tight around her, she was shivering. "I... Could I get closer to the fire—and you? I think there is room enough for me to lie next to you."

Griffin swallowed. This was going to kill him, but how could he refuse? His priority was to make Jane comfortable. It *was* cold out here in the open, even if it could have been worse, considering it was the middle of winter. There would indeed be enough room for both of them in the moss-covered hollow but only if she nestled against his flank.

"Yes. Come."

A moment later, she was lying down next to him. Before he could do anything, she turned to her side and draped herself over him like the most wonderful blanket. And suddenly the cold didn't matter anymore.

Nothing mattered but their proximity.

"I'm used to sleeping with my sister, you see," she said by way of explanation. Though he doubted she entwined her limbs with Siân in the way she had just done with him, Griffin didn't comment. It suited him perfectly to have her all over him, whatever the reason. "Of course now that she's married, we'll never share a bed ever again."

She sounded as if she regretted it and he wasn't sure what to say, or even if he was required to answer. He remained silent and closed his eyes, savoring the feel of her in his arms. This was heavenly.

"Have I thanked you for rescuing me?" Jane whispered after a while.

Eyes still closed, he smiled to himself. "Only about a dozen times."

"Well, then I should do it another dozen more, because I also need to thank you for having stayed with me. I would be cold and scared without you."

The image she was painting was so dire his hold around her tightened. "You need never be scared, or cold, not while you're with me."

"I know. You make me feel safe, brave, and...beautiful."

He blinked. Surely he wasn't the first, or even the only man to do that? She was so stunning he could not imagine anyone not noticing it when they first laid eyes on her. Men, in particular, would fall over themselves to be the first to pay her a compliment. "Do not tell me no man has ever praised your beauty?"

"Yes, they have." She sounded utterly unimpressed, as if the attention had not pleased her. When she spoke again, her voice was hoarse. "But with you it is different. You never give me compliments or comment on my supposed beauty, yet you make me feel like the most precious woman in Christendom, not just beautiful but precious as well. You make me think of forbidden things. You make me..."

Don't ask, his reason warned. *Make sure she means what you think she means,* his body urged.

"I make you...?" his mouth said, making the final decision.

"For the first time in my life, you make me want to do this."

Jane moved, and the next thing he knew, her lips, the lips he had dreamed about for days, were on his. They were so full, so sweet, so perfect, that he groaned deep into his throat. It was just like he had imagined. No, it was a thousand times better. She had climbed over him, as warm and soft and trusting as a kitten. Her weight pressing over his body was stealing his sanity. And then she started to undulate, grinding her hips against his groin.

Stars shot up his spine.

Go drapia! He wanted to kiss her all day. He wanted to stop kissing her immediately and run as far away as he could. He couldn't move; he could only devour her like the forbidden, delicious treat she was. But he had to stop. He could not surrender to temptation with a woman like her. It was not right.

"Jane," he managed to say between fiery kisses. "This is madness. Ask me to stop."

"Never."

Jane was adamant. She would never ask Griffin to stop something that felt so delicious, something she wanted so badly. Finally, after days of longing for it, she was kissing the man she desired above all others. Nothing would make her put an end to the moment. How could she convince him?

Tentatively, she licked his bottom lip—and was instantly rewarded for her audacity.

With a grunt Griffin bucked from under her to reverse their positions. She was now lying on her back, trapped between the soft moss lining the forest floor and the hard, masculine body lying atop hers. Perfect. How had he guessed she'd wanted him taking over, needed him to help her overcome the last of her hesitations? The woman in her, so new to these delights, needed him to be all man, and not let her inexperience ruin the moment. He rose to the challenge magnificently, by giving her a deeper, even more scandalous kiss and then lowering her bodice to bare her breasts to his gaze. His gestures were slow and reverent, as if he could not believe he was being allowed to undress her. Just before her nipples were revealed, he stopped, giving her the opportunity to protest if she wanted.

She did not. He gave the final tug.

"Jesus Christ, Jane," he whispered when she was exposed, his voice trembling with emotion. His eyes had caught on fire; his body was taut with need. "I... Can I?"

Instead of answering, she placed a hand at the back of his nape and lowered his head until his lips had closed around her nipple. "Suck me," she ordered, wondering where she had found the courage to be so shocking. Perhaps he had only meant to touch her. But suddenly she needed his mouth on her, his tongue. "Hard."

He complied all too readily, licking her, teasing her, drawing her taut nipples into his mouth one after the other, behaving as if he could not get enough of her, as if he were the one benefiting from the caress. It was glorious, each pull tightening the knot of fire in her belly a little bit more. Need was gnawing at her core.

"You need to ask me to stop." Griffin sounded agonized, but thankfully he didn't roll away from her, didn't cover her breasts again. "Now. For I am powerless to resist." Another series of licks on her beady nipples made that clear.

"Don't resist," she ordered. Why would he? Couldn't he see she wanted him?

Her lower body started grinding against him of its own volition, in search of...something. Friction? Heat? She didn't know, for this was new to her. The few times men had kissed her, she had not felt the need to press herself against them or search for anything. Then again, she had not been lying under them at the time, with her breasts exposed and her nipples wet from their kisses. Nor had they been anywhere near as irresistible as Griffin.

"Jane, this is wrong. We need to stop." He sounded agonized. "As wonderful as it is, it is wrong."

What was he talking about? Nothing had ever felt so right.

"Please, you can't leave me now. I need you, I need to make the aching stop," she said in a near sob. There was a dull weight tugging at her core, a heat throbbing between her legs. It was unbearable, like an itch she would never be able to scratch on her own, her body's way of telling her she needed a man. This man. "I ache, and I don't understand how to make it stop."

"Hush. I understand." His voice had been reduced to a purr. "And I'll make it stop," he added in Welsh.

A hand stroked along her hip in a loving gesture, then started to gather the hem of her gown. Callused fingers glided over her naked thigh, starting at the knee, creeping higher before settling over the place that demanded to be touched. The relief brought by his warm and assured hand was overwhelming. He understood exactly where she ached, and he clearly knew how to give her the relief she needed.

"Yes, right here," she breathed, lifting her hips higher to increase the pressure over her folds.

"I know. Allow me."

Another kiss prevented her from talking, even supposing she had wanted to. As he started to stroke her, Griffin groaned low into his throat, sending ripples of pleasure skittering over her lips. While his tongue explored her mouth, lower down, his finger probed and stroked, went round in circles and then pushed in, before retreating and teasing her some more. It was not long before every move blended into the next and she lost track of what he was doing. All she knew was that she'd been hot before, she was now scalding, she'd been swollen with need, she was now bursting. She was—

"Griffin!"

"Yes, *cariad*, I'm here, let yourself go."

She did—and her soul spasmed out of her body. Her whimpers of ecstasy sounded like nothing she had ever heard and added to her delight.

When she opened her eyes, her cheeks were wet with tears she wasn't aware she had shed. Griffin was looking at her with fierce, possessive intent.

"I... I..." What was she trying to say? She had no idea.

"I know," he said, nevertheless. "It can be overwhelming."

Yes. That was exactly what it was. Overwhelming. While she lay there, reduced to a pool of satisfaction, he restored order to her bodice, covering her breasts once more then wrapping her cloak tight around her. Had she been cold earlier? She couldn't remember.

A strong arm drew her to his side, which felt like her rightful place. "Come, let's rest a while. We will ride some more in the afternoon."

Jane blinked. How could he think of the afternoon, after what they had done? She would have protested, argued that they should talk but someone had thrown sand into her eyes, and stuffed her mouth with a soft cloth, or so it seemed. She understood she was going to fall asleep and did her best to fight the sensation.

A heartbeat later, she had fallen into delicious oblivion.

Chapter Eight

Griffin could still feel Jane's silky lips on the tip of his tongue. Her taste still filled his mouth. Honey and rose petals, just like he'd imagined, enhanced by a subtle scent of something earthier, like...was it freshly baked bread? Toasted by the fire? With a hint of smoke? It could well be, even if it was a surprising scent for a lady. He'd imagined she'd smell like some exotic, costly spice a farmer's son would never get to sample.

What the hell had happened earlier? One moment they had been about to go to sleep, and the next she'd been draped all over his body, kissing him to within an inch of his life. He had not seen any of it coming. They had shared an expected moment of intimacy, talking about Ffion's betrayal and his sister's inability to accept her heritage, and the next thing his finger had slid inside her wet heat.

How could he have allowed himself to lose all sense of propriety thus?

Admittedly, she had been the one taking the initiative, but he should have stopped her.

Griffin groaned. Stop her? How exactly could he have done

that while his blood was on fire? It had been impossible not to kiss her back when she had thrown herself at him. From then on, it had been only natural to take over and roll her under him. Once she'd been lying on the moss hole like a gem in its velvet box, he had not been able to resist the temptation of baring her breasts. And as soon as he'd seen them in all their glory, he had known he would not move until he'd savored their round perfection and transformed the soft pink nipples into taut little peaks. From then on, what had followed had been inevitable. How could he have refused Jane the pleasure she so clearly craved? She had begged him to make the aching stop, but there had been no need.

He would rather have cut off his own arm than deny her what she wanted.

The oddest thing was that he had not felt any frustration when Jane had fallen asleep in his arms a moment ago. Well, his manhood had been painfully hard, of course, and it still was stiff as a lance now, demanding its prize, but the pleasure of seeing her surrender to his caresses, of gifting her with what no other man had, of feeling her spasm around his fingers had been more than enough to satisfy his mind. His arms wrapped protectively around her, he finally fell asleep, wishing they could remain like this until dusk.

But if one thing was guaranteed in life, it was that all good things came to an end.

Griffin woke up to a sensation of cold after what felt like a very short sleep. His eyes shot up to the sky overhead, which could be seen above the swaying trees. While they'd slept, it had gone heavy with clouds and the wind had started to blow fiercely. Damnation, a storm was brewing. They would have to leave before it descended upon them.

Leaving Jane to sleep a moment longer, he went about saddling Eryr then came back to the hollow to wake her up.

"Jane. My lady." His finger glided over a velvety cheek and followed the delicate curve of her jaw. He hated having to disturb her when she was evidently tired, but they had to leave. The forest would be too dangerous a place to be in a storm.

Slowly, with his caresses, he coaxed her back to consciousness. She hadn't lied about being a deep sleeper. The thought caused a smile to bloom on his lips. Was he destined to find everything about her endearing? It appeared so.

"Jane," he repeated.

"Mm, Griffin?" she mumbled, rubbing her cheek against his hand in an instinctive reaction. "What is it?"

"I'm sorry to wake you, but a storm is brewing. We'll need to find shelter."

Slowly, she sat up and looked around, bewildered. "A storm?"

"Yes." The temperature had significantly gone down, and the branches around them were creaking dangerously. There was no time to lose. "Come. Eryr is waiting for us."

He helped her up on unsteady legs. Coward that he was, he was glad to have an excuse to leave without delay, because he was not quite sure he would have resisted the temptation of another kiss had they woken up in each other's embrace. And now that he knew what kissing the delicious Lady Jane led to, he could not take the risk.

After vaulting onto the saddle, he steered the horse toward a fallen log and hoisted Jane up in front of him, in her customary place. As soon as they'd exited the forest, he nudged the stallion into a trot.

"Where will we go?"

"I remember seeing a village beyond that hill," he answered, talking above the howling wind.

"Yes, so do I. Mayhap someone will agree to let us sleep in the stable for the night?"

Behind her, Jane felt Griffin recoil at her suggestion, as shocked as if she'd just said they could spend the night rolling in pig waste.

"In the stables? A lady cannot—"

"It will be better than being out in the open in our wet clothes," she reasoned. "Sleeping on hay will not kill me. Didn't I survive a night, or rather a day, on the stone floor of a cave? A stable will not be worse."

Jane could sense the struggle going on in his mind and forced herself not to laugh, knowing Griffin would only think she was mocking him. She was not. She loved how determined on offering her every comfort he seemed to be, even while they were on the road, and fleeing men intent on hurting them.

"Very well," he said eventually. "There seems to be little choice. The rain won't hold off for much longer."

"No." The horizon was now a deep shade of purple. The blue sky of earlier had been completely swallowed by the mass of swirling clouds and the sun was nowhere to be seen.

"We won't reveal your identity," Griffin said, launching the horse into a canter. "That way if Geraint and his men ask around, no one will tell them they saw a lady in the village."

Jane nodded. Saying that she was the daughter of Lord Sheridan, who was well-known and liked round these parts would no doubt help convince people to offer them shelter but Griffin was right. In the circumstances, it was better if no one knew who she was.

"So... Shall we just be a husband and wife traveling together?"

It was the obvious solution, considering they were unaccompanied and riding the same horse, but Griffin seemed reluctant to agree, as if fearing she would be offended by the notion. This time she couldn't prevent a smile. How could he be so self-assured and so timid at the same time?

"I cannot presume— " he started.

"You're not presuming anything, I'm the one suggesting it. We don't want to raise suspicion," she reminded him. It was the important part. "I will make sure to speak Welsh within the people's hearing so they don't think me English. Remember, Geraint and his men think I cannot speak the language. If they ask around, they will be told about a Welsh woman traveling with her husband, not about an English fugitive lady and her escort."

"Of course. You are remarkably resourceful, you know that?"

She didn't. At least she hadn't, not until the moment she had been abducted, which was perhaps not surprising. Her life had been free of danger and fear, so there had been no need to resort to trickery of any sort. But it pleased her to see she was indeed capable of taking the initiative when need be, and that Griffin appreciated her efforts. To him, she was more than a beautiful woman, even if he did desire her.

Heat flooded her when she remembered what had happened earlier that day. Because of the storm, they were acting as if she had not thrown herself into his arms and kissed him with all the passion she was capable of. As if he'd not bared her breasts and suckled her for long, delicious moments, groaning his appreciation all the while. As if he'd not coaxed explosive pleasure from her quivering body and left her limp as a rag doll in the aftermath. But these things *had* happened. For the moment they had to find shelter, but she wondered what would happen once they were free to look at one another and talk.

It started slowly, but the fine drizzle drenching the land soon became a veritable deluge. Jane hunched her shoulders and burrowed further into Griffin's embrace.

By the time they reached the village, they were both soaked

to the bone. Griffin led them to the first farm that had a barn at the side. From the way he banged at the door, Jane feared no one would open, thinking, quite understandably, that they might be under attack, but she was wrong. An old lady appeared through the door crack, thereby demonstrating considerable strength of character.

"What do you want?" Despite the abrupt question, she didn't sound unkind.

"Please, my wife and I have been caught by the storm and require shelter for the night."

"We are on our way home after a visit to my cousin in town, and did not see the storm coming," Jane added, making sure to be heard speaking flawless Welsh, as planned. "We set off in the morning, thinking it a fine winter's day."

"Mmpf, fine as it was when it started, anyone could have known it would turn in the afternoon," the old woman said, clearly thinking that young people these days didn't know anything. "Still, I suppose I could allow a poor, exhausted woman and a strapping young man to sleep in the hay tonight in exchange for a favor on the morrow?"

"Anything," Griffin agreed.

"The door of the barn is in sore need of repair. Perhaps you could see to it before leaving?"

He glanced at Jane as if to ask her opinion. She nodded her agreement, even if the repairs would mean a delay. After all, they were not in a desperate hurry to get to Castell Esgyrn. The important thing was to get warm and make sure not to be captured again.

"Of course," she told the woman. "Rhys will set your door to rights in no time."

She had chosen her brother's name for her supposed husband, thinking she had more chance of remembering the fake name if it was one she was familiar with. Griffin wrapped an arm around her waist, indicating he'd understood he was to answer to the name of Rhys from now on.

"If we could bother you with a blanket or two and some food and drink, I will also strengthen this one before leaving," he added, gesturing at the door hiding the interior of the cottage from view. "It looks about to fall apart as well."

"You have yourself a bargain, young man, though I was about to offer food and blankets anyway." The woman's eyes gleamed. "I cannot let your lovely wife freeze and starve, now, can I?"

"Thank you, you're very kind." Jane found it hard not to blush. Though she had been the one suggesting she pose as Griffin's wife, she could not help feeling embarrassed.

They waited, shivering in the rain, while the old woman went in search of the promised items, A moment later, she reappeared, a wicker basket and two blankets in hand.

"Here," she said, handing everything to Griffin. "You'll find all you need in there. Good night to you."

The Lord help him.

Eyes screwed shut, face turned to the door, Griffin was doing his best to control the surge of desire flooding his body.

Behind him, Jane was getting undressed. To his shock, as soon as they had entered the barn, she had announced that they would have to discard their wet clothes and wrap themselves in the blankets before burying under the hay. She was right, of course, it was the only way they would get warm and dry, but...

But there was an obvious flaw with this sensible plan. The thought of her naked under the loose blanket was creating havoc in his mind. And this was nothing. He already knew she would be too cold to remain far from him. Just like she had in the forest, she would want to nestle inside his warmth. How was he to stand it?

"I'm ready," she called out after a short while. "It's your turn."

Griffin started to undress without turning around. Would Jane turn her back like he had done, or would she watch him? Between the storm and the fading daylight, it was rather dark in the barn. Perhaps she would not see much, even if she decided to spy on him. What would she think of his body? Had she even seen a naked man before? Doing his best not to betray his unease, he made quick work of disrobing and putting the second blanket over his shoulders. Damnation, it was too small to cover the lower part of his body as well, the one he most needed to keep hidden from view. Having no other choice, he wrapped the piece of cloth around his loins.

There. Now all he had to do was to will his erection down and he would be quite presentable.

He turned around, hands in front of his groin. Jane was sitting on the straw, her legs folded under her, her wet hair falling over her shoulders. His throat went dry. She looked so sweet and innocent, yet so alluring at the same time. Without her fine gown, she could have been a villager, just like him, a woman he could touch.

A woman he could kiss. Suckle. Lick. Devour. Possess.

"Aren't you cold like this?" she asked, when she saw he was bare-chested.

Well. No, not exactly. His skin was admittedly covered in goose bumps but there was a fire roaring in his veins that warded off the worst of the cold.

"I'll be fine," he grumbled, taking a healthy swig out of the flagon of ale. "The blanket is too small to do anything else anyway." He had insisted on giving her the bigger blanket and he was, well, as the old woman had said, a strapping young man, not a slender lady. No wonder the piece of cloth barely covered him.

"Come in the hay, next to me," Jane suggested, reclining down. "'Tis warmer."

Oh Lord. Didn't she have any idea of the temptation she presented, half-naked and lying down thus? Evidently not.

"I cannot."

"You must. I will not have you catching a chill just because you are trying to preserve my modesty."

He was not, or at least, not only. He was trying to preserve his sanity—and her innocence. If they lay side by side in their current state of undress, nestled in a warm cocoon, he would not be able to resist the urge to do what he'd been aching to do since he had set eyes on her. This morning, by some miracle, he had been able to stop himself, but he was not sure he could be so sensible a second time.

But making love to her was the last thing he should do. Not only, as a lady and a virgin, was she utterly out of reach, but he didn't want her to think he had helped her escape just so that he could take advantage of the gratitude she felt for him.

"Please, Griffin. You know I'm right. Besides, I'm cold as well."

"Very well." If she was cold, then there was nothing more to say. He would not have her catch a chill.

Holding the basket of food in front of him so as to hide the very noticeable bulge tenting the blanket, he walked over to her.

"I might need to get warm, but you need to eat," he decreed, settling himself next to her. Perhaps eating would provide the distraction he needed.

"Yes. I am rather hungry," she conceded, sitting up.

And little wonder. She had barely eaten in the last few days, too scared, he imagined, to have much appetite, and the slice of bread they had shared this morning had been too small to satisfy either of them. In the basket, Griffin found a bowl of stewed turnips, an onion, some bread and the yellowest cheese he had ever seen. Not quite the feasts Lady Jane Hunter would enjoy at Sheridan Manor, but it would have to do. Taking the single knife, he cut himself a slice and handed her the rest of the chunk. He consciously avoided looking at her while she ate, having already seen that the blanket revealed more of her creamy shoulders than was wise. She didn't seem to mind, but he did not need the extra provocation. The temptation to rip the blanket off her gorgeous body was already gnawing at his insides.

All too soon the food was gone and there was nothing else to do but lie back down. Griffin took one last swig of ale for courage and gritted his teeth.

"Let us sleep now," he said, burrowing into the hay.

Sleep.

Of course, that was what they should try to do but Griffin already knew it would be a long while before he could relax. As he'd predicted—or rather, feared—Jane had nestled herself against his flank as if it were the natural thing to do. She seemed to think that because he'd given his agreement to having her in his arms in the morning, it was now the way they would behave with one another from now on. He was not sure it was a good idea, but what could he do? He wanted her by his side, even if he should not.

Besides, he needed the warmth. It was winter, after all, and he was half naked under the paltry blanket.

"Griffin?"

Oh God, the hoarseness in that voice... He knew he would not like the question that was coming but he answered, nonetheless. "Yes?"

"That woman from your village who treated you so appallingly. Was she the only woman you'd ever bedded?"

This was not quite what he'd expected her to say, but the subject was still too intimate for him to be at ease. "No," he said, clearing his throat. He was eight and twenty. He'd not bedded half the village, like some of his friends, but he was not without experience.

"Was she a virgin before...before you?"

"No, which is why I suspect she was already seeing the man she fled with."

A silence. "Of course. I'm sorry, I should not have asked you this, only I'm—"

"I do not bed virgins."

There. It could not be clearer. He did not bed virgins, so he would not bed her, no matter how much he wanted to, no matter how much she begged. Would she accept the idea and put an end to her questioning?

She did not.

"You do not bed virgins, yet you bedded me?"

"I didn't. I only gave you pleasure."

Christ. A spark of need ignited his loins at the memory. Did they really have to discuss what they had done in the forest while they were half naked and lying in each other's arms?

"Yes," Jane sighed. "Pleasure such as I had never dreamed possible." She pressed herself tighter against him. Her hand, light and soft, landed on his chest. Griffin gritted his teeth. He did not bed virgins, he repeated in his mind incessantly, in an attempt to ward off temptation, and he would most especially *not* bed this particular virgin, who was also a lady. "And I want more of it. I want it all, all you can offer me."

The hand snaked a path down his chest, heading to his groin. He grabbed her wrist before she could go past his navel and feel that his body was more than ready to give her what she wanted, even if his reason was urging him to do the right thing.

"Jane, I cannot. You're a lady."

"I'm a still a woman." Oh, undeniably. The most beautiful, arousing woman he had ever seen, a woman he was aching to hold in his arms, a woman who was tempting him like no other ever had, making it impossible to hold on to his resolve.

"But I am a farmer's son," he added through gritted teeth. Couldn't she see that was a problem? "And you're a virgin."

"Being a farmer's son doesn't make you less of a man than being a lady makes me less of a woman. And you're not just any man. You're the man who helped me escape, who saved my father's life, who protected me from Cynan." She paused and he heard her swallow. "Without you I wouldn't still be a virgin, and you know it."

Griffin didn't reply because she was right. Without him, she would have been raped by now. Encouraged by his silence, she leaned in toward him.

"There is only one thing to ask, one thing to take into consideration. Do you want me?"

He closed his eyes like a man in pain. How could she doubt this? "I want you more than the air I breathe."

"Well, I want you too. You've never bedded a virgin before. But there's a first time for everything. We will share this first time together."

Christ on the cross, had he ever met a more determined woman?

"You know the first time will hurt you?" Would the reminder be enough to make her change her mind?

Of course it was not. "I'm not afraid. It might not be so bad as everyone says," she countered instantly. "Or so Siân told me."

"You discuss such matters with your sister?"

Griffin was amazed. He'd never imagined well-bred ladies discussed what went on between men and women with such candor. But he'd already had the opportunity to see that this woman was like no other. One could not trust the serene, polished exterior she presented to the world. Inside lay a passionate, fiery woman.

"Siân and I have no secrets one from the other. And I know that there is pleasure to be had in men's arms. She gets hers with Christopher. Why shouldn't I? This morning was just a start."

Oh Lord, she *was* trying to kill him. "Jane, don't talk like this."

"Why not?"

"Because I'm trying very hard to do the right thing. And this is not helping." Her wrist was still imprisoned in his hand. but he could feel her trying to free herself and resume her caresses.

"And just what is the right thing according to you?" she replied, her eyes sending sparks. "To save myself for someone I don't even know yet? To wait until a man I don't want takes by force what I don't want to give him?"

He clenched his jaw at the picture she was painting. Cynan, laboring over her while she tried to fight him off. Tomos, laughing as he took his friend's place under the eager eyes of the others, a nobleman she had not chosen taking possession of her body on their wedding night while she lay rigidly under him, enduring what he was telling her was her duty.

"It doesn't have to happen that way, though, and you know it," he rasped. "You could experience your first time in the arms of a husband you choose. You told me that your father loved you; surely he would not marry you to a stranger you do not desire?"

"No, he wouldn't, which is why I'm still unmarried. And I say a woman should be allowed to choose who enters her body, especially the first time. I have chosen you, the man who protected me and was selfless enough to give me pleasure without expecting anything in return this morning. Anyway, I don't want to talk about this or anything else right now." With a dramatic gesture, she tore the blanket from her body and sent it flying to the other end of the barn, revealing her naked, perfect body to his gaze. "Griffin, I want you to make love to me. I want you to be the first to possess me. I want you to give me pleasure. Please."

He knew he would not be able to resist such a plea. He might, just *might* have been able to resist his own desire, but he could not deny Jane what she wanted. Before he knew what he was doing, Griffin had taken her in his arms and rolled her under him. Discarding his own blanket, he settled himself where he wanted to be, over her with his manhood poised at her entrance and his mouth hovering over her nipples.

The little nubs, a perfect dusky color in the moonlight, were beckoning to him. He drew the right one into his mouth, groaning as he started to suckle, then moved on to the next one. This was heaven, just as good as it had been this morning, so good he would almost have been content to lap at her all night.

Almost.

This time he wasn't sure he would be able to leave before he'd been satisfied as well.

"Now, please, Griffin." Jane's voice had gone hoarse. "Take me now. I can't wait anymore."

Neither could he. To make sure she was ready, he swiped a finger over her opening. She was wet, and hot, just the way she should be. She hadn't lied. Being suckled had aroused her as much as it had aroused him and she was desperate.

"Open for me," he rasped, taking his shaft in hand to guide himself inside.

When she complied, he pushed in. Determined to take it slowly, he slipped a scant inch in at first, but then the heat wrapping around his hardness robbed him of all thought. His body took over and he pushed all the way in, seating himself deeply in the most wonderful softness he had ever felt. There was a cry and Jane froze under him, placing her palms against his chest as if to push at him.

"Jane?" he rasped, recalled to his senses by her change in attitude.

"I-I... Wait! This is not what— Something's wrong. Siân told me it was little more than a pinch." She sounded strained, her speech was halted, like someone fighting pain and panic. Her arms were still braced against his chest, preventing him from moving. There was no need. The last thing he wanted was to resume his thrusting when she was in such pain. "It's not just a pinch. It's much worse than that."

Griffin thought he might retch. He had hurt Jane; he was still hurting her, merely by being inside her. What the hell was wrong with him? He had known this was a bad idea, and yet he had allowed himself to be persuaded, he had let what his body was telling him overrule his better judgment. He'd suckled her first, admittedly, and ensured she was wet enough to welcome him in, but still he had pushed inside her with one uncompromising thrust. Of course she would be in pain.

"It's all right, sweetheart, we'll stop." Although it was too late to save her reputation, it was the only thing to do. He could not make love to a woman he was hurting.

"No, it's fine, I'm sure it will pass," she whimpered, trying to hold him in.

But there was no way he would continue now, even if he'd wanted to. He had gone soft as soon as he'd seen the grimace on her face. Gently, he withdrew and looked at her, trying to ascertain the extent of the damage. There was the faintest trace of blood on her pale thighs. His heart constricted. This was his doing, *he* had hurt her. He had never hurt a woman in his life before, even unintentionally, and he had never felt worse than he did now.

"Jane," he said to himself, appalled, as he wiped her clean

with a corner of the blanket he'd retrieved. "I'm so sorry. Please forgive me. You know I've never bedded a virgin before. I didn't know it would be that painful or I wouldn't have—"

"No, you couldn't have known, and I don't think it's like that for everyone." Thankfully, she sounded more like herself, not panicked anymore. And perhaps she was right. After all, everyone's body was different. "I told you, Siân felt no more than a pinch. You didn't do anything wrong so there's nothing to forgive."

"No. Still."

Griffin was finding it hard to focus with Jane's womanhood exposed to his gaze, the folds all pink and glistening and perfect amidst the dark curls. He'd gone hard again, and his mouth had started to water at the idea of tasting her most secret place, the one he'd just hurt. This urge he would not fight. It would certainly soothe her and allow him to atone for being too rough.

"Let me kiss it better," he growled, leaning toward the sweet temptation.

Jane lifted herself onto her elbows, a frown on her face. "What do you mean, kiss it b—*ah!*"

The sound she made when his lips landed on her core almost sent him over the edge. It made no sense. What was it about this woman that called to him so? Breathing, he focused on the feel of her heat against his tongue, slick and swollen with need, softer than anything he'd ever put in his mouth. He would make this moment last, the pleasure would not only be for her, but for him also.

His tongue slid upward, lingered a moment over the little nub nestled between her folds, then licked a path back down, all the way to her most secret entrance. Jane did not protest, did not do anything to stop him. Instead, she started to pant. After a few slow, languorous circles around her entrance, he pushed past the muscles keeping her closed, determined to offer her the soothing softness of his tongue where she'd had to endure the painful invasion of his shaft. Jane bucked so hard she sent his head reeling.

"Easy," he murmured. "Let me do this. Keep your legs wide open for me."

"But I'm going to die," she whimpered.

"No, you're going to soar."

Having uttered the words, Griffin stopped talking. He needed his mouth and his tongue if he was to fulfill his promise. Jane's fingers entwined themselves into his hair to anchor him in place. It seemed that despite her protests, she wouldn't do anything to stop him, quite the contrary. Her legs had gone rigid with tension, her breathing ragged. Her release was not far.

Satisfaction swelling in his chest, he closed his lips over her most sensitive place and sucked. It wasn't long before she surrendered. On the fourth pull she gifted him with the most precious gift a woman could give a man. She let out soul-wrenching moans, her body arching and writhing in pleasure. By the time she stopped moving Griffin was out of breath himself.

The world stilled; silence descended back into the barn. Jane opened her eyes, which had gone a shade darker, and said in a breathy voice. "Thank you."

"It was my pleasure." Truly.

"But you... You never..."

"Hush. Forget about me." He'd already had more than he deserved tonight. Smiling, Griffin wrapped a blanket over her, then settled himself next to her, the second blanket covering them both. "Now you need to sleep."

Chapter Nine

G riffin woke up with Jane's hand wrapped around his cock. Outside, dawn was already breaking, and yet it felt as if he'd only been asleep a moment.

"What are you doing?" he croaked. He was hard, possibly harder than he'd ever been in his life. Whether that was due to it being the morning or because her dainty fingers were holding him so intimately, he didn't know, but one thing was sure. As long as she kept holding him thus, his shaft would not soften. They were lying side by side, both naked and she was breathing down his neck, her desire audible. What man would not be aroused in such circumstances?

"I want to try again," she said, her voice barely above a whisper. How long had she been awake, watching him, waiting for him to wake up so they could resume their lovemaking? His whole body trembled at the thought.

"Jane, we—"

She interrupted him by giving his hardness a squeeze. "Since I am not a virgin anymore, it won't hurt. And I want you, even more than I wanted you last night. Please. You didn't reach your release, and yet you brought me untold pleasure twice. I want this. I want to feel you inside me this time, when I..."

Instead of finishing her sentence she hid her face in the crook of his neck—and bit him. It was a gentle bite, but he felt it all the way to his toes. In that moment he knew he would take her. As she'd just said, he had not reached his release last night or the morning before, and his control had been tested to its very limit. He needed her.

"Tell me what you want," he rasped. "We don't have to do what we did last night, there are other ways you might prefer." Would she rather take control? If that was the case, he'd be too happy to let her and watch her sumptuous body while she rode him, breasts jutting forward and back arched.

He felt her shake her head. "I know there are many positions lovers can use, but I want to be under you, I want to watch as you thrust inside me. I want to open my legs wide for you, I want to feel your weight above me, like I did last night. I want you to be the one in charge, because I don't know what I'm doing, and I want this to be good for you also. Please, take me as you need to take me."

Dear God in Heaven, why had he asked her to talk? Never had he heard a woman say more shocking, arousing words. It was as if she had poured liquid fire down his veins. She wanted it to be good for him? It would be good, no matter what.

"Jane," was all he said before rolling over her. Her legs instantly came to cradle his hips, the gesture proving both her readiness and her impatience. "Wait. First, I needed to prepare you." This was going to cost him what was left of his sanity, but he would do the right thing by her. Being in charge didn't mean being rough. "You need to be wet, I'm not risking having you—"

"I'm already wet. I...touched myself as you slept, looking at you, imagining you inside me and it got me unbearably aroused. I'm ready for you."

Bloody hell.

Griffin stared at her; his body taut as a bow string. This had to be the single most erotic thing he'd heard in his life, and he had no idea how he'd stopped himself from coming there and then. Instead, he positioned himself at her entrance and felt on the tip of his shaft the proof that she wasn't lying. The soft folds were soaked, ready to welcome him.

Unable to resist, he pushed in, slowly, inexorably. Ah yes, heaven.

"Christ, you're so hot, so tight," he rasped, his mouth at her temple. "You feel so incredibly good."

He felt incredible too, Jane mused with the small part of her brain that had not been burned up by desire. This was nothing like it had been the evening before, when she'd thought Griffin was tearing her in half. Watching him earlier while he slept, feeling his manhood warm up and lengthen in her hand, picturing him poised over her, his eyes aglow with desire, had sent her to the edge of madness. She had imagined him surging inside her and reaching his pleasure at the same time as her. But as wonderful as the images had been, they could not begin to compare with reality. Her whole body was on fire, and she knew she had made the right choice by asking him to be the first man to take her. This was perfection.

"I'm not hurting you, am I?" she heard Griffin ask, tension in his voice. He had stopped and was holding himself very still inside her.

"No. There is no pain this time." Only wonder.

As if that was all he'd waited to hear, he started thrusting in earnest, bringing his mouth to her neck, where he deposited little, maddening kisses, licking, sucking at her flesh. Jane arched her back, desperate to welcome him deeper, to feel every inch of his member as it plunged in and retreated, bringing her closer and closer to the bliss she had already experienced in his arms, first with his fingers, then with his mouth. This would be different again, but just as spectacular, she could sense it.

"Yes, just like that," she moaned. Now she knew what people meant when they said that making love was the most pleasurable thing a person could experience.

It was ecstasy.

For a moment she allowed her pleasure to build, then Griffin's rhythm faltered slightly. She opened her eyes and saw that his were glazed with indescribable emotion, something like desire and vulnerability combined. Her insides rippled in response, and she knew her release would not be long in coming.

"More!" she urged, arching her body in search of the friction she needed.

"I... I have to withdraw, now, or it will be too late," he said in a desperate rasp. "I need to— I'm going to—"

"No! Wait, just another moment, please."

He couldn't leave, not yet, not now, when the wave was about to crash through her. Jane tightened her legs around him, locking her ankles behind the small of his back to keep him in place. She was so close, she just needed a moment more, just another thrust, another—

It happened without warning. When pleasure finally overcame her, she bit Griffin's shoulder to stop herself from screaming and alerting the whole village as to what was happening inside the barn. He stilled in turn, and groaned, his head thrown back, the sound agonized.

"Oh fuck, Jane, I..."

Heat scalded her insides, prolonging her ecstasy. When he collapsed over her, his breath coming out in short, ragged pants, she understood that her release had triggered his own, and he'd not been able to withdraw in time.

Though she should perhaps worry about the consequences of her folly, she could not bring herself to. The whole thing had been too perfect.

Griffin slid to the side, covering her left breast with a large hand. "I'm—"

"Don't be. If one of us is at fault, it is me."

He had warned her, he had wanted to withdraw, and she had prevented him by locking her ankles behind his back. Well, she thought with satisfaction, at least this time he, too, had reached his pleasure. Her inexperience had not been a problem.

"Sleep," she ordered, just like he had ordered her the night before.

There was no answer, no protest. Smiling, Jane watched as Griffin's eyes fluttered and he succumbed to oblivion.

When he finally came to after the most powerful release of his life, Griffin was lying on his back, with the two blankets wrapped over his naked body—and on his own. He bolted to a sitting position. How long had he slept? And where was Jane? Surely she had not decided to leave for Castell Esgyrn on her own? He knew she felt guilty about him escorting her home, so she might have decided to relieve him of the supposed burden she represented, now that he had ruined her. He knew she had been the one demanding it, but he was still not convinced he should have agreed to bed her.

To think the day he'd met her he had thought he would have given anything to be in the position he was now! He hadn't counted on the guilt that came with the incredible pleasure. He felt like a man who had despoiled a sacred place by entering with his shoes full of mud.

Putting on clothes that were still damp and cold was not pleasant to say the least, but Griffin barely paid it any heed. He had to find Jane, see that she was all right, see that she was still here at least.

Outside the sun was shining over the village, in complete contrast to the storm of the previous day. Frantic, he looked around for a tall, graceful shape dressed in green. Elegant as she was, she would stand out amongst the villagers as surely as an emerald amongst pebbles. Eventually, he found her by the river at the back of the barn, staring into the distance like someone trying to find answers to an unsolvable problem. Relief swept through him. She hadn't left, she was still with him, she was safe. Then doubt replaced relief. How should he behave?

He approached gingerly, unsure what to say.

"My lady, I—"

"Don't you dare!"

Jane swiveled around, eyes ablaze. Griffin's heart plummeted at her forceful reaction. Despite her previous assurances, it seemed that now her body had gotten the release it needed, she regretted having given herself to a poor farmer's son. He'd feared this might happen, and yet when it did, it tore his heart in two. Not her, as well. Ffion had wanted nothing more than his seed; Jane had wanted nothing more than a chance to experience the pleasure her sister was getting with her husband.

She'd not wanted him for who he was. Well, of course she hadn't. He was nothing compared to her.

"I—"

"Don't you dare call me 'my lady' after what we did, do you hear!" She was bristling with indignation and he saw instantly that he'd been wrong. She'd been incensed at his use of her title, nothing more. His whole body relaxed. Thank God. He could breathe again. "I couldn't bear it, not now. I'm Jane to you, always will be."

"So, you don't regret—"

"I regret nothing. I wanted you, and you did exactly what I needed you to do. Everything was perfect."

Perfect. Yes, it had been. And yet... "But you seemed so pensive when I found you."

Her shoulders sagged and she averted her gaze. "Well, if you must know, I'm embarrassed."

"Oh sweet, I'm so sorry." As he'd feared, he had been too forceful, too assertive, he'd made her feel used. As if that were not enough, he'd not been able to withdraw from her in time. When she had closed her legs around him, he would have needed the strength of two men to free himself from the delicious embrace. He hadn't possessed the strength of half a one. "I should never have—"

She cut him off by coming to stand straight in front of him. "I'm not embarrassed by you, or by what we did." She hid her face against his chest, and he thought she breathed in his scent, such an intimate thing to do. His heart missed a beat. "I'm embarrassed by my reaction to it all. I made you stay inside me, I screamed my pleasure, and I was utterly—"

"No." He stopped her before she could berate herself for being too wanton. "It is as you said, everything about what we did was perfect, *you* were perfect. A man's dream." His dream. Just as unattainable. "You could never be anything other than perfect if you tried. And if you are guilty of losing your mind around me, then I am guilty of the same. I'm not myself when I'm with you. Everything about you makes me wild with lust. When you talk, your voice caresses over me. When you laugh, your joy makes my heart burst. When you moan, my groin aches. When you walk and sway your hips, it sends me crazy with longing."

"It does?" She sounded hopeful, no longer ashamed.

"It does."

Jane was amazed. Did she really swing her hips when she walked? She had never noticed. Nor did she think her voice particularly pleasant. Or her laugh. Or her moans. It mattered not, as long as Griffin liked them.

"And *you* are every woman's dream," she said, cupping a hand over his cheek. After almost a week on the road, he was now wearing a beard, the hairs on his jaw a shade darker than the ones crowning his head. He looked just like a Welsh rebel, *her* Welsh rebel, who had risked his life for her.

Her lover, who had just made a woman out of her.

"I don't know about being every woman's dream," he mumbled, leaning into the caress.

Jane's heart broke when she understood that he meant it. His life spent fighting against prejudice had made him think that people despised him; his misadventure with the woman who had betrayed him had made him believe women could not be genuinely interested in him.

"I do," she said earnestly. At least he was the dream man she had never thought to find. "I wish I could—"

"Young man. There you are at last! I believe you have a door to repair? Leave your wife be, she'll still be waiting for you tonight, when my door doesn't let in any more draughts!"

The old woman had appeared from the back of the barn, a walking stick in her hand and a twinkle in her eyes. Jane reddened and drew away from Griffin as quickly as if his body had suddenly caught on fire. With her hand on his cheek, his arm about his waist and their faces inches away from one another, they would indeed appear as if they couldn't keep their hands off each other. Looking caught out himself, Griffin ran a hand through his hair. After their night spent in the hay, it was deliciously mussed. He had never looked better than in this moment.

"Newlyweds, hey, I gather?"

What to say? Mercifully, the kind villager didn't seem to require confirmation. By all accounts, she had made up her mind about the two of them already. Jane noticed her gaze had fastened on a point at the side of her neck and remembered the way Griffin had nibbled and suckled on her skin while he'd pumped inside her. Dear God, had his teeth left a mark? She barely resisted the urge to cover it, not wanting to draw further attention to it.

As could have been predicted, Griffin was the one to put an end to the awkward moment. "I'm coming," he told the old woman, straightening up with decision.

"Give your wife one last kiss if you must, but make sure you leave it at that. We don't have all day. I'll be waiting for you in the cottage to give you the tools you need."

A moment later she was gone and Jane's whole body sagged in relief. She felt like a naughty child caught with her finger in a pot of freshly cooked jam.

"I have to go," Griffin said, looking contrite. "I wouldn't put it past the old woman to beat me over the head with that stick of hers if I dally too long."

Jane let out a giggle, relieved he was helping her get over her embarrassment. "No. You'd better go. After all you did promise to repair the door. Do you want some help?" she asked, as she followed him back to the barn.

He looked amused. "Why didn't I guess you were skilled in carpentry?"

"I'm not, as you know perfectly well. But I can carry planks and hold things up for you."

"Well then, yes, that would be most helpful."

His answer pleased Jane. Most men she knew would have mocked her lack of skills, or insisted a lady had no place handling tools. Griffin saw her offer for what it was, a way of ensuring they wasted as little time as possible, and he was grateful rather than condescending.

When they reached the barn, Griffin stopped and turned to her. Without warning, he removed his tunic, grabbing the collar at the back of his neck and pulling it over his head in one fluid motion. He was not wearing his shirt underneath, so his smooth chest was revealed in all its tanned, muscular glory.

"W-what are you doing?" Jane's heart had gone to her throat at the sight of such beauty.

"It will be easier to work without this, and besides, it will give it chance to dry in the sun. Fortunately, it is a warm day." He nodded toward her. "It's not pleasant to be wearing cold, damp clothes, as I'm sure you'll agree."

"Yes," she conceded, looking at her dress. It had been difficult to put it on this morning, and she did not enjoy the way it was clinging to her body. "But I cannot do like you and remove my—"

The words got stuck in her throat when his eyes sent sparks. "You would not hear any complaints from me if you decided to leave your gown and shift to dry in the sun while you lay naked as the day you were born. I would watch you until my eyes burned."

Jane tried to swallow, found she could not. The image he was painting was so lascivious... "Would you?"

"Yes. But I agree it wouldn't be the wisest thing to do. So let me go get the tools from the woman while you finish what is left of the ale and bread," Griffin said, his voice rougher than usual.

Before she could answer, he turned and left. Shaking herself out of her torpor, Jane did as he'd instructed and entered the barn. There was just enough ale left in the flagon to soothe her dry throat. She drank it gratefully. A moment later Griffin was back, carrying tools—and a woolen dress.

"Here. I'm not certain it will be the best fit but at least it will keep you warm while your clothes dry in a patch of sun."

Jane's heart leapt at the idea of slipping on something warm and dry. She really was quite uncomfortable in the damp dress and shift. "Our friend lent it to you?"

"Yes." He winked at her, stealing her breath. "I think she's taken quite a liking to 'the strapping young man' that I am. She says I remind her of her Alfie, whoever that is."

Of course, he would have charmed the woman. Old or not, she was still a woman. How could she have refused a bare-chested Griffin anything, especially if he'd given one of his bone-melting smiles?

"Thank you. I'll get dressed immediately."

Intent on giving Jane privacy, Griffin disappeared through the door. It had been a good idea to ask the woman—Enid, as she'd told him her name to be—to lend him a dress for his "wife" while her clothes dried.

It was only when Jane reemerged from the barn in the russet dress that he wondered if he had not made a mistake, after all. The kind villager was a wizened old woman, and the dress had been made to fit her. On her small, fragile body it would no doubt look innocuous. On a tall, buxom lady who was femininity itself, it was almost indecent, and he could tell that Jane, though she could not see the effect as well as he could, was aware of it. Her slender ankles were revealed by the frayed hem of the dress, her sensual hips were molded by the thin material, and, most daringly of all, her breasts were threatening to spill out of the bodice.

He could have stared at the glorious sight all day, but he forced himself to look her in the eye, not wanting to embarrass her further.

"I hope it's all right," Jane said, tugging at the top edge of the bodice, which rode very low on her chest. "It's a bit tight."

Mm, yes, and it wasn't the only thing that was tight. The braies plastered to his lower body suddenly felt as constricting as if they'd been made out of iron. Griffin shifted on his feet to try and ease the discomfort.

"It's fine," he said, clearing his throat. Yes. As long as she stayed at the barn with him, it *was* fine. Besides, she needed to dry her clothes. That was the priority. He could not have her uncomfortable or worse, catching a chill because they'd tried to preserve her modesty. "But if you're cold, you could always drape one of the blankets around your shoulders."

"Of course." She gave him a grateful smile that melted his bones. "Why didn't I think of that? Well, I will go and put these next to your tunic and shirt then," she said, gesturing at the gown and shift she was holding.

Leaving him to stare at her swaying hips, she made for the field at the back of the barn. Once she was hidden from view, Griffin focused on breathing again and set his mind on the task ahead.

Forget the lady in russet, he had a door to repair.

"Can you pass me that piece of wood over there?"

Jane made to lift the largest of the planks Griffin had deposited against the wall earlier that morning. His preferred method for reinforcing the crumbling barn door had been to dismantle the whole thing and build it again, using the half dozen planks old Enid had gathered from kind neighbors as a base.

"Sometimes it's better to start anew, rather than try to patch up things that will end up needing attention later on, anyway," he'd argued.

She couldn't agree more, and she had enjoyed watching him

in a carpenter capacity. A noblewoman raised in a castle, Jane had only ever seen men undertake duties and tasks that befell noblemen. Her world was inhabited by knights riding destriers and sparring with swords and maces, by lords reading through ledgers and ordering servants about. The grooms in the stables had been the only men she had seen doing any sort of manual work, but that had always revolved around horses. She had certainly never seen men hammering nails into pieces of wood, roasting rabbits over a fire, patching up their own boots or digging holes in the ground, all things she had seen Griffin do in the last few days.

She took hold of the plank and let out a yelp when a sharp sting hit her. "Ow!"

"What's the matter?" In the blink of an eye, Griffin had dropped his hammer and rushed over to her.

"'Tis nothing. A splinter."

She held her hand to the light to see where the offending piece of wood had lodged itself—in the fleshy part of her left thumb. It was sticking out slightly and would be easy to remove, at least. As she raised her other hand to do just that, Griffin wrapped his fingers around her wrist.

"Let me."

Before she could agree, he'd taken her thumb into his mouth. Her body instantly went liquid, for the sensation was incredible. She felt his tongue move slowly over her skin as it tried to locate the splinter and she remembered what he had done to her with that wicked tongue the night before, when he had soothed the pain of his possession. The place between her thighs, the one he had licked with thorough deliberateness, started to throb in remembrance, then to burn, indicating in the only way it could that it wanted to be licked again.

Griffin didn't seem aware of what was going on inside her. His attention was wholly focused on the task at hand, removing the splinter that was hurting her. He didn't seem to think that having her thumb inside a man's mouth would arouse a woman but, though Jane did not understand why that might be, it was undeniable. She *was* aroused. All too soon, sharp teeth closed over the shard of wood and pulled. Looking her straight in the eye, Griffin spat the offending splinter on the floor. Jane's core spasmed and she groaned in disbelief. Dear God, but she was turning into a veritable wanton.

"I'm sorry, did I hurt you?" Griffin asked, concern in his eyes. He'd mistaken her groan for a sign of pain.

"N-no." With her legs reduced to the consistency of stewed apples and her tongue melted to a puddle, she could hardly stand or talk.

"Is it not too painful?" His thumb caressed over the place where the splinter had been.

"N-no," she repeated, utterly under the spell of the moment.

They stared at one another a long time, him towering over her with his chest golden in the dying winter sun, her with her heart reduced to a quivering mess. She thought of Siân, who'd told her that while she was courting Christopher, he had once licked honey from her fingers, and she had almost passed out from the sensations. Jane had thought at the time that her sister had exaggerated but she now understood that she had not. Griffin had only taken her thumb in his mouth, very briefly, and she had almost swooned. What she would have felt if he'd licked and sucked each of her fingers in turn did not bear thinking about.

"Jane?"

She blinked. "Yes?"

"Are you all right?"

"Yes. I'm all right." Or at least she would be in a moment, when her sanity had returned.

"Are you sure?"

"Yes. I'm all right. I'm sure." He arched a questioning brow. She reddened and then repeated. "I'm all right. Yes. Thank you very much. Please carry on. With the d-door, I mean, not with the... Yes, with the door, I mean."

Looking as if he were fighting a smile, Griffin nodded and resumed the hammering of the wood.

It took longer than she had anticipated, but by the time he declared himself satisfied with his work, Jane was able to think straight again.

"So, you really are left-handed then?" she asked, looking at the hand holding the hammer.

"Yes." He arched a brow. "How did you know I was?"

Heat invaded her cheeks. Why did she have to ask the question when the reason she suspected he favored his left hand was that she had marvelled at his dexterity in the forest, when he had brushed at her folds with such expertise. She had wondered at the time if he would have been as skilled with his right hand. Although, he probably would, now that she thought of it. The man was made to pleasure women.

"I didn't know for sure, but I suspected it from the way you handled Eryr," she lied.

"Mm." he didn't seem convinced, but mercifully, he let it go. "Let us see to the cottage door now," he said, picking up the rest of the tools. "It should not take long, as it's only a case of seeing to the hinges."

"I'll go get our clothes back before the chill of the evening sets in."

They would be dry by now, so she had better bring them inside the barn before they got damp again. Though she had placed them in the sunshine earlier on, she found them in the shade, Still, she was pleased to see that they were indeed dry when she gathered them up.

"*Noswaith dda,*" a masculine voice said from behind her.

Jane's heart stopped for a moment. Was this one of Geraint's men? Had the rebels found her? Dropping the clothes at her feet, she turned around. No sense in trying to run. If this really was one of her abductors, she would not get far. But it was not. A ginger haired man she had never seen before was standing behind her, smiling. Everything within her relaxed. Not one of the rebels who had abducted her, only a villager.

"Good evening," she echoed, smiling back in her relief.

"I'm the cooper's son, freshly arrived in the village. But I don't think I've ever seen you before?" he asked, leaning against a tree.

"No, you wouldn't have. I'm only here because of the storm. Old Enid offered her barn for the night."

"Did she? That's kind of her." He gave a big sigh and smiled again. "Would that you had come to me for help. I would have offered you something more welcoming than a haystack."

In other words, his own pallet—with him in it. Jane was not fooled. The way the man was ogling her, with his gaze lingering on her breasts, reminded her that the dress she was wearing had not been made for a woman as generously endowed as she was. There was a glint in his eyes she had not seen in Griffin's gaze while they worked side by side all day.

Seeing her in a dress too small for her had understandably lit a flare of desire in his body. But after the initial shock, he had made a point of not making her feel ill at ease. Keeping the blanket around her shoulders had not been practical while she'd helped with the door, so she had soon abandoned it. Griffin had already seen all of her, so there was no cause for embarrassment with him, and she had minded more the way the dress prevented her from lifting her arms than she had worried about the way it exposed too much of her bosom.

The man was renewing her discomfort, looking at her as if he were imagining her naked and under him on his pallet.

"Don't worry about me," she said, picking the clothes up again and holding them against her chest to hide her exposed bosom. "The barn was perfectly adequate."

It had been more than that, it had been the perfect cocoon to welcome her and Griffin. It had been the place where she had discovered how wonderful it was to lie in a man's arms, in *his* arms. Nothing could have been more perfect that that.

"I'm sure it was. I'm Cynan by the way." Jane's unease increased tenfold. Why did he have to share his name with the man she was fleeing? With the man who had threatened her with rape? It was time to tell him she had not come to the village alone, but with her husband Rhys, as Enid thought. Why had she not thought of that before? It was the best way to make him think twice about bothering her. "And who might you be?"

"My wife."

The two words answering the question were little more than a growl. Jane wavered on her feet, relief sweeping through her. If Griffin was here, she would be fine. The man wouldn't dare try anything. An arm snaked around her waist, offering welcome support, when her whole body sagged.

"Are you all right, Jane?" he murmured in her ear in English. He'd guessed her conversation with the cooper's son had made her uncomfortable, then. Not that it would be difficult. Placed behind her, he would have been able to see Cynan's face, and he would not have missed the glint of lust in the man's eyes or failed to understand what had provoked it—her scandalously low bodice.

"I'm fine." She gave him a smile and tightened her hold on the clothes.

"Let's go," he said louder, and in Welsh. "Our friend Enid has offered to let us sleep in the barn tonight also. A basket of food is waiting for us. Come, wife."

Without so much as a glance toward the other man, he led her back toward the barn.

~

"The man didn't touch you, did he?"

Griffin sounded mightily aggrieved by the notion but no, the man had not touched her, only made her feel uncomfortable.

"No," Jane assured him. "He'd only just stared talking to me when you arrived."

He mumbled something under his breath, and she thought she heard the phrase *drooling like a bloody dog*. She could not help a smile. Now that she was safe in the barn with only Griffin to see her, she hadn't thought it necessary to change back into her own clothes, even if her breasts were in constant danger of slipping out of the bodice. There was no rush. She could give old Enid the dress back tomorrow when they left, the woman hardly needed it for the night.

Jane swallowed her mouthful of boiled egg pensively. Without knowing why, she guessed that Griffin would not touch her once they'd taken their place in the hay. He might be worried she would be sore after their lovemaking in the morning, but she sensed it was even worse than that. He'd asked her this morning if she regretted giving herself to him. She didn't, and she had told him as much, but it was clear he regretted having given in to her.

As soon as the last bit of the cheese had been consumed, he stood up and started to arrange the hay into a comfortable hole big enough for two. At least he would not refuse to lie next to her, which was reassuring. But when she sat down next to him, he cleared his throat in embarrassment.

"Good night," he said, his voice gruff. "I'm afraid the work of the day has quite exhausted me. I need to sleep."

"Of course."

There was no other choice but to agree, but really, what sort of fool did he take her for? As if a man like him would even register the effort of lifting a few planks of wood. By helping, she had lifted almost as much weight as he had, and she did not feel the slightest strain.

He was signaling, as subtly as he could, that they would not share any intimacy tonight.

After one last nod in her direction, he lay down and closed his eyes. A moment later, he was asleep, and Jane was free to stare at him to her heart's content.

To her delight, he had remained bare-chested and the cracks in the wood were numerous enough to let the light of the bright moon penetrate the dark interior. Fascinated, she watched him fling his arms to either side of his head, the movement causing his biceps to bulge. She imagined the parts of him she could not see. The flat nipples she wished she had licked last night, the muscles on his stomach stretching underneath the blanket. Then her thoughts took on a lewder turn. Just how big was his manhood? Was there a lot of difference between its normal state and when he was aroused? It had felt enormous to her but that didn't mean much, as she had no point of comparison and to an untried virgin, any size would have felt big. But perhaps him being very big would explain why his first possession had hurt? She regretted not having asked to have a look at it before he possessed her.

Would she get another chance? Would he take her again before they reached Castell Esgyrn? Would they even have the opportunity to make love, out in the open? She feared she would not feel his arms around her ever again, because if he was determined not to give in to temptation, she wasn't sure she would find the courage to beg him to take her again. She'd already asked him to take her maidenhead; she didn't want him to think her utterly scandalous and a slave to her womanly desires.

Concluding there was nothing to do but try and sleep as well, Jane placed her head on Griffin's shoulder and her hand on his smooth chest. Without waking up, he covered her fingers with his. She smiled.

It felt as if she had found her rightful place at last.

Chapter Ten

"Goodbye, young man."

"Goodbye and thank you again for offering us shelter."

Old Enid waved Griffin's thanks away. "'Twas no bother. Besides, I really was the one who benefited from your visit. Now both my doors are sturdy enough to withstand an assault from the blasted English should they dare to venture in this valley."

Yes, the doors had been repaired, but Griffin wasn't so sure the kind woman had been the only one benefiting from their halt in the village. By allowing them to sleep in the barn, she had given him what he had never thought to have—an opportunity to hold Jane in his arms and make her his away from prying eyes. The incredible pleasure he had derived from this possession meant that his guilt was not as great as it should have been. He did feel guilty but, as much as his reason agreed it should not have happened, his body and his heart simply could not regret that night with Jane. The memory of it would sustain him until he was too old to remember his own name.

"I'm glad to have been of help," he said earnestly.

The woman cupped his cheek and sighed. "Dear God, but you do remind me of my Alfie. He was just as strong and handsome as you, you know, only he had brown eyes, not blue. I hope for your wife's sake that you are blessed with the same manly appetites as he was." She winked at Jane, who went the color of the flaming sky behind her. "And the same skill."

"I...the—"

"Yes, well, we had better be going," he said, cutting through her embarrassed reply.

Mercifully, the woman didn't add anything else. With one last nod in their direction, she walked back to her cottage.

Jane's cheeks were still flushed when he turned to her, and he found himself hoping she was not trying to decide whether his performance had been as praiseworthy as almighty Alfie's had been. He'd thought to leave her satisfied but one could never be certain... Deciding it was better not to worry about it, he busied himself with the tightening of Eryr's girth. It was time to go. They had lost a whole day already and he meant to take her to the safety of Castell Esgyrn as soon as possible.

He hoisted himself into the saddle then led the horse to an overturned pig's trough that would serve as a mounting block for Jane. At the thought of riding with her settled in front of him, his body gave a jolt. It had been hard before, it would now be torture, because he knew exactly what delights could be found in her silken, womanly depths. Oh, well, served him right for daring to pluck a fruit he had no right to touch. Every punishment he got would be well deserved and might bring some sense back into him.

"F'Arglwyddes," he said, offering his hand.

Jane didn't know whether to be amused or annoyed. Only the day before, she had forbidden Griffin to call her "my lady," and here he was, doing exactly that, but in Welsh. There was no point protesting. If she voiced her disagreement, he would argue that she had not forbidden him to use the Welsh way of address. Besides, he might well be using it simply because he was waiting to hoist her up on his stallion and so looked like a knight attending to his ladylove.

Her heart started to beat hard at the image she was creating in her mind. If only... Well, if he was going to call her his lady, she could call him her lord.

"*Diolch, F'Arglwydd.*"

With a smile, she accepted his hand and settled herself in front of him, in her usual place. A moment later, they were off.

"How long before we arrive at Castell Esgyrn do you think?" Griffin asked once the village had disappeared into the distance.

"It's not that far. Another two days, perhaps."

She suddenly wished it would take weeks. This was the adventure of her life, and she didn't want it to end. With the danger of discovery gone, all that was left was the pleasure of Griffin's company. Besides, what did she have to go back to? Nothing. No one. Now that her sister was living with her beloved husband, Jane feared her life would seem unsatisfying. With her parents who were happy with one another and in love, she would feel more alone than ever.

"Do you know why the castle is called Bones Castle?" Griffin asked. "It seems an odd choice of name."

She nodded, for this was a story she had heard all her life. "When the foundations for the castle were dug more than a century ago, two skeletons were found lying in a shallow ditch. No one knows who they were or why they ended up there, instead of being given a proper burial. Everyone has tried to come up with an explanation since, as you can imagine. My sister, Gwenllian, is adamant they were slaves escaping their dangerous master in the Roman times. When they were caught, they were summarily executed. My father, less dramatically, thinks they are two unfortunate souls who were robbed on the road and left to rot by their attackers. The servants are not above whispering stories about witches, arguing that there was something odd about the skeletons. According to them, they both had six fingers."

He snorted. "Trust people to try and see evil where there is none. What is your explanation then?"

Hers was rather silly, and the last thing she wanted to share with him. Nevertheless, she didn't think of lying. Blushing, she gave her answer. "I've always thought they were two lovers who couldn't be together and decided to die together rather than be separated."

He barked a laugh. "So very dramatic. Two ill-fated lovers, kept apart by their families perhaps?"

No. Rather, she had imagined that their respective situations in life would have precluded an alliance between them. In fact, now that she thought of it, she had thought of a few possible situations not unlike that of hers and Griffin. A lady having fallen for her brother's squire, a rich noble widow in love with her groom and refusing to remarry anyone else, the daughter of a local lord carrying the child of a poor villager.

"I was only seven when I arrived in Wales, remember," she defended. "And such an explanation is not so implausible. There are many things that can keep two lovers apart."

Griffin stilled, as the laughter died in his throat. "Yes. I do know that."

Jane's heart fell. What had possessed her to say such a thing? "I-I didn't mean—"

"No, I know. But you're right all the same. There are too many obstacles to overcome for some lovers. They are destined never to be happy together, no matter what they feel for one another."

Well, if that didn't tell her that she'd been right and he did regret their tryst in the hay, nothing would. Why oh why did the first man she took an interest in have to be someone who thought her too far above himself? She couldn't help where she was born, any more than he could. That didn't mean they could not be together. If life with her parents had taught her one thing, it was that love was the most important thing a person could have and was worth fighting for.

She stared on the road ahead, doing her best to keep her tears at bay. No point in making the moment worse than it already was. For the first time since she and Griffin had started to share a horse, they traveled in silence.

As the sky started to deepen from pale blue to a more intense purple, Jane realized they had almost reached the lake where she had learned to swim—and where once her uncle Matthew had almost died. Already? It seemed that not talking allowed them to travel at a faster pace.

"Let's head toward the village on the other side of the woods," she decided, trying not to dwell on the fact that their time together was coming to an end faster than she would have liked. "Old Myfanwy will be only too happy give us shelter for the night."

"Old Myfanwy?"

"One of my father's tenants. We are not far from Castell Esgyrn now, and she knows me. She will want to help."

"Is she anything like old Enid?" Griffin asked. "I'll admit I've grown wary of stick wielding old women who pass comments on my looks or skill in bed."

Jane let out a tinkling laugh, relieved to see him restored to his usual mischievous self. She had feared everything was irremediably spoiled between them. Reassured, she decided to tease him. "Worry not. Despite her age she walks just as well as you and me. And I'd be surprised if she found you handsome."

"Now, what is that supposed to mean?" He sounded

mightily piqued, as if she'd just said she found him ugly. But surely, he knew she was jesting...surely he'd realized by now how much she found him to her tastes? "Is it because of the beard?"

"No." The beard did not detract from his beauty in any way, quite the contrary. "It's only that she's always been more interested in the female form, shall we say."

"I see." She turned in time to see Griffin arch a brow. "Well then, 'tis a good thing you're wearing your normal clothes rather than old Enid's dress, because she might well have expired from desire upon seeing you otherwise. Do you expect to have to fend off her advances?"

"Silly. She's old enough to be my grandmother!"

"No impediment as I see it. A grandmother still has eyes, does she not?" His gaze heated up and Jane's insides responded in kind. "In any case, I'm glad we'll be able to spend the evening in the company of a nice, harmless old woman."

"Erm... I wouldn't call her harmless exactly." The way he arched his brow again made her explain. "She has an unusually strong intuition and the gift of the sight. More often than not, she gives us odd predictions which always prove true in the end. You've been warned."

"I thank you but I'm not worried. As long as she has some food to spare and a place for us to lie down, she can predict my future to her heart's content. Actually, I would be grateful to know what it holds, for I have absolutely no idea."

No idea. Which meant two things. First of all, now that he had left his village following his lover's desertion, he had no intention of returning there.

And secondly, he did not see Lord Sheridan's daughter playing a part in his life.

"What are you doing here, my lady? I understood from your sister that you had elected to stay behind for the birth of Branwen's babe?"

"I had."

Griffin kept silent while Jane explained that she had changed her mind when she'd realized that she missed her family too much. Interesting. Didn't she trust this Myfanwy with the real reason for her presence here? Or was she loath to place the old woman in danger by revealing too much in case Geraint and his men came sniffing around? Knowing her for the caring, generous woman she was, he favored the second explanation.

"Very well, you decided to come back to Wales. I can't say I blame you. But where is your horse?" The woman craned her neck to look behind Eryr. "Surely you two didn't set off from England on one mount?"

This was a valid question. No one, especially a good rider, would undertake such a lengthy journey on one horse, strong as he may be. But instead of looking caught out, Jane once again demonstrated her resourcefulness by delivering her improvised answer in a natural tone.

"No, of course not. Only, Bluebell cast a shoe earlier this afternoon and I refuse to ride her until she has been reshod. We had hoped to reach Castell Esgyrn shortly after nightfall but it is now out of the question. The farrier we found has gone to the next village, so we had to leave the mare with his wife until he came back. But as, by an extraordinary stroke of luck, we were just a few miles from here, I decided to call on your hospitality." Jane took the old woman's hand and gave it a squeeze, as at ease with her as if she had really been her grandmother. "Do you think we could spend the night here?"

"You know you're always welcome here, my lady. That is

not in question. You can have the room I keep for such eventu-
alities."

Griffin blinked. The woman kept a room to welcome weary
or lost travelers? But surely she didn't expect them to sleep in it
together? This would test his resolve not to touch Jane again to
the limit.

Before he could utter a word, the woman spoke again, not
looking at him but addressing herself to Jane. "Your escort—
Rhys, did you say his name was?—can bed in the barn with my
cow."

He had no idea if he should be more relieved that he would
not have to sleep next to Jane, appalled at the thought of
spending the night away from her, or shocked that the woman
had called him Rhys, when Jane had not yet introduced him.
Rhys had been the name she had given Enid to hide his real
identity. Could it be a coincidence? Somehow he didn't think
so. He'd been warned that the woman was gifted with the sight.
He'd doubted it at first, but he was starting to wonder.

"Thank you." Jane's gaze fluttered toward him. It was clear
she shared his bewilderment at hearing him being called Rhys—
and possibly his dismay at the idea that they would sleep apart.
Still, it was for the best.

"Now, my lady, if it's not too much trouble, would you go
get some water from the well? I was about to put the pottage on
the fire. My neighbor gave me a piece of salted pork to thank me
for the advice I gave him regarding his meddlesome mother-in-
law. We can all enjoy it together with what is left of yesterday's
cabbage."

"I'll go to the well," Griffin offered immediately. What was
the woman thinking, asking a lady to go draw water when he
was idly standing here?

"No. You, young man, will stay exactly where you are. I
need a word with you."

Before he could protest Jane disappeared though the door and Griffin was left alone with the old woman. There was an odd look in her eyes, as if she were seeing beyond where he was, to another, intangible realm. He saw immediately that Jane had been right to warn him. She was about to tell him something unsettling.

"You're a troubled soul, are you not, my boy?"

It was hard not to scoff. After all he'd gone through in the last few weeks, he would not be surprised if the strain of it showed on his face. He'd just spent a week worrying about Jane's safety, he was running for his life, and he was racked with guilt over what had happened the day before. As if that were not enough, he'd recently had a child stolen from him by his cheating lover. No need to have the sight to see he had a lot on his mind.

"Isn't everyone troubled, in one way or another? Didn't you just say your neighbor asked your advice?"

The provocation didn't hit home. Myfanwy carried on as if he had not said anything. "Fret not. What you think to have lost never was."

This time Griffin stared at the old woman in bewilderment. He had indeed lost something recently, or rather, a person. But how on earth could she know about the babe Ffion had taken from him? "What do you—"

Once again, she ignored him. "And beware of the foxglove lurking in the undergrowth. True, 'tis useful for some heart complaints, which is why I suspect you turned to it, but it can quickly become toxic. Much better to aim high, even if it seems unattainable, than to gather the first plant you see at your feet. Eagles soar high, do they not? Why did you name your mount Eryr if you did not agree?"

Griffin had been bewildered at first, but he was now starting to feel uncomfortable. Jane had told him about the woman's unusual abilities, but this went beyond all he had imagined. All he knew was that he had better take whatever the woman was saying seriously. The mention of the foxglove, which was the meaning of Ffion's name, the suggestion that he should aim for unattainable "plants," the reference to his stallion's name... It was as if she knew what was in his past—and in his heart.

Just then Jane came back with a bucket full of water. Old Myfanwy started to prepare the pottage as tranquilly as if she had not turned his brain upside down. While the women chopped onions, he volunteered to go get a couple of heavy logs in the woods. By the time they sat down to eat he was able to behave normally. During the meal, he betrayed none of his inner turmoil. And when the time came to go to bed, he left for the barn without a word.

Chapter Eleven

The night had been a restless one. Griffin had barely slept. A dozen times he had considered going to Jane. Just to take her in his arms, he'd assured himself, and make sure she wasn't cold alone in the room, nothing more. Not to bare her breasts to his mouth and gaze, not to spread her thighs open and taste her intimate honey, not to plunge inside her wet heat and lose himself in a flurry of sensations. He had sworn to himself he would never do any of that again.

Exhausted, he had finally fallen into a deep slumber—only to dream of being with her. They were in a garden, surrounded by hundreds of flowers. Jane took it upon herself to uproot all the foxgloves she could find and throw them in a big fire. Once the plants had been reduced to cinders, he'd started to climb an apple tree with the intention of plucking the branch at the very top, its snowy white blooms as fragrant as honey. When he'd finally deposited the branch at Jane's feet like an offering, she'd thrown her head back and sent her joyous laughter to the sky.

No need to have the gift of sight to know what this particular dream meant...

Still perturbed, he made his way to the well in the predawn

light. Not many people were out and about at this hour, but the few he met didn't even glance his way. Evidently, perhaps because of old Myfanwy's habit of welcoming stranded travelers, they were used to seeing new faces. The shelter where Jane had been led last night was just a few yards away. Was she awake already, or was she sleeping as soundly as she always slept, curled up on her side, her fist held tight in a ball? His heart split in two at the beautiful image.

He was splashing his face with the bucketful of water he'd just drawn for his morning ablutions when a familiar voice hit him from behind.

"Griffin. What on earth are you doing here?"

Slowly, he straightened back up and turned around, readying himself for the confrontation. Over the last few weeks Griffin had often wondered what he would tell Ffion if he ever found himself face to face with her, without ever coming to a satisfactory answer. Now the moment had come, and thanks to Myfanwy, he knew exactly what to say. Forgoing the usual greetings, he launched his attack.

"You were never with child, were you?"

She blanched at the blunt question and placed a hand over her stomach. Her very noticeably flat stomach, when, if her claim to be with child was to be believed, she should be nearing her term. Had she lied to him in good conscience, or had she made a mistake? His direct stare told her she had better tell him the truth.

"No. I thought I... But in the end, I was mistaken. I was only late by a few days."

Intense relief swept through him. Old Myfanwy had been right. *What you think to have lost never was.* What he had feared had never come to pass. He had not lost a child, there would not be a little boy or girl of his loins growing up without their real father.

Thank God.

Griffin bent down and splashed some more water on his face. The nightmare was over. He could breathe again.

"You know...making me with child didn't work then." The ill-placed cheerfulness in Ffion's voice made him turn to face her. What was she up to? Certainly she seemed to have recovered quickly enough from the shock of seeing him and having to admit to the truth of what had happened in the summer. She took a step toward him, eyes ablaze with what he could only identify as lust. "But it might now."

The hand she'd used to stroke her stomach landed on his forearm. Griffin blinked in disbelief. Was she really propositioning him, here, in the middle of the village, after what she had done to him? Was she really thinking he would accept the insulting proposition and drag her into the woods to "make her with child", in her own words?

"Thank you, but I would rather slice my balls off," he said, his voice icy.

"Come. You didn't seem so averse to having me in your arms before. The way you used me certainly indicated you found me to your taste."

"That was before I realized what you were, Ffion." A beautiful, poisonous flower, nothing less than a toxic plant. Myfanwy was right. He'd been so desperate not to be alone that he'd put all his hopes on the wrong person. How ironic. He'd considered building a life with a woman who did not want him and had then fallen for a lady who wanted him but was unattainable.

"You'll regret this!" Ffion hissed, taking her hand away at last. Griffin took in a breath of relief. Her palm had started to burn his skin through the material of his tunic. "All your life you'll think back to this moment and regret not taking the offer I made you. You will end up all alone because you are an abomination that should not be allowed to exist, you spawn of the

English devils! Your father was a traitor to the Welsh, and no one will ever want to be with you because of it."

"Why did you sleep with me if I'm such an abomination?" he asked, doing his best not to let her words hurt him.

"Why do you think? So you could make me with child and give me the one thing Huw cannot give me. I have done nothing to deserve to die childless. I'm a woman like any other." She actually stomped her foot like a petulant little girl. "It's not fair. I should be allowed to have the man I want and a baby."

"Were you that desperate that you were ready to have a child tainted with my half-English seed then?"

Her sneer pierced all the way to his heart. So much scorn! How had he not seen her for what she was before, a selfish, cruel, pathetic woman? "No one would have known who the father of my child really was. Huw and I got married as soon as we arrived here in the village. Everyone would have accepted our word that the babe was his, since the two of you have similar coloring. He was the one who suggested I go to you if you must know, for this precise reason. All the other men of suitable age were noticeably darker and too ugly to consider. I was reluctant to share your bed at first, of course, considering your less than ideal ancestry but then...then I will admit I made my peace with it."

Bile flooded Griffin's throat when Ffion's eyes lit up with lust. He'd been selected as a stud because of the way he looked, and she had allowed the farce to continue despite the contempt she held him in because she'd been happy with the way he'd serviced her. Everything had been planned from the start, by the two scheming lovers. None of it had been real.

He didn't know what to say. Toxic as a foxglove indeed.

"Is your precious Huw aware of everything we did together? Does he know that I gave you more pleasure than he did?"

She made a grimace, and he saw that he had hit a nerve. It afforded him little satisfaction, however. "Who's to say you—"

"Me. Don't think I've forgotten what happened. Should I go to your husband, tell him what his wife let me do? How she begged me to fuck her harder? How she trembled with the force of her releases every time I took her?" He'd never spoken so crudely to anyone, but his rage needed an outlet. "Do you think he would like to hear all we've done together? Things that could never result in a babe? You were certainly not thinking about getting with child when you took me in your mouth or begged me to take you in the—"

"You would never dare speak to him and tell him about that!" Ffion looked panicked at the idea of her wantonness being exposed to her husband. "He would not believe you anyway."

Griffin stared at her, not answering. Let her worry about what he would do, even if he knew he would not bother going to the man. He simply wanted to forget about the whole sordid thing and resume his life free of pain. Just when he was wondering how to put an end to the encounter with his dignity intact, a voice cut in through the tension, as welcome as spring rain over a desolate landscape.

"Griffin, there you are. I've been looking for you."

Jane appeared from behind him and snaked an arm around his waist, coming to stand right next to him. His body instantly responded the way it always did at her contact. His heart started to beat a fierce drum, his cock sprang to attention and his own arm wrapped around her shoulders. It was a shocking liberty to take amidst people who knew her as Lord Sheridan's daughter, but she didn't even flinch, as if she'd expected, or even wanted, this mark of affection.

"Is this a friend of yours?" she asked, smiling at Ffion, who had gone the color of buttermilk. Mayhap she had recognized Lady Jane Hunter and she was amazed to see that the man she had just disparaged had managed to attract such a woman. "Are you inviting her to the wedding?"

What wedding? He blinked.

"The wedding?" The expression on Ffion's face—disbelief and outrage combined—was such that Griffin instantly understood what Jane was trying to do. The wonderful, resourceful, generous woman that she was had come to his rescue. Having somehow overheard his conversation, she had decided to put the woman back into her place. The arm around her tightened in a silent thank you. Ffion would not leave this confrontation the victor. She would see that he would not end up all alone, that someone wanted him, half-English and unsuitable as he was in her eyes. And not just anyone. A stunningly beautiful woman, who had to be one of the most enviable parties around.

His chest swelled in gratitude.

"We decided last night to get married in the spring." In that moment Jane looked every bit the blushing bride proud to announce her upcoming union to the man of her dreams. No one would suspect her of lying. There she was again, improvising with ease. He watched her, utterly awed. "And you are of course invited, if you're a friend of Griffin's."

"I-I'm not, not really."

"Oh? Well, in any case, it's good to see a friendly face in this village. The few people I've met so far are not what I would call welcoming... The old woman in the cottage over there scared me with her nonsensical blabbering about wolves and that man Huw is a pig."

"Huw?" Ffion croaked. She looked about to choke.

"You know him then? Tall, blond, with blue eyes? Like a pale imitation of Griffin, only rougher and dull-witted?" Jane made a grimace and nestled herself closer to him as if in search of protection. "He...well he pounced on me, for want of a better word, just now."

Griffin's head snapped to her. He was no longer amused. "Did he hurt you?" He would kill the man if he had touched a single hair on her head. It was one thing using him in his foul schemes, quite another hurting Jane.

"No. But he was very insistent and refused to take no for an answer. He thought that telling me he was tired of his shrewish wife, and looking for spice in his life would sway me." She shook her head as she looked at Ffion. "Really, some men have no brains at all. As if I'd want such a faithless, lecherous swine to have anything to do with me when I have Griffin. Can you believe it?"

Fully reassured, understanding she was only trying to rile Ffion, Griffin fought hard not to laugh. The woman was truly fearless, instinctively knowing where to hit. There was no doubt a tense confrontation would follow between husband and wife, one where Huw would have to answer for his behavior with women. Good, because now that he thought of it, Griffin wouldn't be surprised if the man did try to sleep with all the women who crossed his path. By all accounts, he did not believe in fidelity. Hadn't he suggested the woman he wanted to spend his life with should sleep with another man? He would have guessed she was getting pleasure from the encounters, and yet he had not minded. Why wouldn't he allow himself the same freedom?

Well, they could do what they liked, as long as they left Jane and himself out of it.

Ffion never answered. Eyes ablaze with fury, she left, storming in the direction of the church, presumably to demand explanations from her husband. A moment later, Griffin was alone with Jane.

"Thank you." He was more moved than he could express. "But how did you know who Ffion was?"

"I was on the bench on the other side of Myfanwy's cottage lacing my boots when she came to you. I heard it all."

"You did?" His heart fell. If she'd heard it all, it meant she'd heard him talk with unforgivable crudeness, allude to acts a lady, no matter how unconventional her childhood had been, should never have to think about.

"I did. That...horrid woman!"

Jane could not credit this Ffion's cruelty. How had she not hit her for what she'd had the gall to do to Griffin, using him so shamelessly and then telling him he was not worth her notice, was a mystery. As soon as the baby had been mentioned, it had been clear who he was talking to, and though Jane should probably have walked away at that point, she had been unable to. She couldn't believe how unlucky they'd been. Why oh why did the woman he was trying to flee have to come live here, in Myfanwy's village?

It had not taken her long to decide to help him. As the one responsible for the confrontation, it was the least she could do. The best thing to do to put Ffion back in her place was to show her that Griffin was loved, that women did want him, half-English as he may be. No one should have to pay for their parents' decision to be together. Jane's own siblings were half-English, half-Welsh and she would take issue with anyone who dared tell her they were less worthy because of it.

"I could not sit there and do nothing," she said, bunching her hands into fists. "I'm sorry if I overstepped the—"

"Don't apologize. Ffion only got what she deserves." His eyes became hard. "But enough about her. Did Huw really pounce on you? I need to be sure." It was clear that if the man had inconvenienced her in any way, he would be made to regret it.

"No. I haven't even seen him. I only thought to hit Ffion

where it hurt. And she'd said you had similar coloring so I thought there was no chance she would doubt me."

Perhaps Griffin was right, perhaps she was unusually resourceful. The claim that Huw had pounced on her to escape his shrewish wife had certainly seemed to strike home. It pleased her to imagine the pair arguing about Ffion's husband's supposed advances on another woman. Besides, she would not be surprised if the man really was sniffing around for opportunities to break his marriage vows. What little she'd heard about him hardly painted him in a good light. A man who sent his lover to another man's bed could not be the scrupulous sort.

Well, as Griffin had said, they only got what they deserved.

"Thank you," he repeated, lowering his mouth to her ear. Their proximity made her head spin. After a rather awkward day in the saddle the day before, she was glad to see the bond between them restored.

"You've already thanked me. No need to do it again," she breathed.

"I'm thanking you for something different." His voice was raw with emotion. "Had you not suggested we spend the night in the village, I would never have seen Ffion. I would never have been able to set my mind to rest concerning the...the babe."

The babe that never was.

Jane placed a hand on his arm, compassion squeezing her chest. "I'm sorry. It must be hard for you to know she lied about something so important, to know she used you so cruelly."

"Yes. But less hard than knowing a child was conceived without my consent and will be raised by another man." This time he lowered his head so much that he actually placed his forehead against hers in a gesture of intimacy. "So, thank you. Now I might be able to get on with my life."

"I hope you will."

Would she be part of it? Now was not the moment to ask.

She instead made sure to enjoy the moment. Griffin had kept his forehead against hers and his hold around her waist had tightened. They remained like this until Myfanwy's exclamation made them both jolt.

"Finally! I see you are plucking the flower you deserve. Well done, Rhys, I knew you had it in you."

Jane drew away from Griffin, realizing they were still entwined, as if they had indeed decided to get married and had every right to hold each other in public. What was the old woman saying now? Was *she* the flower Griffin deserved? Her heart skipped a beat at the thought. After all, why not? No man was braver, more attentive, or more fascinating. No man treated her with more respect or made her feel better about herself. No man made her heart swell and her blood roar.

Why wouldn't he deserve her? Why couldn't he "pluck" her? He had already done so, in a way, by making her his. Could he one day come to accept that there might be a future for them? She dearly hoped so, because she was starting to think that, for her, there would be no future without him.

"We'll be on our way now," she told Myfanwy, eager to put an end to the awkwardness of the moment. "I would like to reach Castell Esgyrn before nightfall."

She regretted the words as soon as the expression on Griffin's face hardened. He seemed to think that whatever was between them would be over once she had been reunited with her family. But that was not what she had meant at all, least of all what she wanted. One way or another, she would have to make him see it.

Behind her, old Myfanwy started to talk, her voice oddly distant. Jane turned around, because she knew that voice. The woman was having one of her premonitions, the kind of visions she could not always explain rationally afterward. If that were the case, they had better listen.

"The giant has been sent to England, but his friend lurks around the bones, hidden in the foliage. Fortunately, the English lord has started repairs on the chapel. 'Twill be easy to slip in undetected if you burrow under the rubble. A diamond can be safely hidden amidst pebbles."

Griffin stared at her, clearly perplexed by the stream of nonsense. Jane stared back, not sure what to make of it either. Before she could ask any questions, a woman came running.

"Myfanwy! Quick, 'tis time. Nia's labor has begun, she's asking after you."

The old woman's gaze cleared, and she nodded at them, no longer a seer lost in an intangible world but a competent midwife ready for action.

"I have to go. Farewell, my lady, farewell, Rhys." She frowned. "*Is* Rhys really your name? It doesn't seem quite right somehow. Ah well, not to worry. I have to go."

"What on earth was that?" Griffin asked, as he and Jane made their way to Eryr, who was waiting by the cottage. "Giants, bones, chapels, diamonds and pebbles?"

Jane shook her head. "I told you she has these visions. We had better heed her words."

"That's all very well, but... Did you understand what she was telling us? I confess I did not."

"No, me neither," she had to concede. Still, she knew it had to mean something, possibly something important.

"Well, perhaps it will become clear when the time comes," Griffin said encouragingly.

"Yes, perhaps. It usually does." Jane could only hope it would not take more than ten years, like it had with her predication about Siân and Christopher getting married. "Let's ride."

They didn't trot once all morning. Was Griffin trying to spare his horse, now that they were assured of reaching Castell Esgyrn before nightfall or was he doing his best to make the day last as long as possible? Whatever it was, she was grateful for it, for she relished every moment spent in his arms and didn't want it to end either.

Then, as they crested a somewhat steep hill, she spotted the familiar sight of Castell Esgyrn in the distance. High atop its own hill, with the elegant north tower guarding over the squat battlements, it seemed to beckon to her, offering safety. And yet as soon as they entered the woods, unease crept down her spine. Old Myfanwy's warning rang in her ear.

The giant has been sent to England, but his friend lurks around the bones, hidden in the foliage.

The foliage—the woods closing around them.

The giant—Cynan, who'd presumably been sent to Sheridan Manor in case she fled there.

His friend—Geraint, who was even now lying in ambush, waiting to capture her before she could get to her father.

Suddenly it was clear as crystal.

"Wait." She seized the reins and pulled, bringing Eryr to a halt before Griffin could question her. They had to leave, now, and ride back the other way.

"What is it?" Griffin asked, alarm spiking through his body. What had he missed? What had Jane seen?

"Let's go back to the river," she whispered, instead of answering the question.

The river? Why? Was she thirsty? No, there was an urgency in her voice that unnerved him. Something was wrong, he just could not for the life of him think what that might be. Trusting her instincts, he steered Eryr back the way they'd come without a word.

A moment later, they were at the bridge spanning the swirling waters. Once they had crossed it, Jane jumped down from the saddle, agitation etched all over her face. He followed suit, knowing she would not keep him waiting for long. She started to pace back and forth, wringing her hands like someone trying to put order to he wild thoughts scattered through her mind.

"I think I know what Myfanwy was trying to tell us," she said eventually. "Geraint is lying in ambush in the woods, ready to block the only path leading to the gate and capture us before we can get to Castell Esgyrn. Remember, we lost a day in old Enid's village, and we cannot gallop. Whatever head start we had, we've lost it by riding double and taking a longer route. Meanwhile, the men rode flat out on the direct road to intercept us. They are here, waiting, I just know it."

Griffin clenched his jaw. How had he not thought of this before? Of course that was what Geraint would do, what anyone would do, try to stop them before they could reach the safety of the castle and warn Lord Sheridan.

"How do we get past them?" He did not even bother to contradict or reassure Jane, because she was right. They were in danger.

She gave him a tight smile. "I know not, only that it will have something to do with diamonds and pebbles."

Mm, yes. The second part of old Myfanwy's prediction. But what the hell did it mean? He still had no idea.

Unable to offer an explanation either, Jane went to the stream to have a drink. Griffin tried to think. Diamonds... How could diamonds, even supposing they had any, help them slip past Geraint and his friends? Because he was certain that Jane was right, and a whole group of men were waiting for them in the woods. The Welshman would have ridden with one or two of the rebels and could by now be at the head of a small group, recruited in the nearest village, the way he'd recruited him the previous month. There would be no fighting them. Even if he had been a knight armed with a sword, there was only so much a single man could do against ten or even five.

Stealth, not strength, would be the solution to their problem.

A noise behind him caused him to turn his head. A cart was heading their way, pulled by a sturdy horse and surrounded by half a dozen men carrying tools. Griffin's whole body surged. He already knew what the answer would be when he asked the men if they were going to Castell Esgyrn.

The English lord has started repairs on the chapel. 'Twill be easy to slip in undetected if you burrow under the rubble. A diamond can be safely hidden amidst pebbles.

The English lord—Lord Sheridan, who was undertaking works in the chapel at Castell Esgyrn, necessitating the comings and goings of workers.

Under the rubble—he and Jane could hide in the cart, under a piece of cloth.

A diamond—Jane, the most precious thing he had on this earth.

Of course. Clever old woman.

When Jane joined him again, he took her hands in his. "I know how to get into Castell Esgyrn undetected."

Chapter Twelve

"It's brilliant."

Griffin gave Jane a slanted smile. It was a rather brilliant plan, even if the merit did not lie with him but with their friend Myfanwy. Without her warning they might both have been captured by now. But thanks to her, they had stopped in time to avoid being taken and they knew how to get to safety.

They would stop the next cart of workers and ask them to transport Jane to the castle, hidden under a cloth. Even if the men thought the request odd, when they identified her as Lord Sheridan's daughter, they would not refuse to help her, knowing they would in all probability be rewarded for what they'd done. Griffin would walk beside them, his face hidden under a hood, as if he were one of them. After having seen carts come and go for days, Geraint would not even take a second glance at the workers walking past.

It was a plan brilliant in its simplicity, but he knew he would never have thought of it without the old woman's strange declaration. It really had been an inspired idea from Jane to stop in that village.

"Once this is over, I will have to go and thank her," he mused out loud.

The halt had not only given them the solution to their problem, but had also allowed him to see Ffion, and put the demons of his past behind him.

"Yes," Jane agreed with a smile. "Without her warning, I'm not sure I would have guessed Geraint was hiding in the woods, which is stupid really, because I should have known he would not give up so easily, especially when faced with retribution from Hywel, who, it is not hard to guess, will not be lenient."

No, he wouldn't be. Geraint would dread presenting himself in front of the rebel without the captive he'd been charged to get. He might very well pay with his life for the failure to bring Lord Sheridan to his enemy. Griffin cared not what happened to Geraint or his men; he would not bemoan the loss of any of them. But unfortunately, the stakes being so high made the man three times as determined—and therefore three time as dangerous. He had to be stopped, as Griffin would die rather than see Jane fall into his hands. Though, ultimately, she was not the one Hywel wanted and would be freed once they had Lord Sheridan in their possession, he still couldn't let it happen. Because then, she would have to live the rest of her life with the knowledge that her father had sacrificed himself for her and been not only killed as a result, but also tortured beforehand.

"Yes, I'm confident the plan will work. But there is one problem. Eryr," Jane said, nodding at the horse who was munching on some grass next to them. "As you say, he is quite distinctive, and not the kind of mount workers would use to pull their cart. He would give us away, as Geraint will be expecting to see him. We will have to leave him somewhere safe."

"Yes. But where?" They could not leave him tethered here

for a whole day, at the mercy of passersby. He would not risk anything happening to his faithful companion.

Jane's green eyes started to sparkle. Was she about to suggest they went all the way back to old Myfanwy's village and entrust the horse into the woman's care? Perhaps. He, at least, could not think of another option.

"How did I not think of it before?" she said, sounding full of renewed hope. "Siân and Christopher live just a bit farther along the stream. They will help, keep Eryr for us and tell us what's been happening at Castell Esgyrn."

Her sister. Of course, it was the perfect solution. He nodded and walked back to the stallion with decision.

"Let's go."

~

"Jane!"

"Siân!"

While the two sisters hugged and kissed with as much exuberance as if they had not set eyes on one another in years, Griffin stood next to a blond man who he guessed was Christopher Harrison. The man looked at the scene, an indulgent smile floating on his lips. Something tightened within Griffin, because he had started to notice that he often smiled for no reason whenever he looked at Jane. Did he look as smitten as Siân's husband appeared in this moment? He dearly hoped not, for she would not fail to draw wrong conclusions from this, or at least, the conclusions he didn't want her to draw.

She could *not* know he was developing feelings for her, had perhaps already fallen in love with her. It would have to be his secret.

"I've never seen two sisters share a closer bond, you know," the Englishman said, crossing his arms over his chest. "And yet they are not related by blood, which I think is obvious when you look at them."

Indeed the two women looked nothing like one another. Siân was slender and almost a hand shorter than Jane, who had a much more voluptuous figure, her hair was neither the same color nor the same texture, her face was that of a lively pixie's rather than that of a serene Madonna carving. Their choice of dress, vibrant red for the Welsh lady, cool green for the English one, their gestures, ranging from wild and impetuous to calm and elegant, the way they laughed, the merry outburst of joy contrasting with the discreet silvery tinkle he was used to, nothing was in any way similar.

"Yes," Griffin said pensively. "It is obvious they do not share blood."

He and his sister were the spitting image of each other, or so everyone had kept telling them when they were growing up, and they definitely had the same parents, yet they could not have claimed to share any sort of bond, close or otherwise. Growing up with her had been almost like growing up without a sibling. It was clear that his childhood had been very different to Jane's, in every way. Would he constantly be reminded that they did not belong to the same world?

"It seems to be a common occurrence in the family," Christopher carried on. "You wouldn't guess from seeing Connor and Matthew Hunter together that they are only milk brothers, even if they look very dissimilar physically as well. But they think and act as one and would die for one another. Such closeness makes you envious, really."

As Griffin had never met either man, much less seen them together, he could not offer any answer. Besides, he didn't feel it was his place to comment. Christopher turned to him, the expression on his face hardening now that he was no longer looking at his wife. Griffin was surprised to see that his right eye, which he had assumed to be blue, like the other one, was in fact brown. The effect was rather unsettling, as was the way he was looking at him. Not like an enemy would, exactly, but definitely with suspicion. This was a man one would underestimate at one's peril. Underneath the polished, carefree exterior lay an indomitable warrior, that much was obvious.

"And who are you, if I may ask?" he asked, straightening his spine. "You're not one of Sheridan Manor's men at arms, are you? What are you doing here, then? Why are you the one escorting Lady Jane to Esgyrn Castle, alone? And why are you both riding on the same horse?"

Griffin had never been subjected to such an intense interrogation, and the man was only Jane's brother-in-law. If this encounter made him feel so ill at ease, he dreaded to think what her father, a mighty lord, would do when he finally decided to talk to him.

"Well?"

The Englishman would not wait a moment longer for his answer but what could Griffin say? It was not his place to tell anyone what had happened, and he didn't want to worry Siân unduly. Jane should be the one deciding what to reveal and what to keep silent. Fortunately, at that moment, she came to his rescue. He could not help a sigh of relief, because he'd had no idea how to convince her protective brother-in-law he was to be trusted without revealing the truth.

"Stop it, Christopher, you're treating Griffin like a criminal when he's done nothing to deserve it. We'll explain everything in due time, but first, we would be grateful for something to drink and eat."

"Of course," Siân instantly agreed, leading the way to the cottage. "Forgive me, I should have thought. Come in."

It was the first time Jane had been inside her sister's new home. The interior was as wild and colorful as she was, nothing like what she herself would choose but cozy and welcoming nonetheless. Bundles of fragrant herbs hung from the wooden beams, cushions of all sizes and shapes were scattered over the low benches and a pewter vase full of greenery was taking pride of place on the solid table dominating the space.

While Christopher busied himself with pouring them a drink of ale, Siân uncovered a wooden plate with her characteristic flourish.

"Try this and tell me what you think. I've been trying to replicate Avice's recipe for honey tarts since we arrived, and I think I'm getting there. At least Christopher seems to like them."

She smiled at her husband, who threw her a look that could only have been described as smoldering. "I like everything you offer me to eat, my love."

Christopher's voice was so husky, the flame in his eyes so scandalous despite the innocent words, that Siân's cheeks went as red as the dress she was wearing, and she handed herthe tart with her gaze averted. Jane accepted it with equal embarrassment. An image of Griffin's head buried between her thighs while he devoured her had just flashed through her mind.

As she bit into the sweet, she made the mistake of looking at him. His eyes were two glittering sapphires. He, too, it seemed, was reliving the moments of intimacy they had shared in the hay and imagining her hands holding him in place against her most intimate place. For a moment, tension sizzled in the room, hot and bright as fire. Jane swallowed her mouthful of tart with difficulty.

"So? What do you think? You will know better than anyone if they taste like Avice's." Siân's voice was little more than a whisper.

"It's delicious," Jane said honestly. The sweet was indeed

reminiscent of the famous tarts they ate at Sheridan Manor. "I do think you are getting there."

A beaming smile stretched her sister's lips. "Oh, I'm glad."

"So, now that you've eaten and drunk your fill, perhaps you could tell us why you are here with a stranger when two weeks ago you decided to stay in England?"

Christopher, as per usual, did not shy away from confrontation. Nevertheless, Jane took the time to finish her tart before launching herself into the tale of her abduction and subsequent escape. By the time she went silent, Christopher's eyes had gone as hard as steel and Siân was aghast. She shot up to her feet and walked over to Griffin, tears in her eyes.

"Oh, my lord, I cannot thank you enough for what you—"

"I am no lord," Griffin cut in, looking uncomfortable.

Siân waved the comment away. "Lord or not, you deserve every praise for what you did, and I'm sure my father will agree. You saved his daughter—and very likely his life too."

"Yes, he will be grateful. The only problem is," Jane observed, "in order to get to him, we have to get past the men lying in wait for us."

"How can we help?" Christopher again, blunt and to the point. He nodded approvingly when she told him what she and Griffin had decided to do earlier that day. "A sound plan."

"I think so. Only, we need you to keep Eryr, Griffin's stallion, here. He is too distinctive not to give us away. Geraint will recognize him as soon as he sees him."

"He can be stabled with Warrior and Angel, that is no problem. And Siân and I will ride ahead of you to warn your family of your upcoming arrival so they can keep an eye on the gate in case there is a problem."

Jane smiled at him. That was a good idea. Given the gravity of the situation, one more precaution couldn't hurt. "Let's make sure we go over the last details before going to bed."

Being so close to victory she didn't want to leave anything to chance. Tomorrow, one way or the other, she and Griffin would be inside Castell Esgyrn—and safe at last.

~

"So. It looks as if you and I are going to sleep on the hard floor tonight," Christopher said, nodding toward the inside of the cottage where the two sisters were chatting merrily.

The women had decided earlier that Jane would sleep with Siân, like they had until very recently. The marital bed was situated in a little room at the back of the cottage, an ingenious arrangement ensuring the couple some welcome privacy whenever they needed it. Except that tonight, husband and wife would not lie in it. Christopher had not raised any objections when Siân had suggested the two men sleep in the main room, even though it seemed to Griffin that the sacrifice cost him dearly. He understood his disappointment all too well. Any sane man would rather share his bed with a warm woman than lie on the earthen floor next to a near stranger.

"Come. Let us drink, so I can forget I won't be able to enjoy my wife's caresses for the first time since our wedding day."

Griffin lifted his cup of mead all too readily, hoping it was strong, for he, too, had something to forget. Tomorrow he would face Jane's father. It was safe to say he did not relish the prospect, as he was not quite the hero everyone seemed to think him. Granted, he had saved Jane from Geraint's clutches, which would earn him Lord Sheridan's gratitude, but he, a humble farmer's son, had also deflowered her, which would almost certainly cause Connor Hunter to erupt in righteous fury when he found out about it. And who could blame him? Say what old Myfanwy might, Griffin had aimed too high in this occasion.

"By the way, I'm sorry for suspecting you of foul play earlier," Christopher said, taking him by surprise. Siân's husband didn't seem like a man prone to offer apologies or even justify his actions to anyone.

"You have nothing to be sorry for. In your place, I, too, would have been suspicious." In reality, he had been reassured to see the man take Jane's safety so seriously. After all, no one here knew him, there was no reason to trust him. Her brother-in-law had been right to be on his guard.

"You know, your English is really quite good for a Welshman. As good as my wife's, which is saying something."

"That's because I'm half-English. My mother was from Nottingham."

The brow over the left eye, the blue one, arched. "Was she now? That's interesting."

Griffin barely refrained a scoff. This was the first time his situation had been described as interesting. But then again, Christopher himself was English, so he was bound not to see any problem with having a mother born in England. Still, it was refreshing not to be judged or mocked or despised, or any other of the things he'd been over the years. Perhaps he had inadvertently found the secret to a more peaceful, satisfying life. If he left Wales or at least found a place to live where his origins would be no reason for contempt, he could be spared the constant criticism. His gaze flicked over to the hill where Castell Esgyrn's tower glowed. Its inhabitants were either English, or half-English. The only two Welsh ones, Siân and Lady Sheridan, had married English men. Clearly in such a place he would be allowed to live his life free of insults.

Damnation, thinking this way was the last thing he needed. Half-English he may be, but he was not noble. He did not *belong* there.

Griffin emptied the rest of the cup in one gulp.

"Time to get some sleep, I think," Christopher said, standing up from the bench. "Are you coming?"

"In a moment."

Alone in the darkness, his mind slightly addled by drink, Griffin started to wonder. Perhaps he wouldn't have to face Lord Sheridan after all. Once Jane was safe with her family, he could leave. There was no reason for him to stay longer than a few moments.

Could he disappear as soon as he had delivered her to Castell Esgyrn? No, of course not, that would be the cowardly way out. Could he ask her not to mention what had happened in the barn to anyone? Of course not, he could not let her face her future husband's ire on their wedding night, when he found out she was not a virgin. Could he repair the wrong he had caused her by offering to marry her? Of course not. He was a nobody. A union between them would be an aberration.

There was no solution to his dilemma.

Racked with guilt, Griffin stared at the star-strewn sky stretching high above him. These pinpricks of light had been around since the dawn of time and would continue to exist long after he was gone. His existence would be a blink in the history of humanity. He was already seven and twenty, he should do his best to give meaning to his life. And here he was instead, stealing a fleeting moment with a woman he had no right to, wasting his time, doing something that would lead nowhere, dreaming of someone who could never be his.

He emptied the last of the mead and went back to the cottage. Tonight he had dreamed his last.

Tomorrow he would be sent back to his rightful place.

Chapter Thirteen

A s agreed the day before, Siân and Christopher left for Castell Esgyrn ahead of the cart to warn the family of Jane's upcoming arrival. At dawn, Christopher had gone to the village on the other side of the river and asked the workers enrolled for the day to come to the cottage first so they could be told what was expected from them. The men had been only too happy to lend their cooperation to the lord of the castle's daughter—and were offended when mention of a reward had been made.

"My lady, it will be an honor to help you. We need nothing in exchange. Lord Sheridan has been more than generous with us already."

Jane had not insisted, knowing the men would be rewarded whether they wanted to be or not. Her parents would see to it.

A hooded garment was found, and a large piece of cloth. Griffin was to walk alongside the workers, his face obscured by the hood, while she huddled in the cart under the cover, amidst the stones and rubble. She settled down with some trepidation but was reassured to see she was completely hidden once the cover was secured.

"The men and I will try and see if aught is amiss in the woods. With luck, we will be able to locate the place of the ambush, so your father can get to the men and have them punished. Whatever you do, do not show yourself," Griffin urged before covering her. Absurdly, she almost reached out for his hand to place a kiss on his knuckles.

It felt like the end of something wonderful, the conclusion of a moment that had been suspended out of time and she didn't know how to handle it. After a few delicious days spent alone in his company, she would go back to her normal life. Would she not think something was lacking? She wasn't so sure.

The men gave the order and the cart started to move. Jane gritted her teeth and focused on staying silent and immobile. Despite Griffin's insistence that they stuff the hole they had created for her with straw from the stables, this would not be a comfortable ride. Stones dug in her back and sides. Well, she would just have to endure it. Soon, she would be safe, it was all that mattered. A few bruises would be small price to pay. Without Griffin, she would have reached her home in a much worse state.

When they entered the forest a moment later, she tensed up. The blanket was thin enough that she was not in complete darkness, but as she couldn't see anything, she had to go by sound alone, which only added to her nervousness. What if, despite their precautions, Geraint recognized Griffin? What if the rebels saw something unusual in the cart's load and decide to investigate? What if they—

No. Jane forced herself to calm down. There was no reason anyone would suspect anything.

The workers started to sing, a good way of indicating they were not nervous in the least and had nothing to hide, she had to admit. At no point did she hear anything worrying, nor did she feel the cart slow down. Still, she could feel sweat trickle down her spine. Only when she finally heard the familiar patter of the horse's hooves on the drawbridge did she start breathing again. The plan had worked.

They had made it.

~

"Jane! Finally, thank the Lord!"

"Are you all right? You look a mess."

"Siân and Christopher told us what happened. Dear God, *are* you all right?"

Everyone gathered around the cart and started to talk at the same time when Jane emerged from under the covers, looking, for once, slightly worse for wear and disheveled. Still unfathomably beautiful. Griffin's chest tightened. Now that they were inside Castell Esgyrn, and safe, she was not his to protect and look after anymore. She didn't need him.

And so began the second part of his life, the one after his meeting with Lady Jane Hunter. What would it bring?

Looking overwhelmed by the flow of questions and comments addressed to her, she turned to face him. "This is Griffin ap Madoc, the man without whom I wouldn't be here." Once everyone had expressed their heartfelt gratitude, she pointed at different people, introducing them in turn, omitting only Siân and Christopher, whom he already knew. "My parents, Lord and Lady Sheridan. This is my sister, Gwenllian. My other sister, Seren. My brother, Rhys. Our friend, Bethan."

It was odd to finally put a face to the names he had heard mentioned so often in the last few days and he did his best to greet them with the proper amount of deference, but he wasn't sure what else to do. Jane was the only other noble he'd ever been in contact with. With her, everything had been easy from the start, maybe due to the unusual circumstances of their meeting. With these people dressed in their finery, looking at him as they would to a savior, he wasn't sure how to behave.

"You have the biggest beard I've ever seen," little Seren said, coming closer.

"Have I?" He couldn't help a smile. The girl was adorable. At least it was not difficult to know how to be with her, she was just a child. "Well, it certainly feels enormous, and I cannot wait to shave it off."

"Are you really all right, Jane?" The blonde woman he now knew to be Jane's mother was not so easily distracted, understandably so. There was a haunted look in her eyes, as if she was imagining what could have happened to her daughter.

"Perfectly all right. But I will need to speak to you and Father," Jane answered, throwing him a glance he had difficulty interpreting. Did she want him to come with her? Was she apologizing to him because she preferred to be alone with her parents to discuss what had happened? What did he prefer?

Before he could decide, Lord Sheridan took Jane's hand and tucked it in the crook of his arm. "Come, indeed we have much to discuss."

Everyone started to disperse. The workers, having been thanked profusely for their help, headed for the chapel to start on their day's work, Jane's siblings made their way toward the main hall in their parents' wake. Only Christopher remained in the bailey, appraising him with a frown on his face.

"Come with me, we'll put you to rights before your confrontation with Lord Sheridan. He's bound to want to speak to you next. And you're right, you do need a shave. You're also in sore need of a bath and clean clothes."

After days on the road, he probably was, but Griffin was dismayed that it should be so obvious. Had Jane noticed how filthy he looked? Did she mind? Please Lord, let her not be disgusted by him.

His heart heavier than ever, he followed the Englishman to a small room next to the stables. It was obvious Christopher had asked for everything to be prepared as soon as he'd reached Castell Esgyrn, for there was all a man needed to make himself look presentable, including clean clothes. He guessed they belonged to Christopher, who seemed to be of similar height and build to him. The water in the shallow tub was lukewarm, a luxury a farmer's son had rarely indulged in. At any other time, Griffin might have lingered and taken the time to appreciate that it was all over and he had delivered Jane home safely, but his stomach was tied up in knots at the idea of what was to come, the confrontation with Lord Sheridan and, more to the point, the pending separation from Jane. Now that she was safe with her family and didn't need him anymore, he didn't see why anyone, her included, would ask him to stay.

Christopher nodded and left him to his ablutions, saying he would be waiting outside when he was finished.

"Tell me, is there any reason why you should be so nervous?" he asked once Griffin had come out of the room dressed in a dark hose and velvet tunic that fitted him like a glove.

"Nervous?"

"Nervous." The Englishman crossed his arms over his chest and fixed him with his disconcerting eyes. "I don't understand why you would be. You've saved Lord Sheridan's daughter from a band of ruffians who intended her to use her to get to him and would, I imagine, have raped her at the first opportunity. You're a hero, and the man will be sure to thank and reward you for what you did. Yet you look as if you feared he would slice you open. It makes no sense. Unless..."

Yes. Unless.

Griffin averted his gaze.

"Unless you took liberties with the Lady Jane while she was alone with you and at your mercy and you feared retribution for assaulting her yourself?" In a flash, the affable, slightly mocking man was replaced by the lethal warrior. "I hope to God this is not what happened, because if you so much as—"

"No!" Griffin was horrified to be mistaken for what he was not, but he did not take a step back, more worried about establishing the truth than protecting his face from the punch he felt sure was coming. "Of course I did not assault her, or anyone! I would never do that. I took her away from the group of men precisely because I wanted to spare her that fate."

Christopher relaxed. "Very well. I believe you. She doesn't seem wary of you, now that I think of it, rather the opposite." His face underwent another transformation as understanding dawned. "You did not assault her, but you did sleep with her," he asserted, leaning in as he lowered his voice. "Which is why you're nervous at the idea of facing her father."

Could Griffin lie? Yes. Unless he spoke to Jane, who would more than likely refuse to discuss something so private with him, Christopher had no proof anything untoward had happened. Was it a good idea to lie though? No. Griffin lifted his head. He might feel better for admitting the truth that was crushing him. Besides, he sensed that his new friend might understand.

"Yes. We were forced to take refuge in a barn after being caught in a storm one night. She was cold, so we lay side by side, and one thing led to another. When I tried to push her away, she told me that she wanted me to...well, be the first man to take her in her arms and I didn't find the strength to do as I should have. I know it was not—"

"Say no more." A gleam passed in the Englishman's blue eye. Compassion? Had he experienced the same thing with his little wife? Had she been the one initiating the seduction? It would not surprise Griffin. He'd had the chance to see that Siân was a fiery little thing, even more impetuous than Jane. "If that is what happened, I can only sympathize. These Hunter girls are determined not to be thwarted when they want something. And if that something is a night in a man's arms, then the poor bastard doesn't stand a chance. Never has surrender felt sweeter, though."

Exactly. Sweeter than honey. *If* you forgot the guilt racking through you afterward, of course...

"I don't know what to do." He ran a hand through his hair.

Christopher didn't seem to share his dismay. "I'm not sure there's anything to do. These things have a way of resolving themselves all on their own." Did they? Just how many farmers' sons who had bedded a lord's daughter did the man know that he could be so confident? His and Jane's situation was unusual to say the least, and he could not see how it could end in a satisfactory manner. "Trust me, the less you meddle, the better."

Griffin had no idea whether to be reassured or not, but what choice did he have? "If you say so."

"I do. Now, come. Lord Sheridan should be ready to see you."

"Who do I thank for the rescue of my daughter?"

The look on Lord Sheridan's face was clearly not meant to be intimidating but Griffin felt his blood slow down all the same. Tall and broad-shouldered, with raven black hair and piercing green eyes, Jane's father was a formidable man who had evidently handed down his coloring and innate elegance to her. The resemblance between the two of them did not help Griffin to hold on to his composure.

Nevertheless, he straightened his spine, doing his best to appear undaunted. "I'm Griffin ap Madoc. I come from a village on the coast, west of Castell Esgyrn. My father was a Welsh farmer and my mother an English maid at the employ of a lord from Nottinghamshire come to settle here after the conquest in '82." He suspected that Connor Hunter, who was English himself and married to a Welsh woman, would not hold his origins against him. Indeed, the green eyes betrayed no disapproval, which did ease his discomfort somewhat. "But please, there is no need to thank me for doing what any man would have done in my place."

Lord Sheridan exchanged a look with his wife, who was standing on the dais with him. She nodded, as if to indicate they were thinking the same thing.

"There is *every* need to thank you. And I'm not sure I agree with you. Not every man would have done what you did, the majority would only have thought to obey orders, either through fear of retribution or hope of dubious reward. It takes a man of honor to stand up and do what's right, despite the danger." Lord Sheridan spoke with certainty, and perhaps he was right. None of Geraint's men had seen anything wrong in the abducting and the using of Jane as hostage. "Now tell me, why did you decide to betray your friends, and risk your life for my daughter, a woman you'd never met before?"

Even though he understood why people would assume Geraint had been his friend, Griffin could not help a burst of outrage at the notion. His spine stiffened further.

"Begging your pardon, my lord, but none of those men were my friends. They came to my village last month asking for someone who could speak English. As I had already made my mind to leave, I volunteered for the task, imagining they wanted some papers translated or something similar. I only discovered their intent when they brought me in front of Lady Jane so that

I could relay their threats to her." Remembering his shock at seeing what was required of him, he clenched his jaw. "I was horrified, and decided I would do what I could to help her. I would have done the same for any woman, regardless of whether I knew her or not."

Lord Sheridan nodded. He didn't seem to doubt his words, at least.

"So, you spirited her away as soon as you were able?"

"Yes. Unfortunately, the opportunity didn't present itself immediately, and the men kept her captive for almost five days. I wish I had acted sooner but she was under close guard, as you can imagine. One night, I took my chance." Griffin thought it best to keep to himself the conversation he'd overheard between Cynan and Tomos. It would only add to Jane's parents' distress. Besides, they seemed to have guessed what the vile men had had in store for their beautiful hostage. The miracle was that Cynan had not pounced on her sooner. "I will add that the Lady Jane was a model of bravery throughout the ordeal. You can be proud of her. She never showed her fear and tricked the men into thinking she couldn't understand them, thereby gaining precious information for you."

"Indeed. She's already told me all I need to know to find and punish those bastards. My men are as we speak scouring the woods to capture the ones lying in ambush. Others will be sent to England as soon as we know where to look for the rest of the gang."

Griffin could not help a grim smile of satisfaction at the idea of what was in store for Geraint. The man would be questioned and made to reveal where Cynan and the rest of the men had gone. Sheridan Manor, in all probability, in case Jane had decided to go back there first.

"You know who is behind the abduction then?"

The green eyes hardened. "Yes. I had heard that Gruffydd

ap Hywel had a son, but I had not expected him to be as foolish as to try to pick up the fight. His father is long dead, killed for daring to abduct Siân, who was only a child at the time, and causing my wife untold distress." Griffin noticed that Lord Sheridan didn't mention the fact that the old rebel had tortured and almost killed him, just for being English. It seemed that, in his mind, this was a minor offense compared to what his wife and daughter had endured. "Rest assured that none of the men involved in this affair will get away with what they did. I cannot afford to be lenient and place my family in any danger. They will have to face the consequences of their actions."

"You're right." Though in the end the men had not really hurt Jane, Griffin felt no compassion for them. They had abducted an innocent lady in order to pressure her father into handing himself over so he could be killed for a crime he had not committed. Two of the men had even planned to rape her together. The others would either have watched and cheered or joined in. None of them deserved any mercy.

"And now it is my turn to thank you." Lady Sheridan, a beautiful woman with hair of gold in which a few silver strands were dancing, stepped down from the dais. Her husband followed, and suddenly they were both standing in front of him. "Because we all know your bravery saved not only my daughter but also my husband. Connor would have had no other choice but to surrender himself to the rebels had they been able to state their demands with Jane as their hostage. He would not have left her in their possession a heartbeat longer than necessary. And then Hywel and his men would have killed him, just like Gruffydd tried to do all those years ago. And I... I would not have survived the loss."

When her eyes filled with tears, Lord Sheridan drew her to his side with an arm around the waist and murmured soothing words in her ear. The love between them was so obvious, so beautiful to watch, and in that moment, Griffin did feel some pride at having spared the family so much grief.

"Please. As I said, I only did what I thought was right."

Lord Sheridan cleared his throat but kept his wife against him. "Spoken like a true man. I'm not surprised Jane spoke so highly of you."

The pride Griffin had felt bloomed into gratitude. Jane had praised him? He had not dared hope as much, because he truly felt he had done the only thing he could have done. But she had told her parents, two powerful nobles, that he was a worthy man. What was more, she seemed to have kept their dalliance, for want of a better word, secret. Could it be that he would not face her father's wrath for touching a woman he had no right to? He didn't know whether to be relieved or be honest and confess everything.

"You will sleep here tonight and be our guest for as long as you wish," Lord Sheridan spoke before he could reach a decision. "Jane has already told me I should under no pretext let you leave the castle until she's had the chance to thank you for what you did."

"There is no need. She has already thanked me a dozen times." In more ways than one.

"I do not doubt it. Still, she clearly intends to do so at least once more so you will indulge us."

Griffin agreed, relieved he would not be parted from Jane just yet.

He didn't, however, get to see her before going to bed. As he was leaving the hall, Lady Sheridan had informed him that her daughter had gone to bathe and change. He'd nodded, hoping he would get to see her sometime in the afternoon.

It was not to be. Shortly after, Geraint and five men were brought to Castell Esgyrn under heavy guard. Lord Sheridan requested his presence to translate his words to the rebels, as his own knowledge of the Welsh language was not as good as Griffin's and he wanted him to identify which of the men had taken part in the actual abduction. The three villagers who had been recruited to lie in ambush in the woods, youths who had been lied to about the true purpose of the expedition, were sent away with a warning never to involve themselves in such dealings ever again. Geraint was questioned until he had revealed where they could find Hywel and what had happened to Cynan and the others. As Griffin had suspected, they had ridden back to Sheridan Manor in case Jane decided to flee back there. They still thought her with child, and at odds with her father, so it did make sense she would have run to her lover instead of her family.

After the long and painful interrogation, Geraint and his two friends were led to the dungeon until Lord Sheridan decided what to do with them. By the time it was all over, it was late and the women, they were told, had already retired to bed, which meant he would have to wait until the morning to see Jane. After days in her constant company, her absence was painful.

Refusing Lord Sheridan's offer of a drink, Griffin made his way to the bedchamber he had been allocated and found himself staring at the white-washed ceiling in disbelief. The whole day had been a whirlwind. Still, he was not tired and even lying in the most comfortable bed he'd ever lain on in his life did not help him fall asleep. He would have gladly swapped the down mattress for a barn full of hay if it meant lying next to Jane. He was plagued by thoughts of her writhing under him, moaning her pleasure into his mouth, welcoming him inside her heat.

Dear God, this had to stop. But how? And what would he do once he finally left Castell Esgyrn?

He didn't want to return to the village where nothing but

painful memories awaited him and he didn't have anywhere else to go, no one he wanted to be with. Or at least, no one he *could* be with.

Because, yes, there was someone he wanted to be with. Someone who was even now sleeping a few doors from him, more unattainable than ever.

Chapter Fourteen

"You'll never guess. I'm betrothed."

Jane and Siân looked at one another in stupefaction. At fourteen, Bethan, Gwenllian's friend, was two years older than their sister but still very young to be betrothed. She was also extremely beautiful, which perhaps accounted for the fact that she had attracted a man's attention and moved him to offer for her hand.

"Do we know the lucky suitor?" Siân recovered first, as usual, and asked the question burning Jane's lips.

Bethan made a face that left no doubt about what she thought of her husband-to-be. This was definitely no love match. "I doubt it, as I don't know him myself. His name is Dougal Campbell. He's a Scot."

"A Scot? How on earth did a Scot find you?"

Bethan sighed. "Our fathers met in '77 at the start of the conquest. Dougal's father, then a young man of twenty, was shocked by King Edward's invasion. Fiercely attached to his own land, he decided he could not stand idly by while the English tried to force a country that did not belong to them to submit to their governance. Having just become laird of a

powerful clan, he had means at his disposal. He quickly assembled a contingent of men and rode to Wales to help the fighters.
There, he met my father, who saved his life in battle."

Jane thought she understood where this was going. This
union with a powerful clan would be a way of restoring the
family's lost prestige by calling in old debts. Bethan's father, a
brewer's son who'd gained standing by his efforts, had been
dispossessed of his lands in 1283, like many other local lords. In
the wake of the conquest and in order to establish his domination and quell any rebellious intent, the English King had given
lands to his most trusted advisers. Jane's own father had been
one of these lords.

And now poor Bethan was going to be the instrument with
which her father regained what he had lost. She could almost
sympathize with him, as the man had done nothing to deserve
being stripped of all he'd worked so hard to earn. But still she
found it hard to condone the using of his daughter thus.

"What does this have to do with anything?" Gwenllian,
being younger and somewhat naïve, had not understood the link
between this story, which had happened more than thirty years
ago, and her friend's current predicament.

"When I started to bleed, my father declared he would find
me a husband whose fortune could help rebuild the one he had
lost. But all the lords he's approached over the last year have
made it plain that a match with the daughter of a man whose
own father had been a brewer, and Welsh to boot, would by no
means be advantageous to them. Ambitious men are now
turning their gazes toward England for useful alliances. That's
when he thought of Laird Campbell. He hoped that being a
Scot, his old friend would not refuse to wed his son to the
daughter of the man who had saved his life and was..." Bethan
blushed as she repeated her father's words. "Who was an
acknowledged beauty. He did not. We received the letter this

morning, confirming his agreement. And so I am to marry Dougal Campbell and end my life in a foreign country, far from everything I know and love."

Jane's chest constricted. Having known Bethan since the day she was born, she was aware her father was nothing like Connor Hunter, who had allowed his daughters to grow into healthy women before considering marriage and even then, had not tried to force them into unions they did not desire. In the last ten years, Gwenllian's friend had spent more time at Castell Esgyrn than in her own home, accompanying them to England on more than one occasion. She was almost like a fourth sister. Hearing that she was being treated so callously was hard. No doubt her father was doing what he thought best to ensure her future, but in typical male fashion, had not taken into consideration what his daughter might feel.

A child bride, married off to a stranger, sent alone to an unknown country, was no cause for concern in most people's mind, and he would have thought only of his family's prestige in this affair.

"Dougal is thirteen, even younger than me," Bethan continued, her voice flat. "Because of our age, the wedding will only take place in three years, at which time he will come to get me. My brother, Siaspar, is furious but he cannot do anything. He cannot go against our father's word."

Of course, the boy was only twelve, he didn't have any say in the matter, any more than his sister did. If Bethan's father and his Scottish friend had agreed on this alliance, then there was nothing she, Siaspar, or anyone could do.

"I'm going to miss you terribly." Gwenllian sounded on the verge of tears at the idea of her friend leaving for remote Scotland to be the wife of a man she didn't love or even know.

"Me too." Bethan fell into her arms, sobbing. "Oh, I wish my betrothed won't come for me until I'm an old maid!"

Deeply affected by the scene in front of her, Jane walked over to the bay window to restore some calm to her tumultuous thoughts. Unfortunately, she couldn't claim to be shocked at Bethan's father's decision. Most, if not all the women she knew, had been married off to strangers they didn't like for strategic reasons. Very few were lucky enough to marry men they had chosen, much less loved. The women of her family, though, seemed to have avoided that dreadful fate. Branwen, Carys, Siân... All of them had made love matches. Even her mother, who'd been forced to wed an English knight, had found happiness in the end. Jane vowed she would be the next one to marry a man she loved, as, mercifully, her situation was nothing like Bethan's. Her father was not trying to ally himself with rich lords and make people forget his humble origins. He was also a loving, generous man. As a consequence, she was free to choose her husband, and she would not settle for less than what the other people in her family had.

Just then the door behind her opened on Christopher and Griffin—and it all became clear.

If she married him, she would avoid Bethan's fate and have a husband she loved.

Because yes, she loved this man, she realized. This man who had saved and protected her, shown her that there was more to her than beauty, who had made a woman out of her with skill, patience and generosity. That he had appeared in the room at the exact moment when she had been pondering her future union had to be a sign. She was destined to marry none other than him.

Arglwydd Mawr.

Griffin's heart fell to the bottom of his chest when he saw Jane standing in the shaft of light piercing through the window.

No woman had ever looked more alluring than she did today. In her sumptuous clothes, she was a vision. The gown of soft velvet, with its straight, narrow sleeves embroidered at the cuff, drew the eye to her delicate wrists and beautiful hands. The blue of the bodice, deep and shimmering, was the perfect foil for the inky black tresses cascading over her shoulders and the generous breasts he had not been able to forget. Even without any jewelry around her neck or at her ears, she was breathtaking, every inch a nobly born lady.

He saw it all with painful clarity.

They could never be together. Any foolish thought he might have entertained about wooing her vanished like mist under the glaring sun, because everything was different now. As a hostage, she had relied on him for her protection, and while they'd been on the road at the mercy of the elements, the gulf between them had not been so wide. Restored to her usual magnificence, surrounded by her family, she was no longer the naked lover he'd been allowed to possess, no longer the approachable traveling companion, no longer the captive woman who'd needed a protector.

He stared and stared, knowing this might be the last time he would ever see her.

Then, after a while, he saw that for a reason he could not fathom, Jane seemed as stunned as he was. She was looking at him as if she had never seen him before. Yet he knew he would not appear anywhere near as striking as she did. Christopher's clothes were finer than any he had ever owned, admittedly, but still nothing like those of Lord Sheridan.

While Christopher and the three ladies by the fire started a conversation, he waited for Jane to speak first, as was proper.

"You've shaved," was all she said.

"Yes." She'd made it sound as if this was the most extraordinary thing he could have done when they both knew there was nothing more normal for a man than to shave in the morning. He cleared his throat, unsettled by her scrutiny, and ran a hand over his smooth jaw. "I prefer it that way."

"I like it both ways."

"Being clean shaven is more comfortable."

"I can imagine. You must have wished you could shave while we traveled."

"I did."

Griffin blinked at the unlikely exchange. Were they really talking about his beard in such a stilted manner? Was that all that was left to them? He should be asking her how she felt, now that she was reunited with her family, and safe, he should beg her not to send him away but to find him a position at Castell Esgyrn, anything but talk about the bloody hairs growing on his face. But he didn't know how to recapture the ease between them. In front of old Enid and Myfanwy, he had not felt out of place. Here, in a lavishly decorated castle, surrounded by noble people, he did.

Behind him, Christopher let out what sounded like a chuckle. Was he amused at the awkwardness of the exchange he'd overheard? Griffin wouldn't put it past him. Blast it, but the man was mischief personified.

"Ladies, we've been sent to get you," the Englishman said, offering his arm to his wife. "A veritable feast awaits us in the main hall. Shall we?"

"Yes. I'm famished," Siân said, beaming at him.

Gwenllian and Bethan followed them, arm in arm, and Griffin had little choice but to offer Jane his arm in turn. She took it with her usual grace and a smile that tugged at his heart. Here he was, behaving like a nobleman when they both knew who he was in reality.

Perhaps he should leave at the first opportunity. This unfortunate delay would only end up causing him more heartache.

"Married life suits you. You're positively glowing."

Jane smiled at her sister as they completed the first turn about the list. The change in Siân was incredible. She had only wed Christopher a month ago, but even in that short amount of time, the difference was obvious. It was as if she had finally found her rightful place in life.

"Yes. Being Christopher's wife is just as wonderful as I'd imagined. And there is a reason for my glow, as you call it... I think I might be with child."

"Oh, Siân! Congratulations! *Llongyfarchiadau!*" Having children had been her sister's dream from a young age, Jane knew. How wonderful to see it happen so soon. "Isn't it a bit early to tell though?"

She remembered Ffion saying she'd been mistaken because she'd been a few days late. Would her sister not suffer a similar disappointment? Jane dearly hoped not.

"It is early, you're right. But I can already feel that something has changed within me." Siân bit her bottom lip. "I have missed my courses, which is why I think this babe might have been conceived before our wedding, on the night Christopher and I were reunited."

Jane remembered that night perfectly. The couple had just announced they were to be married without delay, despite the fact that Siân had been widowed very recently. That union had been brief and in name only. In fact, Jane herself had been the one suggesting they celebrate their reunion in each other's arms. Apparently, they had followed her instructions to the letter.

"I guess then that Christopher did what I instructed him to do, and gave you the pleasure he owed you?"

The color spreading on her sister's cheeks was an answer in itself. He had done that and more, since he had also given her the child she'd craved all her life. A burst of gratitude toward the man swept through Jane. He might have made her life a misery as a child, but he was apparently the husband Siân needed. Perhaps if she kept that in mind, she would learn to get on with him.

"He did. Every time he touches me, I melt."

Melt. Two weeks ago, Jane would not have known quite what her sister meant by that, but now she knew exactly. A question crossed her mind, a question she would only ever dare ask the woman in front of her. Since they were discussing intimate matters anyway, there would be no better time.

"You know you told me that being taken for the first time didn't hurt?"

"Yesss..."

"Well," Jane pushed on despite the sudden note of suspicion creeping into Siân's voice. "Do you think it's the same for all women? Or would some feel the pain more keenly?"

Like being knifed through the gut, even if you desire the man, even if he's gentle with you?

There was a pause while Siân considered. "I suppose, like with most anything, it can vary from woman to woman. I know I'm probably lucky my first time didn't hurt, and I'm glad of it, because I would have hated to worry Christopher."

"Yes." Exactly. The pain had been one thing. The anguish in Griffin's eyes when he'd seen her reaction, quite another. He had not deserved to be made to feel so wretched, when she had been the one begging to be taken. Her body had been untried, something he had not been responsible for.

"Don't fret. It's not your fault, just the way your body was made. I'm sure he was very understanding."

"No, I know it wasn't my fault, but I cannot help—" Jane froze when the meaning of the words hit her. Siân had said "was," not "will be." She was not talking about a hypothetical situation and a non-existent man, she was talking as if she knew her sister was no longer a virgin, and she had guessed Griffin had been the one to deflower her. "You know? How?"

"It's not hard to guess what happened since I last saw you." Siân took her hand and gave it a squeeze. "You, too, are glowing."

Jane placed a hand on her heated cheek. *Was* she glowing? Perhaps. She certainly felt different, at ease with herself, conscious of her body in a way she hadn't been before. Still, there was no denying that what she had done was shocking.

"You...you do not think less of me for—"

"No. I would never think less of you for anything. How can I condemn you when I myself made love to the man of my choice before marriage? And I doubt you behaved as scandalously as I did?"

The heat on Jane's cheeks reached an alarming level. The day before her wedding, her sister had explained how she had once tricked Christopher into making love to her outside in a meadow, seducing him in the most shocking way when he had tried to resist her advances. Compared to that, Jane had to agree that she had behaved with the utmost decorum.

"No, it wasn't quite as scandalous as that," she conceded in a breath. There was a pause, while they entered the herb garden and sat on a stone bench. "Can I ask you another question?"

"Since when do you need my permission to ask anything?"

Indeed. The two sisters had always been very open one with the other. That she hadn't just asked the question went to prove how nervous she was. "I know you've only seen him briefly but what do you think of Griffin?"

Siân stared at her, understanding what she was really asking. When her sister had confided she was in love with Christopher last summer, Jane had been less supportive than she should have been, allowing rumor and prejudice to cloud her judgment. She regretted it now, because even if she'd had her reasons to dislike the man, she understood how her lack of enthusiasm would have hurt Siân. Now that she needed her approval, she wasn't sure how she would bear to hear that Siân thought Griffin less than perfect for her.

Siân smiled her warmest smile and nudged at her shoulder in a playful gesture. "He's perfect for you."

Relief washed through Jane, but she forced herself to voice her concerns out loud, knowing that, unfortunately, not everyone would be as understanding. "He does not have a title."

"Neither does Christopher. He's no longer Lord Ashton."

"No, but he was still nobly born." She hated having to insist, but she needed to hear that her unconventional choice could be accepted. "Griffin is only the son of a farmer and a maid."

"Mayhap. But his children will still be Lord Sheridan's grandchildren. Not that it matters, anyway."

"I've known him for less than two weeks."

"It makes no difference. When you know, you know, there is no point dragging on the proceedings, it will only make you miserable. I knew immediately when I met Christopher that I wanted to marry him. Believe me, I wish I hadn't had to wait for more than ten years to finally make him mine. Two weeks would have been perfect." She gave a little chuckle. "Well, perhaps not, as I was only nine at the time, but you know what I mean."

Jane gave a taut smile. She knew what Siân was trying to do but she would not be distracted so easily.

"Griffin has never—"

"Listen, do you really care what he's never done, where he's never been or whom he's never met?" Siân interrupted. "He's perfect for *you*, and that is all that matters. Or are you telling me you don't actually want—"

"No! I want him!" The words burst out of Jane, and she shot

up to her feet in her vehemence. "I want him more than I have wanted anything in my life. I burn for him like I've never burned for anyone. I think, no, I *know* that I am in love with him. And nothing will change that."

The sound of someone skidding to a halt made the two women turn toward the opening in the stone wall. Griffin was standing under the stone arch, staring.

At *her*.

Jane fell back on the bench when her legs crumpled from under her. Had he heard her heated declaration about being in love with him? Of course he had. Why else would he have gone as pale as a ghost? She knew he would hate to hear that she had such strong feelings for him, and seeing that she was discussing them so openly with someone else, be that her sister. Hadn't he taken fright after their night together? Hadn't he been acting odd since they'd arrived at Castell Esgyrn? He was worried their difference in status would mean the death of whatever had started between them. Not wanting to rush him, she had purposefully kept silent and allowed him time to come to terms with everything.

And now he'd heard that, for her, it was not merely a blossoming relationship. She'd declared out loud that she was burning for him, that she was in love with him.

He couldn't deal with it.

"Griffin," she started, not knowing how she could reassure him.

He turned and was gone before she could call him back.

Chapter Fifteen

I want him more than I have wanted anything in my life. I burn for him like I have never burned for anyone. I think, no, I know I am in love with him. And nothing will change that.

Griffin ran a hand through his hair, barely resisting the urge to pull on it. Could he fool himself that Jane had been talking about someone other than him? Did he want to? Though he dreaded to hear that she had feelings for him, feelings they would never be able to act upon, he could not bear the idea that she was actually in love with someone else, burned for another man.

No, he reasoned, it could not be. She would not have gifted him with her maidenhead if she was in love, or even merely interested in someone else, she would not have begged him to take her, she would not be looking at him with such longing in her eyes, she wouldn't smile at him as if he were the answer to all her prayers. Because such was the way she looked at him, such was the way she smiled at him.

Damn. If that was really how she felt, then she might not let him go. It would be up to him to find the strength to do the right thing and leave.

As if he could sense his master's turmoil, Eryr nudged at his chest in reassurance. Griffin gave the horse a stroke on the neck.

"Ignore me, my boy, I'm being a fool," he murmured. "You're lucky to be a horse, in many ways. Come on, it's time to pick your hooves."

Better to focus on something he could actually do than obsess about someone he had better forget. He took the hoof pick from the bucket and sighed. What a mess he'd landed himself in. He had accepted Geraint's offer to escape heartache and disillusion, and here he was, being forced to see that what he'd felt for Ffion had been nothing more than lust. He had not felt anything special for her, rather he had tried to persuade himself they could have a future together. The difference with what he felt for Jane was glaring, and made him see that he would easily have gotten over the loss of the villager, especially now that he knew she'd never been with child or even wanted him.

Having cleaned all four of Eryr's hooves, he straightened back up—and found himself staring straight into Seren's green eyes. How long had the little girl been standing there? He smiled at her, and she smiled right back.

"Is that your horse?" she asked, eyeing up the stallion with the air of someone who knew what they were talking about. Griffin was not surprised. He'd already had a chance to see that Lord Sheridan only kept splendid animals in his stables. His daughter, young as she was, would know a destrier in his prime. "He's beautiful."

"Thanks, I think so too. His name is Eryr."

"Have you had him long?"

"No. Only a few months."

"How old is he?"

"Eight, I think."

"I'm eight as well!" she piped up, eyes sparkling. The unusual color of her irises reminded him of Jane's, even if the shade was slightly darker, more like Lady Sheridan's. The little girl would grow up to be a stunning woman, just like her sister. "Maybe he and I were born on the same day!"

Not wanting to disappoint her, he agreed. "You never know."

"No, you never know." She nodded sagely, then seemed to remember what she'd come to tell him. "I was sent to tell you that we're all waiting for you in the main hall. The food is ready."

"Thank you. Just let me wash, and I'll be there."

As he scrubbed his hands clean, Griffin wondered what to think. What were the Hunter family doing? Treating him like a prestigious guest when he was a farmer's son, behaving as if it were normal that he sit at table next to a lord, waiting for him before starting their meal? And what was he doing, going along with the farce, instead of insisting he should eat with the grooms and the servants?

He was doing the only thing he could, he reflected, as he entered the hall and saw Jane smile shyly at him. Delaying the inevitable parting for as long as possible.

Was Griffin avoiding her? Was it because of what he'd heard in the herb garden earlier that morning? Was it because he'd lost all interest in her now that his mission was over?

Jane picked up her embroidery basket and sighed. Did it matter why? What mattered was that he *was* avoiding her. After the meal, where he had seemed rather uncomfortable sitting between her and her mother, he had disappeared back outside, claiming he needed to exercise his horse. It was clear he thought he had no place anywhere in the castle, except in the stables with the grooms. She would have to go find him, talk to him in private before he decided he could not bear it anymore and left for good.

Yes. And tell him what, exactly? That she was in love with him? No. It would be a terrible idea, since he already knew and the notion clearly frightened him. She would have to give him time to absorb the information before she did anything else. He'd told her as they were finishing their meal that he was thinking of going to England next, for want of a better alternative. Should she suggest he go somewhere near Sheridan Manor, so as to ensure she knew where to find him when the time came to confront him? She wasn't sure.

More confused than ever, Jane picked up her needle. Just then the door opened, and hope surged through her. Had Griffin come back to his senses? Had he decided to ask her to go for a ride with him?

Her shoulders sagged in disappointment when Christopher entered the room with his usual saunter. Having lost his title of Lord Ashton in the summer had not affected his spirit. He was still the most irreverent rogue she had ever seen, nothing like Griffin, who, despite his masculine presence, could not hide a certain vulnerability. She knew which she preferred in a man. Christopher's immovable confidence grated on her.

What was wrong with her? Why couldn't she be at ease with him now that he was her brother-in-law and she'd seen he made her sister happy? Despite the difference in status between them, Siân had accepted Griffin with no hesitation, because she could tell he was the man for her. So why could Jane not get past her childish resentment and accept Christopher?

"Little Lamb."

Before addressing or even looking at anyone else, he placed

a kiss on the top of his wife's head. There was so much love in that gesture Jane's insides constricted. In the last two days, she had discovered a new side to Christopher Harrison, one he only allowed to shine with his wife. Perhaps she would eventually forget the insufferable braggart he'd once been, if she spent enough time with the devoted husband he was now.

"Are you all right, my love?" Siân asked, cupping his cheek with her hand.

Evidently, she had detected something in her husband's demeanor that warranted the question. Jane had not seen anything amiss, but she could not claim to know him as well.

"I'm perfectly all right. But I wanted to show you this." He handed her a folded parchment complete with red wax seal. It looked rather official, almost ominous. "A missive from Throckmorton Castle arrived earlier this morning."

Jane instantly understood the enormity of the announcement. Lord Ashton, Christopher's half-brother, was his declared enemy since he had tried to kill Siân for daring to resent the way he had made her believe Christopher was a liar and usurper. He was the last person who should want to write to him.

"What does Thomas have to say?" Siân sounded nervous. Evidently, she agreed with the ominous aspect of the letter.

"I know not. I wanted to open it with you."

Well. Attentive, tender, willing to share his most important news with his wife, the man really was a model husband. If she kept witnessing such behavior, Jane might have no choice. Against all odds, she might end up liking Christopher Harrison.

"Shall I leave?" she offered, making to get up.

"No," Siân answered, giving her a quick smile. She slipped a shaky finger underneath the seal and opened the letter. Together, husband and wife started to read and then stilled, looking at one another in stupefaction.

Jane waited, certain an explanation was coming.

"This is from Lady Ashton," Siân said after a while, shaking her head in disbelief at the news she was about to impart. "Her husband is dead, killed in a fit of rage by a local lord who caught him in bed with his daughter."

Jane did not comment. What was there to say? A despicable lecher full of his own worth, a would-be murderer himself, the man had finally gotten his just deserts. She could not begin to feel sorry for him, and she saw that neither Siân nor Christopher were devastated by the news.

"There is more," her sister said slowly, smoothing the piece of parchment on her lap. "Their ten-year old son Henry died the following day, having caught a chill during a sword training session in the snow."

"Oh no! Poor Lady Ashton." The death of her wayward, cruel husband might not have crushed her, but the loss of her child, especially in a manner so absurd as this one, would be terrible for a mother.

"I'm certain Thomas was the one who insisted on his heir training in such harsh conditions, determined as he was to make him a man and a suitable lord when the time came," Christopher spat, contempt for his brother audible. "I should have killed him when I had the chance, when he tried to strangle my wife. If I had, little Henry would still be alive."

A silence followed. Then Siân spoke, her voice low.

"Yes. But don't you see, my love, if they are both dead..." She sounded unsure how to say what she wanted to say. "It means that, as the only male left in the family, you are now Lord Ashton."

Oh Lord, she was right. How had Jane not thought of that?

How ironic. The previous summer Christopher had been told the title he'd thought was his all his life had been taken away by an older, legitimate son of his father's no one had known about. The revelation had been a shock and had almost ruined his and Siân's life. And now, it seemed he was going to be Lord Ashton again.

It was quite a reversal in fortune, but Christopher didn't seem particularly happy to hear the news. It was as if, now that he was married to Siân and about to be a father, he had everything he wanted, anyway. She could understand the feeling. Indeed, the love of a good person was all one needed to be happy.

He walked over to the window, bracketing the sides with two powerful arms while he absorbed the enormity of the revelation. Jane stole a glance at Siân, who appeared nervous herself. What would her husband decide? Would they have to go back to England?

Hand in hand, the two sisters waited.

"We will travel to Throckmorton," Christopher announced after a while, turning back to face them. "But only to tell the lady I won't reside there ever again. I have a home and a family in Wales now. Why would I return to a place where I was so lonely and unhappy?"

Jane's heart melted when he walked over to Siân, placed a hand over her stomach and smiled. Yes, she could get used to this new side of the man...

"What about Lady Ashton?" she asked. The woman shouldn't have to pay for her husband's villainy. "What will happen to her?"

"She's welcome to stay, but arrangements will have to be made. That is why it's simpler if I go in person." Christopher frowned, looking at his wife. "Unless you don't feel well enough to travel, my love? I don't want you to suffer when there is no need."

Siân let out a giggle. "I only found out this week I was with child. I don't think I should take to my bed just yet, do you?"

Her husband was not impressed by the teasing. "Sometimes women feel unwell at the start of their pregnancies."

"I know, but thankfully, I do not feel any different than usual. I will be fine."

"I will accompany you, if I may," Jane declared, standing up. "Though Father has already sent a missive to them to explain my sudden disappearance, Uncle Matthew and Aunt Branwen will be reassured to see me safe and sound. And I want to see the new baby, who should be born soon."

These were only convenient excuses. As she'd said, her uncle and aunt's minds would have been put at rest by the message sent the day of her arrival in the cart, but this was an opportunity not to let pass. She would ask Griffin if he wanted to travel with their retinue. Since he'd decided to go to England anyway, he would have no reason to refuse. That way she would ensure herself more time in his company and maybe find a moment to talk to him away from her father's formidable presence.

She could only hope it would be enough to convince Griffin that they could not throw away what they had started to build together.

Chapter Sixteen

T he retinue left early the next morning.
Riding at the front were Siân, on her gray mare,
Angel, and Christopher, on his copper-colored stallion, Warrior. Jane had chosen to take Prince, her favorite
chestnut gelding. Next to her, Griffin was riding Eryr. Gwenllian and Bethan had decided to join the expedition. They, too,
wanted to meet the new baby, and provide Bethan with a
distraction from thoughts of her recent betrothal. They were
accompanied by the groom's two sons, who would start working
at Sheridan Manor. Four men at arms were bringing up the rear.
All in all, it was a company of twelve that set off as the pale
winter light started to brighten the horizon.

All throughout the day, Jane wished she could ride double
with Griffin again. It had been so good to be held against his
warm, strong body. Without him she felt cold and lost, which
was odd considering how much she usually loved riding.
Besides, riding with him would have made it easier for them to
have the conversation they needed to have. What did he intend
to do once they had reached their destination? Would he stay a
few days, or leave immediately? She still didn't know. They had

been granted an unexpected reprieve with this trip back to England, so she had better make the most of it and find the opportunity to talk to him before they arrived.

Thankfully, mindful of his wife's comfort, Christopher had ordered the company to go slowly. Jane could tell Siân would have protested, but unfortunately, the morning after they had set off, she had felt queasy. Moments later, she had run to the nearest bush and cast her accounts on the forest floor.

"I'm so happy," she'd said once she'd joined the company again, walking on shaky legs. Despite the pallor on her cheeks, she'd looked radiant with joy. "For this means I must indeed be with child."

It did. And so, from that moment on they had taken every precaution to ensure Siân's well-being, only setting off in the middle of the day, once she'd eaten something to settle her stomach. After all, Christopher had ruled, they were not in any hurry. It suited Jane fine, as a slower travel meant more time with Griffin.

Of a common accord, they agreed to stay well clear of Sheridan Manor and go straight to Throckmorton Castle. Cynan, Tomos and any others who were waiting for them would have to be found first. It was decided that the men at arms accompanying them would be sent to Uncle Matthew, who, with a contingent of his own men, would uncover the rebels lying in ambush. Only once the way was clear and the threat removed, would Jane and Siân go to see their aunt, who might well be delivered of the child by the time they got to her.

Finally, on the afternoon of the third day, Jane did manage to find some time alone with Griffin.

They had reached a big town and a halt was decided, so that everyone could take the opportunity of buying items they could not easily get in Castell Esgyrn. While Siân went to buy cloth to prepare for the arrival of the baby, Jane asked Griffin to escort her to the tanner's shop. In truth, she could not think of anything she needed to buy but she wanted to get him away from prying eyes and ears. To her relief, he agreed. She had half expected him to ask one of the guards to go in his stead, but he merely nodded and followed her.

Before they could reach the tanner's shop, however, he stopped by a forge.

"What are we doing here?" she asked, smiling, when he started to finger various daggers. They were simple, their handle unadorned, unlike the jewel-encrusted ones she was used to seeing, but beautiful in their simplicity. The smithy was clearly a gifted craftsman.

"We are getting you a blade. You need to be armed, my lady."

My lady. The two words, pronounced with such ease, cut through her as surely as if he'd pushed the blade he was holding into her heart. She could tell he had not meant to create any distance between them, but rather that he felt that distance in his bones, which was even worse.

She was losing him, more surely than if he'd ridden to the other end of the country.

"Try this one. It's small enough that it should fit into your palm nicely." Griffin had not even noticed her dismay—or he was ignoring it because he didn't know how to deal with it. When he pressed the blade into her hand, her fingers automatically closed around his.

"Griffin. Please."

He misunderstood the reason behind her plea. "I know you will hate the idea of hurting someone, but I need to know you have some way of defending yourself."

Defend herself from what? Not from the pain of his rejection, which was the only thing she needed defending from right now. She shook her head, feeling on the verge of tears. How could what they had shared end in this way? Though she had met Griffin only a fortnight ago, she felt that they had a future to share. They could not part ways now, in such an unsatisfactory manner.

When you know, you know, Siân had told her. Well, she certainly did, and so did Griffin, in all probability. The difference was, he refused to accept it. She tightened her grip on the dagger, wishing it were as easy to master her emotions.

"Having a weapon is all well and good," Jane said once she had herself under control once more. "But for it to be of any use, I need to be taught how to wield it. Who do you suggest can teach me?"

He lowered his gaze. "I don't know. Christopher maybe."

Well, that certainly answered her question. She had asked the question specifically to see if he would offer to stay to teach her. He had not.

"I don't want Christopher to teach me," she said in a low voice. No one but Griffin himself.

Griffin heard the defiance in Jane's voice when she told him she refused to deal with her brother-in-law. He'd noticed how she always seemed ill at ease in the man's presence. It had bothered him for days and here was the perfect opportunity to ask her about it. Knowing how close she was to her sister, he'd imagined she would love the man Siân had chosen as a husband. But she seemed oddly shy in his presence, nothing like her usual self.

"Why not? Why are you so wary of Christopher?"

"W-wary?" she stammered, looking caught out.

"Yes, wary," he insisted when she didn't answer. He needed to know, and he'd rather discuss that than the fact he would not be around for much longer. He'd not missed her reaction when he'd called her "my lady" earlier. But try as he might, he just could not see how the two of them could have a future together.

Heart beating hard, he waited. Would Jane answer, or would she force him to address the matter at hand?

She returned the dagger to its place on the bench and took a few steps toward the church, leaving him to follow if he wanted to. Of course, he did. The buying of the weapon could wait another day. This could not.

"I'm not wary of him, exactly," she said after a while. "But I am ill at ease. I suppose, to my shame, that I cannot get past what he made me endure when we were children."

Endure? Griffin's jaw tightened. This was not what he had expected to hear, and far more worrying. Would he have to take his new friend to task? Christopher had not seemed the kind of man who would hurt a woman but evidently, something had happened between the two of them. "What did he do to you?"

He must have looked ready to go confront the Englishman and use the dagger she'd just discarded to slice him open, for she shook her head and hastened to reassure him. "It's nothing as bad as you're imagining. He grew up not too far from me and we often met, by accident or during various festivities and banquets organized at Sheridan Manor. Whenever he saw me, he liked to tease me and make me feel bad about the way I behaved, all prim and proper in his opinion. And though it has been years and he has since apologized for it, I cannot seem to forget the pain he caused me. I really wish I could, because it's not fair to Siân. I can tell she wants us to be friends."

He nodded in understanding. The notion that she could not fully accept her beloved sister's choice would weigh heavily on her mind. Siblings were not supposed to question or disapprove of one another's decisions. Griffin understood better than most how she felt because he'd always hated the fact that he did not get on with his own sister.

"I see."

"It's silly, and I'm sure with time I will forget the nonsense.

Especially when I see how well he takes care of Siân and how much he loves her. I'm sure once the babe is born and I see how he dotes over it, as he's certain to, the last of my resentment will vanish."

Once the babe was born.

The words caused a tightening in Griffin's chest. That would not happen until after the summer. Where would he be then? He had no idea. He wasn't even sure where he would be at the end of the month. Well, one thing at a time. First, they had to reach Throckmorton Castle and see about capturing Cynan. At least he knew he would not leave until he was certain the danger lurking in the shadows had been removed. He would do nothing until he knew she was safe.

"I'm certain you'll find a way to forgive Christopher," he agreed. Jane was nothing if not a generous soul, ready to give people the benefit of the doubt.

"I hope so," she murmured. "All the more so that Siân has explained that his taunts stemmed from his unhappiness. He was jealous of the love and attention I received from my father. He grew up in a crumbling castle, you see, ignored and unloved by his dour old grandfather, whereas I—"

To Griffin's dismay, she burst into tears before she could finish her sentence. Ignoring the voice in his head urging him to stay away, he took her in his arms. There was no way he could stand here while Jane cried and berated herself for her inability to get past the pain the young Christopher had inflicted on her all those years ago.

"Hush," he soothed, one hand draping over her nape. It felt so delicate under her silky soft hair that he almost groaned. What was he doing? This was precisely why he could not afford to get into such close proximity to her, because it put unholy thoughts in his head and unwelcome feelings in his heart. "There is no shame in having had a happy childhood."

"No, I know," Jane sobbed against his chest. "But it makes it impossible for me to imagine ending my life on my own, without anyone to love me."

Without you.

The two words didn't pass her lips but he heard them all the same. His insides twisted and he just held her until the tears dried out because there was nothing he could say. He could not imagine his life without her either, but the difference was, he could not see a way to make a union between them work. Eventually she calmed down and stepped away from him. Her eyes were red rimmed, her lips swollen and wet with tears, her cheeks blotchy. She had never looked more precious to him.

"Come. Let us join the others," he said, gesturing toward the square where they had left the horses. He wasn't sure he wouldn't resist the temptation of a kiss if they stayed alone much longer.

Jane stared at him a long moment, then eventually nodded.

The retinue reached Throckmorton Castle on the evening of the eighth day, after an uneventful journey.

Gwenllian, Bethan, the two grooms and the four men at arms, having nothing to fear from Cynan and his friends, had gone ahead to Sheridan Manor.

As they entered the bailey shortly before dusk, Griffin looked around in amazement. The place was not just bleak because of the eerie light; it was falling to pieces. Half the merlons on the battlements had crumbled to dust, the door of the barbican was missing, and grass had started to grow at the foot of the keep. No wonder Christopher was in no hurry to come live here. Who in their right mind would swap such a gloomy castle for the warm, cozy cottage he shared with his wife? What was the point of being a mighty lord if it got you such an uncomfortable life?

Perhaps being humbly born was not such a bad thing, he mused, taking in his gloomy surroundings. He could choose where he lived, he wasn't burdened by responsibilities and no one wanted him dead because of the power he wielded. Yes, perhaps he was better off than men like Lord Sheridan and the new Lord Ashton.

The only problem was that his origins placed him well below the notice of the woman he wanted. Or, at least, it *should* do, because it was clear Jane was determined to behave as if the two of them could have a future together. Before leaving, she had told her sister she was in love with him. It was such a ridiculous thing for someone like her to say that he had hoped she would come back to her senses and understand that, in the relief of being reunited with her family, she had mistaken the gratitude she felt toward him for something else. So far it hadn't happened, and he was starting to doubt it would.

"This way." A tall, lean man led them to the solar where a woman Griffin assumed was Lady Ashton—or rather, the late Lord Ashton's widow—was waiting for them. A rider had been sent in advance to warn her of the arrival of the retinue and what looked like a veritable feast had been laid on the trestle table, a welcome sight after a long day on the road. That was one of the significant advantages of being a noble. You never had to wonder where your next meal would come from.

"Lord Ashton, you are very welcome," the blonde woman told Christopher, before bowing to him in turn. "My lord, please have a seat. You must be weary."

Griffin cleared his throat in embarrassment. "Thank you, but I am not a lord."

"Oh, forgive me, I thought…"

Christopher brushed over the moment in his typical flippant

manner. "Griffin is a dear friend of Siân's sister. He kindly agreed to travel with us. The more capable men the better when it comes to my wife and sister-in-law's safety, as I'm sure you'll agree."

Well, Griffin mused, that was not exactly a lie, but he'd conveniently forgotten to mention who his parents were.

"Of course." The relief in the woman's voice was obvious. Her mistake was forgotten. "Come, let's eat."

The fare they were offered was just like the castle itself was, abundant but sorely lacking in refinement and even taste. Of course, it was still markedly better than what he was used to, but Griffin could not help but note the difference with Castell Esgyrn. The food there had been exquisite, rich in flavors he had never tasted in his life and cooked to perfection.

Later that night, he found himself alone with Christopher. Lady Ashton had excused herself as soon as was decent, and the two sisters, tired by the journey and eager to sleep in a comfortable bed for the first time in a week, had retired not long after.

Alone in the great hall with Christopher, Griffin poured two cups of ale and mentally prepared himself. There would never be a better opportunity to ask what had been bothering him for days, ever since his discussion with Jane outside the blacksmith's forge that day in town.

"I heard you tormented Jane when she was young." He could not help to snarl the words. Though he liked the Englishman, who treated him like an equal, the idea of anyone causing her any discomfort enraged him. Jane had assured him it hadn't been that bad, but he needed to know. "Is it true?"

"It is." Christopher sounded cautious, somewhat wary, a most unusual attitude for him, who was brazenness personified. "Are you going to take me to task over it?"

"I should. I want to." He clenched his jaw, because in that moment he did want to pummel him to the ground and the intensity of his feelings worried him. After days spent trying to tell himself he could not return Jane's feelings, he was forced to see his heart had not heeded his reason, and he didn't like it. "What did you do to her?"

"*Do?* Nothing! God's bones, what do you take me for?" The outrage on Christopher's face was enough to tell Griffin he had never raised a hand to her or even treated her half as badly as he had feared at first. "I mocked her for always being poised and happy, everything I was not. I called her Perfect Little Jane Hunter, which never failed to grate on her."

The tension in Griffin's body relaxed marginally. It was just like Jane had said, not Christopher's proudest moment but it could have been worse.

"Well, she *is* perfect," he said more calmly. "If you wanted to mock her, you should have chosen another name for her. Stating the obvious hardly proved your cleverness."

Christopher stared at him, his cup of ale half-way to his lips. "Bloody hell, man, you're smitten."

Oh, he was not smitten. He'd been smitten that first day in the blue room, when he'd first seen her. After two weeks with her and their tryst in the hay, he'd catapulted straight past infatuated into a whole new realm of emotions.

"It's much worse than that," he mumbled. "I think I'm in love with her."

There. He'd finally admitted out loud what he had struggled with for days. Perhaps the darkness helped. Perhaps he simply needed to let his secret out for fear it would suffocate him. Though he had the impression he had just loosed an arrow that would rip damage through everything he knew, Christopher didn't seem perturbed by the revelation.

"How is that worse?" For once there was no mockery in his voice, only genuine bafflement.

"How? Well, just look at me!" Griffin gestured at himself

angrily. "I'm wearing clothes that don't belong to me. My only possession in this world is a horse that was given to me, while Jane is Lord Sheridan's daughter, a man so far above me I should never even have met either of them."

"But you did meet them. You did much more than that. Connor Hunter owes you his life and Jane gifted you with her favors." An eyebrow arched above the blue eye. "Or have you already forgotten about all that?"

Forgotten! He let out snort. He would sooner forget his own name.

"What we did doesn't change the fact that I have nothing and I am no one."

"You are not no one in her eyes, it is all that counts." Christopher sounded unusually serious. He leaned in to rest his elbows on his knees, like a man about to impart great wisdom. "Listen to me. Siân fell in love with me, arrogant, unbearable fool that I am, and made her mind up to have me when all her family was set against me. She forgave my mistakes and the hurt I caused her and her sister. She married me even though I had been stripped of everything I had."

"What does that have to do with Jane and me?"

"Do the Hunter girls a favor and remember that they are not like the rest of the women you might have met before or will ever meet again. They see beyond what other people see and are not afraid to take what they want. Siân was the one who seduced me. I should have known then it would not be worth fighting what was inevitable."

The man had a point. Jane was like no one else, certainly like no lady he imagined, and she had given herself freely to him.

"Be that as it may, I cannot—"

"Don't you dare even contemplate leaving her now and doing what kills you for 'her own good.' It will only end in disaster. I once tried to do what I thought was best for Siân and ended up causing us both untold misery." Christopher gritted his teeth. "Believe me, you do not want to have to watch her being married off to another man."

No, Griffin could only imagine the torture that would be. But what other option was there? He could not very well marry her himself!

"Do you think—"

He stopped, not knowing what he wanted to say and stared at the dying fire. Darkness had started to engulf the room, and he was worried it would spread to his soul as well.

"You know," Christopher started slowly. "Now that I am Lord Ashton in truth, I could make you a knight."

The announcement fell between them like an axe blow on a log, splitting it in half. Griffin stared at the Englishman in disbelief. Him become a knight? On what grounds? He had not earned the honor by any extraordinary feat, he'd not helped the king win a victory in battle, saved a member of the royal family, foiled a treasonous plot or done anything remotely remarkable. It would be ridiculous. Did he even want to become a knight? Simply the fact that he was asking himself that question showed him he probably didn't. Only earlier that day he'd congratulated himself on being unburdened by responsibilities and free to live his own life. Besides, accepting Christopher's offer would solve nothing. Being made a knight was all very well and good, but it wouldn't give him a fortune or a place to live, and that was what he needed to be worthy of Jane. As Sir Griffin, he still wouldn't be able to give her the life she was entitled to.

He was prevented from saying as much when the door opened on the tall man he guessed had been the late Lord Ashton's squire. The stealthy way he slipped in told Griffin he had not expected anyone to be in the great hall at this hour and had not seen the two men sitting in the high-backed chairs by the hearth. When the man removed both his tunic and under-shirt in one fluid motion Christopher cleared his throat to signal their presence. Evidently, he had no desire to see more of the man and Griffin could only agree.

"My lord!" The squire gave a strangled squeak and brought the discarded clothes up to cover his chest. "Apologies, I-I had no idea you were here with your friend."

No. That much was clear. It would seem that the man had an assignation with someone and had not counted on the room being occupied by two strangers. Griffin felt sorry for having unwittingly disturbed his plans.

"I'm sorry, but we got to talking and forgot the time. Stephen, is it?"

"Y-yes, my l-lord." The man was stammering hard, possibly due to his surprise at seeing that the new Lord Ashton knew his name—or the fact that he was standing half naked in front of him and his friend. "I will leave you now."

The door closed with a creak. With a boyish chuckle, Christopher helped himself to another cup of ale.

"Poor bastard. I hope he can find whoever was supposed to join him and take her somewhere else. I would hate to have deprived her of the pleasure he wanted to give her." He sounded highly amused, and not at all sorry. "I wonder who that might be?"

Chapter Seventeen

Another dead end.

Jane let out a sigh of frustration. Just how big was this castle? No wonder it was hard to maintain to an acceptable standard. Although now that she thought of it, Castell Esgyrn was almost as big as Throckmorton, but thanks to her parents' careful administration, it was kept in prime condition. It did not surprise her to see that Thomas Harrison had let his inheritance go to ruin. Nor did it surprise her that Christopher, even though he had been restored to his title, had decided to remain in his cottage in Wales. It was much more comfortable and welcoming. Why, she herself wouldn't mind—

A shuffling noise at the end of the corridor caused her to slow down. In the absence of burning torches to light her way, she could not see who, or what, was hidden in the darkness. Used to her home castle's comforts, she had not thought to take a candle with her, even though it was a gloomy day. A mistake, clearly.

"Hello, is anyone here?" she called out, edging forward.

There was no answer, but more shuffling noises. Jane skidded to a halt when the two people huddled in an alcove drew away from one another with a haste betraying their guilt. It seemed that the castle's lack of adequate lighting encouraged illicit trysts in its dark corners. That was perhaps to be expected. What was not was the identity of the two lovers.

"My l-lady, oh, my lady," the former Lady Ashton stammered, bringing her hands to her chest to hide her lowered bodice. "Please don't...don't think this is..."

The man, whom she recognized as the squire who had welcomed them the previous day, planted himself in front of his blushing lover, doing his best to shield her while she recovered her wits, and restored order to her clothes. The gesture was enough to tell Jane the man was a man of honor; despite what the situation might lead her to believe.

"My lady, please, do not think ill of her ladyship. I'm afraid I took liberties I have no right to take. If you must punish someone, then I am the sole—"

"No, Stephen, I cannot let you lie and take the blame for this." The lady stepped from behind him, all shyness forgotten. There was a defiant gleam in her eyes. "And there will be no punishment, for you have done nothing wrong, nor taken any liberties. What happened here happened with my full consent. I'm sure Lady Jane will understand."

Jane inhaled sharply, for she did understand. The lady was looking at the man by her side as if he held her whole life in his hands, and the squire was carrying himself with pride but a hint of vulnerability, as if he thought deep down he didn't deserve to touch the woman taking his defense so bravely. It was all too reminiscent of another couple she knew. Caught in a compromising position with her, Griffin would do exactly the same, try to protect her against malice and judgment, and she would take his defense, and look at him in the same adoring way.

She swallowed, moved by the scene unfolding in front of her. "Yes. I think I understand."

A silence, heavy with tension, settled over the corridor, then Lady Ashton stepped forward, every inch the dignified lady despite her state of disarray.

"I was never happy with my husband. Thomas was a petulant, violent man who thought nothing of bedding all the women who crossed his path. From the moment we were wed, aged seventeen, he made my life a misery. When he became Lord Ashton last year, it only became worse. The title, predictably, added to his already insufferable arrogance. He railed against me, hating the idea that he was saddled to such a useless, lowly wife when he could, as a lord, have aspired to a much more advantageous match. Stephen, who was appointed as his squire when we came to live here, saw it all, saw how my husband treated me and my poor Henry..."

There, talking about her recently dead son, her voice broke, and she buried her face in her lover's chest, hiding, while great sobs racked through her body.

Stephen held her throughout the storm, solid as a rock. When he lifted his head to look straight at Jane, there was agony in his eyes. It was clear he blamed himself for the death of the child and his lover's grief. But how could he be responsible for such a thing? The letter Christopher had received had mentioned sword fight training in the snow. Perhaps Lord Ashton, too lazy to see to his son's lessons himself, had asked his squire to supervise them and Stephen had been unable to refuse the order, resulting in the poor boy catching a chill.

"Shame on me, I never dared speak up for her, or little Henry, all these months." His voice was bleak, matching the emptiness in his eyes. "I should have been the one to die that day."

"No, Stephen," Lady Ashton whimpered.

"Yes. Anything to spare you the pain of losing your child."

Jane could understand the guilt weighing on him, but she

also knew that a mere squire would have had no choice but to hide what he thought of his master's behavior and what he felt for his mistress. A man as violent and unreasonable as Thomas would have killed Stephen had he challenged him in any way or hinted at the feelings he harbored for his wife, unsuitable as he deemed her.

"The shame is all the late Lord Ashton's, for mistreating his wife and causing his son's death, not yours. You have done nothing wrong." A glance to the dark corner made her meaning clear. *You have done nothing wrong by being with a woman you love and who loves you and needs you.*

"I swear I never did anything that would compromise her honor, only loving her from afar all these months," Stephen added, nonetheless. "If was only after..."

Lady Ashton had rallied by this point, and she left her lover's embrace to face Jane when Stephen's voice trailed. Her face was a mask of determination, her eyes, still red rimmed, held a fire that spoke of the depth of her feelings.

"When my husband died, I rejoiced, do you hear? I rejoiced. Finally, I was free of that despicable tyrant. Finally, I could be with a good man, a man I love and who loves me." She straightened her spine and took her lover's hand in hers. "I care not what people will say about me. With my Henry dead anyway, I have nothing left to live for but Stephen's love and support. I will not let anyone deprive me of it. I am not ashamed and will never be, of wanting to be with him. If you want to spread the word about our liaison, then do."

"Your secret is safe with me," Jane said slowly. How could she do anything to thwart two people who were so obviously meant to be together, when she was yearning for her own happily ever after with a man people would deem unsuitable? It would be plain hypocrisy. "But I will say that I do not believe it should remain a secret forever. You are a widow now, and

Stephen does not owe anything to anyone. In a few months' time, you will be able to marry."

The look the two lovers exchanged twisted her heart. There was hope, joy, and longing in that look. And love. So much love. They knew the difficult times were behind them, and soon they would be together for good.

"Thank you, my lady. This means a lot." Stephen's voice was hoarse with emotion. "And I hope you find your own happiness soon."

"Yes. I hope so too."

Perhaps she had found it already, but the man who'd planted the seed of her future happiness in her heart refused to let it bloom. He was only staying because he wanted to make sure Cynan and the men were stopped. But she didn't know how she would stop him from leaving once she was safe. Ironically, being no longer in any danger would be the death of her.

Unable to contain the tears burning her eyes, Jane turned and fled.

Later than afternoon, a group of riders led by a white horse were seen galloping on the road leading to the gate. From her place at the top of the battlements, Jane recognized Raven, her uncle's stallion. Her heart seized in her chest. Matthew was coming, with a contingent of men. Was he bringing news of Cynan's capture? Unable to wait a moment longer, she rushed down the wooden ladder and was in the bailey in time to see him dismount.

"Uncle Matthew!" She threw herself in his arms.

"Jane. Dear God, we were so worried. Are you all right?"

"Yes, yes, I'm all right, thanks to..." At the thought of Griffin, of all he had done for her and with her, of all he refused to accept, she burst into sobs.

"Hush, don't worry," Matthew soothed, putting her reaction down to the ordeal she'd endured at the hands of the rebels. "It's all over now."

At this she looked up at him, then at the men behind him. Were Geraint's friends amongst them? She couldn't see any. These were all guards from Sheridan Manor. "You mean... You've captured the men?"

He made a face that clearly indicated he was not satisfied with the result of his expedition. "Come. Let us find everyone so I can tell you what happened."

A moment later she, Christopher, Siân and Griffin were seated in the solar, listening to her uncle's tale.

"As soon as we got the missive Gwenllian delivered, explaining you believed men were lying in ambush waiting for you, William and I mounted an expedition. He scoured the forest to the east, and I headed west."

Jane nodded. It was as she'd expected. The squire, who'd arrived at Sheridan Manor at the age of seven as a page, was an exceptionally brave man, and would have volunteered immediately to help her. Between them, and the retinue they had assembled, the two men couldn't have failed to capture the rebels. Or...

"You didn't get them, then?"

Blunt as ever, Christopher asked the question everyone was dying to ask.

"I was the one who happened on the rebels hiding in the deepest part of the forest. There were a dozen of them, mostly villagers who had no idea how to defend themselves. But I'm sorry to say two riders galloped away while we gathered everyone round, probably their leaders who used them as distraction to allow themselves a chance at freedom."

"Was one of them a giant of a man with wavy brown hair and impossibly broad shoulders?" Griffin asked.

He was right. Cynan was the one who mattered. Tomos, even if he did know how to fight, was a weakling only following orders and the others, villagers who had been recruited at the last moment, would never mount a second expedition. This was not their fight. But Cynan would not be defeated so easily.

"I know not the color of his hair," Matthew said, shaking his head. "But he certainly seemed too big for his poor horse."

Jane took in a shaky breath. If Cynan was still out there, then she wasn't safe. He would not rest until he'd captured her. Not because he meant to hand her over to Hywel, but because he wanted to avenge the humiliation he'd suffered and would hate to be denied the opportunity of raping her. A shiver crept down her spine. Griffin saw it, and he made to take her hand. At the last moment he froze and bunched his fist instead.

Was he wary of being seen doing something too familiar in front of her family? Or did he think he had no right to touch her?

"What did you do with the other men? Did you interrogate them?" Thank God Christopher was asking the questions she should be asking because she was in no state to do anything.

Matthew sighed. "Of course, but they are simple villagers, who could only tell us where they had all agreed to repair to in case of a problem. A castle to the north, which is the direction we saw the two riders take. Most likely they have gone there to recruit more men and mount another expedition. I sent William and six men there, to try and catch the two fleeing rebels before they can disappear again."

"What did those damn villagers think they were doing, lying in wait to capture an innocent woman?"

To say that Christopher was not impressed was an understatement. He looked positively fuming on her behalf. Such protectiveness surprised her. But hadn't she already remarked that he'd changed? Apparently, his apology a few months back had been sincere, and he now truly considered her as family. Her chest warmed at the thought.

"They were told they were here to help a spurned suitor secure a meeting with the lady of his choosing, nothing more. It was obvious they had been misled and possibly even paid to help the bastard, and didn't think anything would happen to the lady in question. In the end, we had to let them go with a promise they would not take part in such underhanded dealings again."

Yes. Jane could only agree. As Griffin himself had been kept in the dark about the true purpose of Geraint's men, she could not condone the punishment of men whose sole mistake had been to believe the lies of a man without scruples.

"Thanks for coming here to tell us," she murmured. If Cynan had gone north to regroup, then they had a few days to come up with a plan. "And please thank William for helping you."

Her uncle nodded. "I also came to deliver other, happier news."

At this Jane sat up, excitement bubbling up her chest. "Aunt Branwen had the baby then? Oh, that *is* wonderful news! Are they both all right?"

"Yes." Matthew smiled, his face alight with pride and joy. "You have a new niece. Alys was born last week, in the hours just before dawn. Branwen was wonderful, as usual. I held her hand throughout and the labor was not as long as the other three were, for which I'm grateful."

Jane's lip started to wobble and she wished she could do like Siân had done, place her hand over her stomach and rejoice in the life she was harboring. But, unlike her sister, she wasn't with child. Or... Suddenly she wondered when the last time she had bled was. With everything happening around her, she had not kept track of her courses. But she was not a virgin any longer. She had been with a man since her last monthly courses, and that man had spent his seed inside her. And since that day, she had not bled. Could she be...?

"I hope to see them both very soon," she murmured, torn between hope and dread. What would happen if she was with child? Griffin had panicked at the idea of her being in love with him, he would be horrified to hear she was going to give birth to his son or daughter.

"Yes," her uncle said, oblivious to her musings. "But if I were you, I wouldn't come anywhere near Sheridan Manor at this time. You must be careful while those two men are free. I doubt they will be able to do anything before they recruit more men, and at the moment, they have no reason to suspect where you are. For all the rebels know, you sent us a message from Esgyrn Castle. You are safe here, with all the men around, so it's better you don't venture too far away from Throckmorton until we find your captors."

"Yes."

Indeed, no one but her family knew where she was. Even if Cynan had not gone to his hideout, which was doubtful, he wouldn't know to look for her here.

"I will leave in the morning, to go and see if William has found anything but my men will stay behind to ensure your protection."

At this, Christopher nodded. "Thank you. I know not how much trust can put on the guards Thomas employed. They seem to be a lazy lot who have no idea what a real fight is. I will feel better having reliable men around at this time, what with my sister-in-law being under threat and my wife with child."

"Of course. May I offer my most heartfelt congratulations on this happy news and the restoration of your title?"

"You may."

Jane exchanged an amused look with Siân. Not so long ago, Uncle Matthew had seen Christopher as a rogue of the worst kind and forbidden him to set foot in Sheridan Manor. It seemed he had come to accept the new family member whole-heartedly. Could he extend the same trust to Griffin, who hadn't done anything wrong, quite the contrary? She dearly hoped so, for, just like her sister, she would feel more comfortable having her family's approval regarding her choice of man.

Of course, she would first have to make Griffin himself accept the idea of a union between them. Marrying a man like him was an extreme step, but she could not see another way forward. She was in love with him, she would not stop being in love with him just because it scared him, just because he'd happened to be born on a farm instead of a castle, especially now that she had started to wonder if their tryst in the hay had not made her with child.

Somehow, she would have to make him see that there was only one possible future for them.

One as husband and wife.

Chapter Eighteen

Early the next morning, Jane's uncle left.

Griffin had liked the man immediately. Matthew Hunter was personable; he had treated him as an equal even after being told who he was. His ability as a warrior was obvious, as was the affection he felt for his nieces. This alone would have been enough to ensure Griffin's approval. Anyone ready to defend Jane was assured his good opinion. If only he could be the one to do it...

The parting was emotional, with Jane promising that she would visit Branwen and little Alys as soon as she could leave Throckmorton safely, and her uncle assuring her they would be waiting for her. Griffin wished she could go see her newest cousin straight away, but the man was right. While Cynan was still at large, she was safer here.

After one last hug, Matthew Hunter left in a thunder of hooves, no doubt eager to be reunited with his wife and child. Griffin could not blame him, or be surprised; his love for her had shone through his every word. Were all the members of the Hunter family happily married? He had yet to hear about one who had not made a love match.

Once everyone had gone back inside the hall, he went to the stables on the pretext of seeing to Eryr.

He'd barely finished picking his horse's hooves that two villagers came to the gate, asking to speak to Lord Ashton. Christopher, who'd joined him to check on his own stallion, Warrior, gestured to the guards to bring them forward. Intent on giving him privacy, Griffin made to leave, but he was asked to remain.

"I hardly think this will be an intimate conversation," Christopher said with his customary side smile, "rather a boring one centering around some recrimination or other. Welcome to the life of a lord, my friend. I will admit I haven't missed this. Perhaps you're right not to want to become a knight."

As if on cue, the older of the two men, a grizzled old bear of a man who doffed his cap before addressing himself to him, started to talk.

"My lord, begging your pardon for the inconvenience but a tree fell on the bridge yonder during the night, due to the strong winds. It is stopping us from crossing the river and getting our sheep back. Would you have a strong man or two to lend a hand moving it?" He eyed Griffin none too subtly while he spoke. Evidently, he had identified him both as a menial and strong, in other words, ideally suited to the task.

"I will come and ascertain the damage now," Christopher said, every inch the patient, benevolent lord he was supposed to be, even though Griffin knew he could have done without the imposition, as he'd announced his intention to leave Stephen and the late Lady Ashton in charge of Throckmorton Castle. "You can come, Griff," he added with a smirk, enjoying himself. "I daresay you're strong enough to lift a tree."

There was no other choice but to agree. Besides, some exercise would do him good. Lifting trees might help expend some of the powerlessness he'd been feeling for days.

Before following the two villagers, Christopher went to the foot of the keep, where his wife had just appeared, arm in arm with Jane. "My love, Griffin and I are going to the bridge down below. A tree has fallen in the night and needs to be removed. You ladies can watch us from the postern gate if you want. It should prove an amusing spectacle."

"We will, as we're in dire need of distraction," Siân agreed, before telling Griffin in Welsh. "Christopher is not forcing you to go do the work of a menial, is he? Don't hesitate to send him to hell if he is."

"No, he's not," he assured her in the same language. He really liked the woman, who was as mischievous as she was kind.

"Very well. Though I daresay you men would fare better by removing your tunics, and mayhap even your undershirts for this endeavor."

"Siân, please! You're impossible," Jane protested, going redder than a ripe berry, and just as tempting.

"What?" Her sister gave a naughty giggle. "Don't tell me you would object to the sight of two men—"

"Am I the only one around here who speaks only one language and cannot understand a word of what is being said?" Christopher interrupted, his mock offense highly amusing.

"Yes, you are," his wife answered, reverting back to English for his benefit. "You had better learn, for fear of not being able to understand what I tell our son when I suckle him later on in the year."

A growl was all the warning Siân got before she disappeared into her husband's embrace. Apparently, the image of her feeding their babe was enough to make him lose his mind. While his friend whispered a heated declaration into his wife's ear, Griffin's blue gaze crossed Jane's green one. There was a gleam in hers that he could not account for.

Then he saw that she had placed her right hand over her stomach, and her fingers were holding the velvet of her dress in a tight grip. His heart started to beat twice as fast as usual. What the—

"Come," Christopher said when he finally released Siân, who looked rather flushed and disorientated. Griffin sympathized. He felt rather odd himself. "Let's go and see what we can do about this tree before I decide I would rather spend the day in bed with my wife, learning all the parts of the body in Welsh."

The two men made their way down the slope without a word. Christopher seemed in very high spirits but as soon as they drew neare the bridge, his smile disappeared, and Griffin instantly understood why. The tree hadn't fallen down because of the wind, unlike what they had been told. Rather it had been felled. The axe cuts at the base of the trunk were obvious, even from here.

Christopher turned to the villagers, a frown on his face. "What's the meaning of this? The wind is not responsible for the falling of the tree, any fool can see that. Someone hacked at it."

The old man, who still had not put his hat back on his head, started to stammer. "D-di they? We didn't realize..."

"No? It's rather obvious, I should say, even from here."

Christopher led the men to the stump, and crouched down, gesturing at it. Griffin waited where he was. It was not his place to argue with the men, but his friend was right. Being a lord was not something to be envied.

Suddenly there was a rustle in the undergrowth behind him, then a woman's scream in the distance. Had it come from the castle? Griffin turned around, only to find himself face to face with Cynan. His whole body lurched. What the devil was the man doing here? Wasn't he supposed to have ridden to the north? Was he alone? Why hadn't anyone heard his approach? There was no time to face all the questions bursting through his mind.

The big man bunched his fist—and a heartbeat later, stars exploded into Griffin's skull.

From their place outside the postern gate, Jane and Siân watched the progress of the four men. Christopher was leading the way, Griffin by his side, while the two villagers followed at a respectable distance. Walking with long, fluid strides, they soon reached the bridge, which was only about a hundred yards from the lists, at the bottom of the slope. Before they could reach the tree, they stopped and turned to look at the villagers. After a brief exchange, Griffin was left a few feet behind while the three others went to examine the stump.

It all happened in the blink of an eye.

A dark shape emerged from the bushes behind Griffin, and crept forward, shoulders slumped. Even from this distance, Jane recognized Cynan's wavy hair and imposing bulk. Dear God, what was the rebel doing here? None of the four men, with their attention focused on the tree, had seen his approach.

Before she could think, she shouted a warning and started to run.

By the time she'd reached the group of men, Cynan had sent Griffin to the ground with a punch to the head and five more rebels had come out from the undergrowth. Four of them held Christopher off while the older villager who, Jane now understood, had to be an accomplice, bound a barely conscious Griffin's hands together with ropes he had extracted from his pockets. His son then helped him lift Griffin's limp body off the ground.

"I told Geraint you'd betray us, English, and help the lady escape! But did he listen to me?" she heard Cynan growl. Then a sinister laugh escaped his lips. "You'll pay for it, never fear. I'll enjoy showing you where your loyalty should lie, you cur."

"No! Leave him!" she shouted, only to be stopped by the fifth rebel, a blond man who'd taken her by the wrist. Tomos. His eyes lit up in recognition when she turned to him and he saw who she was.

"Well, well, if it isn't the lady herself," he hissed in her ear, before shouting to Cynan. "Hey, I've got Lady Jane here! Let's take her along too. We never had the chance to get between her milk white thighs. Methinks 'tis the perfect opportu—"

"No!" Griffin roared. He was being hoisted up a horse the youngest villager had retrieved from the undergrowth, but he had heard the vile declaration and found the strength to rear up. "Christopher, for the love of God, take her away! Make sure she's not hurt in any way. It's me they want. I can't—"

A blow to the head silenced him.

Christopher, who, being the only one armed with a sword, had finally managed to rid himself of the men holding him, didn't need to be told twice. Shouting in righteous anger, he slashed at Tomos, who howled and stepped back, cradling his bleeding arm. As soon as she was free, Jane made to run to Griffin. He was draped over the back of the horse, unconscious and bleeding. She didn't make it further than a few steps, however. Grabbing her by the waist, her brother-in-law started to drag her back to the postern gate.

"No!" She screamed. "I can't leave him!"

"You must. 'Tis what he wants. I—" He interrupted himself to slash at a man coming at them. The man shrieked and fell to his knees, blood soaking his hose. The others, seeing that they would only end up cut to ribbons if they tried to stop his retreat, backed away.

Jane didn't stop fighting when Christopher threw her over his shoulder and ran up the slope to the safety of the castle. "I haven't got a horse. I can't save him. But I can save you, and I will," she heard him say, his breathing coming fast and ragged.

A moment later, they were at the postern door. Jane threw a desperate glance at the scene of the attack when Christopher dropped her back to her feet. One man was lying by the bridge, immobile.

Of Griffin and the others, there was no trace.

Jane stared at the flames dancing in the hearth without seeing anything. Where was Griffin? Was he still alive? If he was, it would be a miracle. And it was all her fault. He'd done nothing wrong. He'd been captured, punished and possibly killed because of her. Because he'd wanted to save her from the rebels. How would she bear it?

Siân placed a cup of spiced wine into her hands. "Drink," she encouraged when Jane looked at it as if she had no idea what to do with it.

She drank. The first sip made her wrinkle her nose. The second caused her stomach to roil. She put the cup down.

"I'm sorry, Jane." Standing next to his wife, Christopher sounded agonized. "I couldn't stop the men from taking Griffin away. Eight was too much for me to overpower but I should have—"

"No. You did what Griffin told you to do, you saved me," she said in a dull voice. She knew her safety would have been his priority, and she was glad that in his distress he'd been able to rely on a trusted, strong friend to prevent her from being taken too. "You have nothing to blame yourself for."

"Mm." He didn't sound convinced. "But now that I have you safe, and a horse at the ready, I will go back to him. I cannot stay here while he's in danger."

The three people in the room looked at one another in help-lessness. Go back where? No one knew where Griffin might be, that was the whole problem. The rebels had not let slip any clues as to their destination. Still, they could not admit defeat so easily, not yet, not when they had not even tried. Christopher was right. They had to do *something*.

Jane stood up and started to pace around the room as she expressed her thoughts out loud. It was a habit she'd had since she'd been a child. It had always helped her see things more clearly.

"I don't think they will have killed him just yet, only to throw his body in a ditch. Cynan did say he wanted his revenge and would enjoy making him suffer. I believe him. He will not kill him until he has made him pay for his supposed betrayal." She forced herself to think rationally, even if the thought of Griffin in the arms of the brute was horrifying, and she really thought they had a bit of time before the irreparable happened.

"No, he won't," her sister and brother-law said in unison, as if to infuse her with the strength this assurance would give her.

"I think they will have brought him back to the place where I was detained myself when they captured me, because there they can be assured of the privacy needed to put their vile plan to execution. Geraint seemed to have an understanding with the lord living there, an Englishman who did not question his actions and had been rewarded by Hywel for his help. Only... I have no idea where that place might be. I was unconscious when they took me there and then for the first part of the journey to Wales, they took a route I didn't know, so I cannot situate it. It cannot be too far away though."

"Can you recall anything that might help us identify the place?"

Christopher had started pacing also. He sounded full of renewed hope, which gave her the surge she needed. Could she recall anything? Perhaps. She closed her eyes, imagining herself in front of the bay window while waiting for Geraint to come to her to explain why she was being detained. It seemed a long time ago now, but there had to be a clue somewhere.

"From my room I could see we were quite high up. So a castle on a hill. And I think there was a lake in the distance." The stretch of water she'd seen peeking between the trees could not have been the sea. She opened her eyes and turned to face Christopher as something flashed through her mind. "Wait, they mentioned the name of their hosts before we set off, thinking I could not understand them. Sir William? Lord Wilt? Something like that."

Christopher's unusual eyes lit up in recognition. "Lord Wills?"

She nodded, heart in her throat. Yes, that was it! "Do you know him?"

"No. But I think I know the place you mean. During my weeks of hopeless wandering after the tourney where I met with your sister again, I happened upon this castle. Lord Wills agreed to have me spend the night there."

Hope surged through Jane. If he knew where it was, it was as good a place to start as any. "Is it far from here? Could you get there in—"

"I will take Stephen, and a dozen men with me," he cut in. "We'll be back as soon as we can. There's no time to lose."

Before he left the room, Siân drew her husband into her arms and gave him a passionate kiss. Jane watched on, fighting the urge to throw herself into his arms as well. If he succeeded in saving Griffin, she would forever be in his debt.

"Thank you, my love," Siân said, her voice shaky with emotion. "You will be careful, won't you?"

Christopher placed a hand over her still flat stomach and smiled reassuringly. "Always, Little Lamb. Worry not about me.

You have our child to think about and protect. That is plenty already."

Jane hated herself for placing her beloved sister's husband in danger at this critical time, but she had no choice. Without him, she was helpless. He, unlike her, knew where Cynan and his men had gone. He, unlike her, could wield a sword and defeat the scoundrels holding Griffin captive.

It didn't take long to assemble the retinue. Through tear-misted eyes Jane watched Christopher, Stephen, her uncle's men, and a couple of Throckmorton's guards mount their horses. They looked like men on a mission. She tried to tell herself that such a formidable force could not fail and almost managed it. When the beat of the hooves had vanished into the distance, however, she fell to her knees, her sister hugging her tight against her own trembling body.

Please, please, please, Lord, let them get to Griffin in time.

Chapter Nineteen

Griffin was dead.

The men were dead. Christopher, Stephen and the others, they were all dead, reduced to a bloody heap of limbs.

It was the only way to explain the fact that they had not come back yet. Jane kept staring at the door of the solar, unblinking. She had not moved from the chair, drunk or eaten anything since the retinue had left hours ago. She had barely taken a breath.

Why weren't they back yet?

"They're all dead," she whispered to herself, feeling like her head would burst if the awful thought didn't get out.

"Of course, they're not," Siân said from behind her, her tone sharp. "Stop thinking like this, it will only send you mad."

Jane let out a snort of incredulity. "I will go mad if they don't come back soon, whatever I think about. Don't you see? The man I love is out there, facing—"

"Please." Something in her sister's voice made Jane turn around. Siân was standing in the middle of the room, her eyes huge in the fire light, her hands flat over her stomach, her lips wobbling. She was on the verge of tears. "The man I love is also out there, and I am doing my best not to go mad myself, imagining what could have happened to him, imagining my baby never meeting his father."

"Oh, Siân, forgive me! I'm such a fool!"

"You're not a fool, you're only worried, with good reason. But it will not help. We need to stay strong for when the men come back. They will need us then."

Jane fell in her sister's arms, sobbing. How could she have been so selfish as to allow her anguish to show thus? Of course, she was not the only one worrying herself to death. Siân would be racked with fear as well. Her husband, the father of her unborn child, was in mortal danger, because Cynan would not go down without a fight, and there was no telling how many men he had at his disposal. The ones they had seen by the bridge might not be the only ones he'd recruited. Others might well be waiting at Lord Wills castle.

Oh, she would make sure her father and uncle made the foul Englishman pay for all he had allowed the rebels to do!

"Listen to me." Siân, almost a hand shorter than she was, but magnificent in her determination, held her at arm's length, her blue eyes sending sparks. "Our men are *not* dead, and they will be here soon. They had better do, because if they don't, I'll kill Christopher myself for the worry he's caused us."

Jane could not help a laugh at this spirited answer, so typical of her sister. "Oh, Siân. You're the best—"

A noise interrupted her. Her heart tripped in her chest when she identified it as the one she most wanted to hear. Horses' hooves. At last! With a gasp Jane bolted to the door and ran down the spiral staircase, followed by her sister. In the bailey, the group of men were already dismounting, Christopher at its head. The usually impeccable Lord Ashton appeared as disheveled as she had ever seen him. His tunic was cut in various places, his long hair was in disarray, and his left cheek was cut. In the torchlight, the crusted blood appeared a dull brown, as if he'd been rolling in mud.

With a scream Siân threw herself into her husband's arms. Eyes closed, Christopher held her without a word.

It was then that Jane saw Griffin. No wonder she had not spotted him at first. He was being lowered from his horse by Stephen and two of her uncle's men. She ran to his side, panic overwhelming her when she saw he was barely conscious and had to be held upright. If Christopher resembled a knight returning from the crusades, Griffin looked like a man who'd gone to hell and been spat out by the devil himself. His clothes were in tatters, his hair was matted with blood and his right hand was roughly bandaged, as if the men had done their best to cover a grave injury before setting off. He was pale as death, and slick with sweat.

"Oh, my God, what did they do to him?"

Christopher drew to her side, his shoulders stooped in contrition. Siân was still holding him close, with both her arms wrapped around his waist. "I... I'm sorry to say they had started torturing him when we arrived." He was breathing rather fast, like a man fighting pain. Evidently the cut on his cheek was not the extent of his injuries. He was very pale himself, paler than the rest of the men. "His right hand...the two smallest fingers are missing. On his chest—"

"I will see, worry not."

Jane knew she would be sick if she heard exactly what the Welshmen had done. This was a grim repetition of what had happened to her father fourteen years ago. Instead of just killing him outright, Gruffydd had taken pleasure in drawing out Connor's suffering. It seemed that the son had inherited the father's taste for cruelty.

Not that she was overly surprised.

A sob escaped her lips. "I don't know how to thank you for getting Griffin back," she told Christopher, overwhelmed by the enormity of what he had done. He was the one who had saved Griffin.

Without him she would never have known where to look. Even supposing they had eventually found out where Cynan had taken his captive, it would have been too late. The rebels had wanted to amuse themselves by torturing him, but they would have quickly tired of the sinister game and ended up killing him. Or a weakened Griffin would have succumbed to the torture. Either way, it was a miracle they had gotten to him in time.

"Please." Christopher gave her a tight smile. "Finally, I feel I have atoned for what I made you go through when we were young, Perfect Little Jane Hunter. We'll talk no more of it. Go see to his injuries, while my wife sees to mine."

Indeed, it seemed as if the will not to worry Siân unduly was the only thing holding him upright at the moment. Jane nodded, as eager to get to her man as he was to lie down. "Of course. Thanks again."

When he left, supported by Siân, Jane knew she would never think ill of Christopher Harrison ever again. He had given her her life back by rescuing the man she loved and had almost lost his in the process. They were now linked by an inextricable bond.

On her orders, Stephen and the two men carried Griffin to the room she had been allocated, next to the solar. Having settled him on the bed, they left, assuring her they would bring back everything she needed to see to him without delay.

Once she was alone, Jane drew near the bed, intimidated in front of an unconscious Griffin in a way she had never been when he'd been at the height of his potency. Bracing herself, she started to unwind the bandage around his hand—and recoiled in horror when she saw only a bloody mess where his little finger and ring finger should be. Christopher had warned her about the injury, but stupidly, she had not paused to think what it actually meant. *Two fingers are missing* was what he'd said. The simple, impersonal description did not begin to describe the horror of what had actually happened. But at least the wound was not bleeding anymore.

Taking heart from it, she placed a light kiss on his thumb. As the damaged hand was the right one, her guess was that Cynan had not known Griffin was left-handed and had naturally started the torture with his supposedly more useful hand, so as to inflict the most damage. This was some consolation. Of course the pain of the mutilation would have been felt just as keenly, but at least now he would be able to live his life with less inconvenience than if he had lost the fingers of his leading hand.

Jane threw the soiled bandage on the chest lining the wall and set about removing Griffin's undershirt. Encrusted with blood, covered in dirt, cut in dozens of places, it was already damaged beyond repair so, deciding it was the best way not to hurt him, she simply tore it from his body, uncovering the wound on his chest Christopher had warned her about. It was deep enough to warrant stiches, but it too, had stopped bleeding.

In preparation for the men's return, she lit as many candles as she could find. Better keep busy than stare at the dozens of cuts crisscrossing his honeyed skin and go mad with anguish.

A moment later, true to their word, the three men were back, carrying water, bandages, a needle and thread, a tray laden with food and some clean clothes, everything she needed to make Griffin more comfortable.

"Here. Should you need anything else, you only have to ask, my lady," Stephen told her.

Not trusting herself to speak, she thanked him with a wobbly smile.

Once they were gone, she started tending to Griffin. He had still not recovered his senses, and was thrashing on the bed, like a man fighting demons. Was he in physical pain, or reliving the torture he'd endured at Cynan's hand? Both? Tears started to run down her cheeks. She had forgotten to ask Christopher what had happened to the rebels, but she didn't doubt for a moment that they were finally free of them.

"Oh, my love," she murmured, running a cloth over Griffin's sweaty brow. "I'm here, it's over. I'm here. Now all you have to do is to get better."

~

Griffin was swimming in an ocean of pain.

The only thing preventing him from drowning in it was Jane's presence by his side, Jane's voice in his ears, Jane's hands on his skin. She was wiping his brow, stroking his cheeks, cleaning his chest, talking sweet nonsense all the while, as if she feared silence would bring his demise. And she was right to be worried. Without the anchor to reality she was providing, he was in danger of slipping into the dark, dangerous oblivion beckoning.

But why was she here with him? How had she found him, in the dank castle cell he'd been thrown in? He hadn't dared hope anyone would come to his rescue and had resigned himself to the idea that he would die, alone and reduced to a bloody mess. He didn't even mind so much. It was the torture he had found hard to stomach. The humiliation of it, the powerlessness, the pain...

Yes, the pain. His hand was throbbing, his chest was on fire, his throat had been scraped raw. He was so thirsty... He tried to talk, found that it was too painful and gave up, focusing on the pleasurable sensations Jane was creating in the few parts of his body that were not hurting. He felt her wet his hair, brush it with soothing, tender strokes, her love evident in every gesture. He allowed himself to bask in it. She was telling him everything would be fine, that the pain would soon stop. He could only hope.

Then her words started to take a new direction. No longer soothing, meaningless reassurances, they took on a new urgency. How long had they been in that room together? It wasn't the cell, he had established that much, and it seemed to him that it was no longer dark outside, that light was trying to pierce his eyelids. He wished he could put his arm over his face to stop it, but his body was too heavy.

"Griffin, please, you have to wake up," Jane was saying, her voice tinged with panic. "You cannot die, not now, I need you, you cannot leave me... Us."

"Us?" he croaked. If ever there was a time to make an effort, this was it. Had he heard her right? Who was this "us" she was talking about? He didn't have anyone in the world except her. Something started to niggle at the back of his brain. Hadn't something been bothering him when he'd been attacked?

"Oh, thank God!" Jane fell against his chest, sobbing, relief audible in her voice. He closed his eyes again, exhausted by the effort it had been to open them. "You're not dead!"

No, he was not quite dead yet. And he dearly needed to hear what she had to say. "Us?" he repeated, unable to say anymore. Hopefully she would understand what he meant.

A silence. He fought to stay awake.

"I haven't had my courses since we..." She stopped but there was no need to continue. Since they'd slept together, she meant. "Since we arrived at Castell Esgyrn. I think I may be with child."

Jane was with child.

His child.

Dear God. This was exactly what he had dreaded to hear after their encounter in the barn—and what had been bothering him before the attack. An image of Jane's hand cradling her stomach while Siân had talked about feeding her son tore through the haze in his mind. He'd wondered at the evocative gesture. Now he understood what it meant. The world stilled around him; all the lights dimmed at last. And then... And then the ocean won.

Griffin fell into a deep, black void.

Chapter Twenty

For two long days and two awful nights, Jane had to watch Griffin fight off the fever holding him in its grip. At first, she'd been relieved to see him succumb to unconsciousness, since it would only help him to get over the worst of the pain while she stitched the cut on his chest. It had been as emotionally hard for her as it would have been physically painful for him, and it had helped not to have to see him fight to remain stoic. Once the last stitch had been cut, she had retched into the bowl of bloodied water. Then she had burst into tears, dissolving into a puddle at the foot of the bed. No, it was best Griffin had not seen any of the pathetic display.

But then when he had failed to fully regain his senses she had started to worry. Fever and infection were the real danger for someone in his situation, everyone knew that.

On the second night her eyes grew blurry with fatigue, and she started to wonder how she was going to carry on. To add to Jane's despair, the evening after the fever had taken hold of Griffin, she had started to bleed. It would seem that, unlike what she had thought, she was not with child, but only a few days late, perhaps due to the strain she'd endured since her abduction. And now she was losing hope of seeing the man she loved get better. Would she lose him moments after being forced to accept she was not carrying his child?

She didn't see how she would survive it.

The only good thing to come out of these dreadful days was the news that Christopher had recovered from his wounds. The cut on his cheek would leave a scar, but otherwise, he was as well as could have been hoped. It had been a relief to hear it. She certainly didn't need any more cause for concern. He had also informed her that Cynan and his men were dead. Lord Wills would have had a visit from Uncle Matthew by now and she could be certain the man had been made to regret his part in the whole affair.

As dawn broke on the third day, Siân entered the room, carrying a tray of food. Jane took a sip of ale and nibbled at some cheese while her sister looked on, worry etched on her face.

"You need to get some rest," she urged, putting the tray away when it became obvious the pottage would not be eaten. "Stay in the room if you must, I understand you do not want to leave his side. I would do the same if it were Christopher. But you need to sleep, so I asked for a pallet to be brought in."

"I must—"

"You must rest. 'Tis the most important thing. Griffin is not going to be pleased when he wakes up and finds you half dead from exhaustion. I do not want to have to answer to him for not looking after you properly." Despite the chiding, it lifted Jane's spirit to hear her sister talk about the moment Griffin would wake up as if it were a certainty. She had started to doubt she would ever see him recover. "I promise to wake you the moment there is news."

Jane would have protested, had not servants brought in a bundle of furs and some straw in at that precise moment. The prospect of a few hours' oblivion was impossible to resist. Not bothering to remove her dress, she fell on the welcoming pallet and lost consciousness.

She woke up in the bed next to Griffin, who was looking at her with clear blue eyes. Such a piercing stare could only mean one thing. The fever had broken at last. The worst was over. He was finally on the road to recovery. Everything within her slackened. It was over, he—

Then she bolted upright, relief eclipsed by dread.

"Don't tell me you lifted me from the pallet and carried me to the bed!" she shouted. With his injuries, it was the last thing he should have done. "Your stitches, the—"

"No. I woke up this morning with Siân by my side, watching over me. She told me you had fallen asleep not so long ago. Between us we agreed you needed your sleep, so she didn't disturb you. But I wanted you next to me, so we had Christopher bring you to the bed." He gave her a tender smile, the kind of smile she had feared never to see again. "You never even stirred once."

No, she wouldn't have. She always slept soundly, as he knew, and after three days with little to no sleep, her body would have needed to recuperate. But he'd wanted her next to him... It was the best thing she could have heard. Reassured, she lay back down and snuggled into his all too delicious warmth. Christopher had placed her on Griffin's left side, she noticed, so she could not hurt him when she moved.

"How long have I been asleep?" He'd mentioned the morning and it was now dark. On the chest by the window a single candle was burning, casting gold light onto the stone wall.

Griffin gave her cheek a stroke. "Not as long as I have by all accounts, but long enough. How do you feel?"

"How do *I* feel? I should be the one asking you that question. You've been delirious for days, your injuries—"

He shook his head. "Forget about me. I'll be fine, thanks to you all. How are you...both?"

His good hand, tentative, landed on her stomach. Of course. He didn't know. He still thought she might be with child, perhaps he even *hoped* she was with child. Jane crumpled from the inside, because now she would have to tell him there was no babe. Would he think she had deliberately misled him, like Ffion had done a few months ago? Would he not resent her for the pain she had caused him by raising his hopes yet again?

"I'm sorry, Griffin, I'm not with child," she sobbed, hiding her face in her hands. "I thought I might be, but I was mistaken."

And she was heartbroken. It was only when she had started bleeding that she had realized how much she had wanted to carry Griffin's baby. Not just because it would have meant they had no choice but to discuss a future together, but because she had wanted the baby. Unlike Siân, she had never been obsessed with children, but at the idea of holding a babe who was the image of the man she loved, her heart had melted.

Besides, she knew Griffin wanted children, and she wanted to be the one to give them to him.

"I'm so sorry. I didn't mean to—"

"You have nothing to be sorry about," Griffin assured her, holding her tight against him. "It's not your fault."

But she did feel guilty. She should have stayed silent. Panicked at the prospect of having to raise their child alone, even more panicked at the idea of losing him, she had blurted out her fears instead of allowing him to focus on his recovery with his mind unencumbered by worries and false hopes. She had only been a few days late, everyone knew such things happened, and it was no cause for concern. Mentioning it to Griffin would only have raised his hopes without achieving anything. Whichever way you looked at it, she had made a mistake.

So, Jane was not with child, after all.

Eyes closed, arms tight around her, Griffin wondered how the news made him feel. Only a week ago, he might have been relieved to hear that their tryst in the hay hadn't had any consequences. Now he was crestfallen. During his fever, the only thing that had sustained him was the knowledge that Jane needed him, that she was waiting for him to recover so they could welcome their child together. And he had sworn to himself that if he survived, he would not let anything or anyone get between them, even himself, even his doubts.

Well, he had survived. And so, it was time to make good on his promise.

He took in a deep breath, feeling like he imagined a knight might feel when about to throw himself into battle.

"Worry not, *cariad*. In time, I will give you a babe. If not this year, then the next, or the one after, but I will give you children because I intend to bed you as often as I can. In the meantime, I will give you my heart and my love." His chest constricted. Would it be enough? "I cannot give you anything else for it is all I have. Will you—"

"It is all I want!" Jane cried out, nestling herself even closer to his chest before he could actually ask her to marry him, as if to say she was prepared to live with him in sin as long as they were together. "Your heart and your love are all I need. Griffin, you know I love you."

"I do." He draped his good hand over her nape, circling the soft skin under her ear in soothing gestures. "And it doesn't scare me anymore. But being without you does. So please, marry me before I come back to my senses and flee as far as Eryr can take me."

Instead of giving him the answer he wanted, she sat up in

outrage, much like she had done earlier. Dear Lord, he was really making a mess of this marriage proposal. Weren't women supposed to swoon and agree? Instead, his bride-to-be was glowering at him.

"Flee! You will do no such thing, and I will go get the priest if you persist in your folly, and have him marry us right now, in this chamber, do you hear me, Griffin ap Madoc?"

Oh, he heard her, he heard all the love and determination to have him for a husband. He smiled. Messy as it was, this was the best marriage proposal he could have dreamed of, because it was to this woman and she was agreeing.

"Don't get the priest now, please. I would rather stand when I make you my wife, Lady Jane Hunter."

Her whole body relaxed and she gave him a radiant smile. "Aye. I would prefer that too, and let the whole world see us."

"Does that mean you accept?" Was she really going to marry him? He still could not believe it.

"Yes. I was your lover, now I will be your wife and, in time, the mother of your children."

His throat tightened. "You know..."

Griffin hesitated. Should he tell her that Christopher had offered to make him a knight? He didn't feel worthy of the honor. He was a simple man, he hadn't had any training, and a knighthood usually rewarded valor in battle. These men were squires, nobly born. No matter what name was bestowed upon him, nothing would change the fact that he'd been born of a maid and raised by a poor farmer. But if Jane thought she would be more comfortable with being Sir Griffin's wife, then he would put his misgivings to one side. Anything to avoid causing her discomfort.

"The day before I was abducted, Christopher told me he could make me a knight now that he is once again a lord. Would you rather—"

"No."

His heart sank when the word darted out of Jane's mouth. So, she didn't think him worthy of the honor either. "I see."

"I will not have you being anyone else other than who you are, becoming anything for my sake," she said hurriedly, when she saw his face fall. "If you think I would rather marry a knight, then let me tell you that I don't. I fell in love with you, not Sir Griffin. I want to marry *you*. I believe I would marry you even if you were elected to be the next Prince of Wales."

Even if...

He drew her into his arms. "Oh, Jane, I love you." After such a declaration, how could he not?

"And I love you too. Now, let me go and announce our betrothal to Siân and Christopher. I don't think they will be overly surprised."

~

In the end, no one was in the least surprised.

Jane had the pleasure of seeing everyone, from her sister to her uncle, accept her choice of a husband. They started to plan for the wedding that very day, but it took three weeks to organize everything, give Griffin time to heal, write to her family at Castell Esgyrn to inform them of the impending ceremony and allow them time to travel to Sheridan Manor.

For once, Jane and Christopher had been of one mind. Though a wedding in Wales might have been the couple's preference, she had been adamant Griffin was not to ride such a long distance after the injuries he had endured, and Siân's husband had refused to let his wife travel when she was sick every morning. And so the wedding would take place in England, in the castle of Jane's birth. It was just as good a solution, even if the wait was excruciating.

Fortunately, little Alys was here to help pass the time until she became a wife.

Finally, the day came.

That morning, just before dawn, Jane was awoken by a weight pressing down on her. A warm, delicious, masculine weight, one she would know anywhere.

"Good morning, my lady."

"Griffin! You...you shouldn't be here." The rebuke lacked conviction, because there was nothing she liked more than feeling his body against hers. It was a feeling that had become very familiar in the last few weeks. Of a common accord, they had decided not to wait until they were married to worship one another's bodies but despite their numerous encounters, he had not yet dared come find her in her bed at night.

"With you, I have done many things I shouldn't have been doing. One more is hardly going to matter, don't you think?" He nipped at her earlobe, the gesture as playful as it was arousing.

"How many times will I have to tell you it is your right to do what you will with me?"

"At least a dozen more."

"You said the same thing the last time I asked, and the time before that." She sighed. Was it his way of saying he would never feel her equal? She dearly hoped not.

"Stop arguing with me and listen. Today we are going to get married." His mouth at her ear purred the words. He had never sounded more enticing. "Which means we will spend the day either in the chapel in full view of everyone, or in the great hall, surrounded by dozens of guests." He started to grind his groin against her buttocks in a deliciously provocative manner. "We will then have to accept their heartfelt congratulations, eat our way through a sumptuous banquet, and even partake in some dancing, I believe. All this while you wear your finery and look more alluring than words can express." She felt him reach between them and unlace his braies. Her whole body caught on fire when she felt how hard he was. "Which means I will only be allowed to whisk you away to our bed in the middle of the night. There is no way I can last until then without going mad. I need you now."

A moan escaped her lips. "Yes. I need you too."

After this display of sensuality, she could not imagine having to wait all day to feel him inside her. They had made love many times since he had recovered, of course, but somehow it was never enough. A lifetime would never be enough. Well, they could always start now.

Eager to welcome him inside her heat, Jane made to turn around. A hand between the shoulder blades stopped her. "No. Stay where you are. Let me."

A finger lifted the hem of her shift, exposing her buttocks, a knee parted her legs, making room for a hard body, a mouth landed a kiss on her nape, causing goose bumps to scuttle along her spine and then Griffin settled himself between her thighs. How wonderful to feel him take care of her thus. She loved it when he took charge, not just because it never failed to arouse her, but because it showed that, at least as her lover, he did not feel unworthy.

If he was not afraid of who he was in bed he might, in time, come to forget the difference between them in life.

"Are you wet for me, my lady?" A hand landed between her legs and started to tease her, the gentle strokes sending sparks deep in her belly.

"Can't you feel it?" she rasped. Didn't he know her by now? It only took a few words from him, and some naughty caresses to get her aroused beyond bearing.

"Mm, yes, I can. Wet and hot, ready for me, the best feeling in the world." The tip of his manhood replaced the probing finger, promising her untold delights. This was always her favorite moment, when she felt him poised at her entrance. Knowing he was as desperate as she was and about to push inside, never failed to make her insides melt. He always made sure to stay there a moment and let her enjoy both the sensation and the anticipation. "Do you want me inside?"

"Yes! You know I do. Stop teasing me!"

A chuckle. Why did the wretched man think this was in any way funny? "Raise yourself on your hands and knees."

Jane's breathing caught in her chest. This was new. They had made love in various ways over the last few days but never like this. However, as he had yet to do something that did not send her wild with ecstasy, she was only too happy to comply. Had he asked her to stand on her hands that she would have agreed.

"You will feel me deeper than usual in this position," Griffin rasped, his mouth at her ear, his body folded over hers. "Tell me if it becomes too much."

He sounded already on the verge of losing control, which, in turn, sent her arousal to dizzying peaks. Within moments, he was sliding in and out of her body with scandalous ease, pinning her in place with his hands at her waist. Dear God. Nothing had ever felt so good. Held in a strong grip, she had little chance to move, which she loved. There was nothing guaranteed to make her feel pleasure more than to be at the mercy of the man she loved. In that moment, she knew he didn't feel he was lacking in any way.

"Not too much?"

The question was little more than a growl.

"Not enough," she moaned, already knowing she would beg him to take her in this position again and again. Pleasure was building inside her with worrying speed, and she sensed her release would be explosive. It would also have to be soon or she would go mad. "Please. I need... Now. Please."

She needed to survive this so she could get married to him this morning.

"As my lady commands."

Griffin reached around to the sensitive place screaming for attention and pinched it lightly, before starting to rub it in time to his thrusts. Perfection.

"Yes!" she cried out.

"Yes," he echoed. The hand still holding her waist tightened the grip further, forcing her back so she could take him even deeper. "Jane, dear fucking Christ!"

They erupted at the same time, their moans melding into one another.

Stunned by the exquisite release, Jane fell flat to her stomach. Griffin followed her, careful to land next to her as always. He stayed a long moment behind her, panting, holding her tight against his heaving chest.

"Now, my love, now I believe we can go and get married."

"Christopher tells me he didn't find Griffin in his bed this morning," Siân said as she entered the room, carrying the wedding dress. "Do you have any idea where your groom might be? I don't wish to worry you but my dear husband, who takes his responsibilities as host very seriously, is wondering if he fled during the night, unable to face the day."

Jane flushed red to the roots of her hair. Griffin had not taken fright, thank God, he'd only left his bed to come gift her with the best lovemaking she had experienced thus far.

"I... Erm, no, he did not flee. He's here, in the castle." She could still feel his heat inside her and the sheets around her were all in disarray, testimony to the wildness of their coupling. "I saw him earlier."

"*Saw* him did you?" Her sister's eyes started to sparkle.

"I, erm, we..." Actually, no, she had not really seen him, considering the manner in which he had taken her. But she was not about to talk about that. Fortunately, Siân put an end to her embarrassment by placing the dress on the coverlet.

"Well, if you saw him, then the wedding can go ahead. It is all I need to know. Shall I ask for a bath to be prepared?"

"Yes. 'Tis perhaps a good idea." She could not go to the altar smelling of the man she loved, could she? Or... She shook her head. Of course she could not, and she was a fool for even entertaining the possibility.

Soon she was dressed in what Griffin had called "all her finery." The dress was new, a wedding present from Branwen's mother, Carys, and a stunning creation of pale pink velvet embroidered with stars along the hem and collar. In it, she did look like a lady about to be presented at court, so Jane could not help a moment of trepidation when she thought of what Griffin's reaction would be. Would he love it, or would it remind him that they did not belong to the same world?

Well, there was only one way to find out.

"Here," Siân said, handing her a bunch of snowdrops tied with a ribbon the same shade of pink as her dress.

"Oh! They are beautiful! Where did you find them?" She was touched at the thought, all the more so that was not easy to find flowers so early in the year.

"I didn't. Christopher did, this morning, at the foot of the ramparts. He wanted to—"

Siân didn't get to finish her sentence because at that moment Jane dissolved into tears. "I cannot believe I ever thought this man a rogue. I'm so sorry for not understanding before how right you were about him, and how wonderful he really is." This delicacy was the mark of a good man. Not to mention that he had not hesitated and saved Griffin's life. For this alone, she would have opened her heart to him.

"Yes, he is wonderful. As is your husband. We can only hope Gwenllian, Rhys and Seren will be as lucky in their choice of spouses. For Bethan, unfortunately, it is too late." Siân gave her hand a squeeze. "Now, let us go. I assume you don't want to keep your groom waiting?"

"No." Causing him to worry because he feared she had changed her mind was the last thing she wanted to do.

After one last hug, the sisters made their way to the great hall, where the rest of the family was waiting. Jane thanked Christopher for the flowers, and he surprised her by rubbing the back of his neck in embarrassment, mumbling that it was nothing. Her mother was the first to hug her, then Gwenllian and Seren both threw themselves into her arms. Having just turned twelve, her brother, Rhys, merely gave her a manly nod.

Once everyone had left for the chapel to join the waiting Griffin, her father placed a kiss on her forehead.

"My Jane. It feels like yesterday I first held you and your sister in my arms, and here I am, about to entrust you to another man." His voice had gone hoarse and his eyes were shinier than usual. He, too, was thinking of Elspeth, who should have been here with them. "I wish for you and Griffin all the happiness Esyllt and I found in our union."

Jane tilted her head, too moved to speak. It was all she wished for as well.

"Come," Connor said, straightening his spine. "It's time to go."

Wiping her cheeks, she took his arm, and they crossed the sun-filled bailey to the little chapel on the northern wall.

Twenty-two years ago, her father had married his first wife in this very place. Less than a year later, she and Elspeth had been christened there. Only a few weeks ago, Siân had married

Christopher in front of the marble altar. Now her sister was with child and it was her turn to marry a man she loved.

It was perfect, another piece in the family history.

When she walked in through the door and saw Griffin waiting for her, Jane's heart exploded. He had not fled, plagued by last doubts, he was here, and his eyes shone with love and pride. He was magnificent in a tunic of blue velvet that showed his muscular physique to advantage. Jane had to force herself not to break into a run and throw herself into his arms.

Once her father had given her one last kiss, she took her place by his side. This was it. By the time they left the chapel, the lover she had chosen for herself would have become her husband, and her life would never be the same.

The ceremony was over in the blink of an eye. The banquet, however, seemed to last an eternity. Had wedding feasts always been that long? Jane didn't seem to remember it going on so late into the night for Siân and Christopher. But right now, all she wanted to do was leave and be with her new husband—alone.

"Let us leave now, wife," Griffin said in her ear, as if he'd read her mind. "People will understand. We still have a marriage to consummate."

"Griffin! We...we already have!" she said in a scandalized whisper. "No later than this morning, mind you."

He arched an innocent brow. "Have we? I cannot recall a thing."

A giggle escaped her lips. How could he tease her so? "We had better leave then and do it again. This time I'll make sure you remember every single moment, every single kiss, every single thrust. And I won't stop until you have begged me to put an end to your suffering."

Sapphire eyes darkened. "Is that a promise, my lady?"

"Yes. A promise."

Epilogue

T wins.

Jane still could not believe it. When the midwife had told her she was to prepare herself, as a second babe was coming, she had almost fallen into a swoon. Another child? No, surely she couldn't go through the excruciating labor again? But she had, because there had been no other choice. And so, while Siân held her blonde little daughter in her arms, she had given birth to her son. Once the black-haired little boy had been cleaned, she had asked the midwife with a trembling voice if she was sure there wasn't a third child.

Mercifully, there hadn't been.

Heart filled with a joy such as she had never known, Jane stared at the two babies lying side by side on her husband's smooth chest. It was not long before her eyes started to burn with another wave of tears. It really seemed she had done little else but cry this day.

Griffin had insisted he be the one looking after the babes, while she slept. Exhausted by the long labor, desperate to escape the pain gnawing between her legs, she had been all too happy to comply.

But now she was awake, and ready to start on this new part of her life. Siân had given birth to her daughter six months ago, less than a day after Jane had announced she was with child. Every time she had taken her niece in her arms, she had imagined how she would feel when she finally met her own child, but she had failed to anticipate such a rush of love—or that she would have to split this bounty in two. No, not split it, she reflected, but multiply. She had more than enough love for each babe, and the ones who would follow, as well as for their father.

"My love. How do you feel?" Griffin whispered when he saw her awake and looking at him.

"Much better." Still not perfect, but a lot better.

There was a pause before he spoke. "I've been thinking while you slept and, if you agree, I'd like our daughter to be called Elspeth."

"Oh, Griffin!" The tears she had been fighting since she'd woken up finally fell down her cheeks. He wanted their little girl to have her sister's name, to make her part of this joy. She was more moved than she could ever put into words, because she'd had the same thought. It seemed the only fitting name for a twin girl of her loins.

"Don't cry, please *cariad*, not when I cannot hold you." He nodded at the two babes huddled on his chest, their foreheads touching. His meaning was clear. He did not want to risk moving while they were resting so peacefully.

"These are happy tears," she assured him, nestling herself against him. If he couldn't move, then *she* would. "And we will have to find a name for her brother. I was thinking of Llywelyn, like you'd imagined you would name your son. Now that you have one, you can... Unless you'd prefer Madoc, after your father?"

"Llywelyn is perfect." He sent her a fiery look. "I love you, my lady, you do know that?"

"I do." And she loved when he called her "my lady" because she knew in his mind it was now the most meaningful term of endearment.

They stayed lying side by side for a long moment. Jane could feel herself falling asleep again. Then the babes started to squirm, the reason for their unrest obvious. They were hungry. With Griffin's help, she settled herself in the bed and then put the twins at her breasts. A giggle escaped her lips. Heavens, this would take some getting used to, but she could already tell she would cherish the connection with her children.

Griffin crossed his arms over his still naked chest and looked at her, his eyes filled with love.

"You know, I don't think the two skeletons they found in the castle ditch were those of two ill-fated lovers," he said, looking through the window to the imposing structure crowning the valley. From their cottage by the river, it was all they could see. "I think Castell Esgyrn is too happy a place for that."

"Yes," Jane agreed, placing a hand over her daughter's head. "You're right."

Certainly she had never been happier than in that moment.

Next
A Scot for Bethan

About the Author

As far back as I remember, I have been attracted to the Middle Ages, to knights in shining armour and their ladies in spectacular dresses. Now I get to write about them, I feel like the luckiest woman in the world. Being French and married to a Brit makes each book I write extra special, as our countries share a long and sometimes painful past. But in the end, in life as well as in fiction, love conquers all!

I have published several medieval romances under my own name, including series, and also have a pen name, Judith Falcon, for spicier projects, still in historical romance.

Join my newsletter and check out my other books on virginiemarconato.com.

Also by virginie marconato

The Welsh Rebels

A Husband for Esyllt

A Savior for Branwen

A Second Chance for Carys

A Rogue for Siân

A Lover for Lady Jane

A Scot for Bethan

The Noble Norsemen

Taming the Wolf

Soothing the Beast

Wooing the Devil

Baiting the Bear

Tempting the Saxon

Seducing the Warrior

Loving the Blacksmith